I0736495

INCUBUS 2

By Brandon Varnell
Art by Orendi Laran

Incubus 2
Copyright © 2020 Brandon Varnell & Kitsune Incorporated
Illustration Copyright © 2020 Orendi Laran
All rights reserved.

To see Brandon Varnell's other works, or to ask for permission to use his works, visit him at www.varnell-brandon.com, facebook at www.facebook.com/AmericanKitsune, twitter at www.twitter.com/BrandonbVarnell, Patreon at https://www.patreon.com/BrandonVarnell, and instagram at www.instagram.com/brandonbvarnell.

If you'd like to know when I'm releasing a new book, you can sign up for my mailing list at https://www.varnell-brandon.com/mailing-list.

ISBN: 978-1-951904-13-5

DEDICATION

This page is made in dedication to my amazing patrons.
Without them, my characters would never get lewded by so
many wonderful artists:

Aaron Harris
Alarinnise
Alexander Rodriguez
Amando Pastrana
Benjamin Morgan
Brennan
Bruce Johnson
C.L. Holgrahm
Chace Corso
CosmicOrange
David
DeseriDeri
Dhivael
Edward Lamar Stephenson
Emery Moore
Feitochan
Forrest Hansen
Ine Airlcana
Jacob Flores
Jacob Wonjo
Jason Davis
Jason Grey
Jeremy Schultz
Jessica
John Patton
Joshua Garrett
Kevin
Lucid Fact
Mark Frabotta
Matthew Wallace
Max A Kramer
Michael Moneymaker
Nathan

Nathan S
Nicholas
Omegapudding
Patrick Burns-popieniuck
Phillip Hedgepeth
Rafael Eriksen
Red Phoenix
Red Viking
Samuel Donaldson
Sean Gray
Seismic Wolf
Shotgunr12
Saudi Corp
Starwarsscout Jon
Thomas Jackson
ToraLinkley
Travis Cox
Trevor Ward
Victor Patrick Baur
Virgil Gardner
William Crew
Yuriy Snyadanko
Zachery

CONTENT

PROLOGUE

Secilia stood under the hot spray of the shower head. Her eyes were closed, so she couldn't see them, but she could feel the droplets of water as they pelted her face, shoulders, chest, and stomach. If she concentrated enough, she could make out the individual droplets as they ran down her body. Several of those adventurous little droplets ran down her stomach, over her crotch, and descended down her inner thigh.

She had been created with incredible perceptions, which was why she made such a great magical engineer. Her ability to perceive things others couldn't allowed her to find mistakes in devices even experts in magical engineering would have missed. Some people might have even called her ability magic, but that wasn't it, not really.

"Hey, sis! You almost done in there? Some of us would like a chance to shower too," a voice came from the other side of the bathing room door.

Secilia sighed. "Yeah. I'm almost done. Don't get your panties in a twist."

"The only one with twisted panties here is you." There was a dramatic pause before Alex spoke again. "By the way, this lingerie is pretty damn racy. Were you hoping to win Anthony over with sexy underwear?"

A small haze of red caused Secilia's vision to boil; she couldn't stop herself even though she knew he was saying that to rile her up. She turned off the shower, stepped out, and grabbed a towel from the nearest rack. After making sure she was properly modest and her long locks of hair were wrapped in a towel, she stormed over to the door and slammed her fist against the unlocking latch, which emitted a soft beep before the door slid open.

She glared at the man standing on the other side.

Alex wore the same cocky grin he always did, which complimented his swept back blond hair and made him look like a true delinquent. His green eyes were not the same as her blues, and his blond hair was the complete opposite of her black. He wore several piercings that made his appearance seem even more rakish. Her brother truly looked like a rogue.

"Hey there, sis." Alex's grin broadened as he waved at her. "You didn't have to stop on my account. I was just admiring your undergarments. I'm sure any man worth his weight in gold will drool when they see you in this, especially a certain incubus you know and love."

"If you're trying to be funny, then I recommend you stop. You have the comedic sense of a senile sea monkey." Secilia stepped into the changing room. The cold tiles felt so different from the warm ones she'd just left, but she ignored the slight jolt traveling up her legs as she moved over to the sink. "Hurry up and get in. The shower is all yours."

"Thank you, sis!"

With a broad smile like a kid who'd been told it was his birthday, Alex adjusted the towel around his waist and marched into the shower. The door closed and locked behind him.

Secilia sighed as she turned away from the door. She knew her brother was trying to lighten the mood, to keep her optimistic, to keep her mind off her worries, but he didn't seem to understand that nothing he said or did could stop the worry she felt from invading her mind.

"Anthony? Who are these two?"

A voice rang out inside of her head. It was the voice of that woman, Brianna, a member of Custodes Daemonium. That voice haunted her dreams, both waking and asleep.

Secilia removed the towel from her hair, placed her hands against the sink, and stared at her reflection in the mirror. Her long locks of curly dark hair had a glossy sheen as they traveled down to her butt. The color of her hair presented a stark contrast with her alabaster skin, completely unblemished and smooth. Many men had complimented her on her skin, among other things. Her dark brown eyes were set on a small face with a pert nose, pink lips, and dimples.

She was well-aware of her own attractiveness. After all, she had been created this way. Her design was based off the woman who... well, Secilia supposed that woman could be called her mother. She'd always thought of her as such at any rate.

Grabbing a hair dryer and a comb, Secilia began the laborious process of drying her hair, which always took so much time that Alex finished his shower before she was even done.

"You know it would be much easier if you cut it short," Alex said as he dried off and dropped his towel without a care for his own modesty.

Secilia rolled her eyes. "I prefer having long hair."

"Do you really prefer it, or have you not cut your hair because you think Anthony likes it long?" asked Alex as he slid on his boxers and pants.

"I'm warning, Alex. If you don't shut up about Anthony, I am going to remove your testicles with an engineering laser."

"All right. All right. I'll stop. I guess now isn't really the time to joke about that." Alex scratched his head and released a weary sigh. "Anyway, I'm going to make us some breakfast. You want anything specific?"

"I'm fine with whatever," Secilia mumbled.

"Right. I'll have breakfast ready by the time you get out."

Alex left the changing room, leaving Secilia alone to her thoughts, and she had a lot to think about.

Her mission here was a failure. Her entire purpose in coming to Academy Island alongside her brother was to seduce Anthony Amasius, smuggle him off the island, and take him to the Nametech headquarters located in the Americas—formerly known as the United States of America and Canada.

Unfortunately, her creators had forgotten to take several important factors into account. The first and probably most important was that she had not been built for seduction. Her beauty was merely the result of good genetics. She'd originally been made for a completely different purpose. It wasn't until Nametech somehow caught wind of Anthony's existence that they decided to send their secret weapon and her handler to Academy Island.

Because she knew nothing about seducing people, she had been unable to make Anthony hers, which led to the second factor her creators hadn't taken into account. They had not considered the possibility that she would fall in love with him instead of him falling for her.

While Secilia might be the result of several decades worth of experimentation, it did not change the fact that she was, at heart, still a girl. Even being kept in isolation for most of her life could not change that, especially after coming to Academy Island. No, she might not live for love and romance like people in those ridiculous movies she sometimes watched, but she did think it would be nice if she could meet a good guy, fall in love, and start a family.

It was a pipe dream, but it had been one of the small hopes she had kept secreted in her heart.

Meeting Anthony had caused her desire for romance and family to bloom. It had nothing to do with his pheromones. Anthony had been so weak when she met him that he wasn't even capable of emitting any pheromones at all. And while he was attractive despite being skinnier than a twig—she quickly realized it was the result of mana starvation—it hadn't been to the point where she would drop her panties for him. What she had fallen in love with wasn't so transient.

Her intentions toward Anthony upon meeting him had been completely impure, but Anthony, who couldn't have possibly known about her real objective, had treated her with a great deal of respect. He was helpful, kind, and dedicated. She had grown to admire his dedication to helping his brother, had come to love how kind he was to the people he knew, and admired how he was willing to lend a hand to others.

He also had a really great wit. She'd never met someone who could trade banter with her like that.

Of course, even that was not enough to make her fall for him. What had really done it was simply interaction. Meeting with Anthony every day, talking with him every day, seeing him constantly, getting to know him better, bonding with him over their shared interests.

Secilia closed her eyes and brought up a memory, one of many featuring her and Anthony.

Secilia could still remember the first time she'd gotten sick. It was about two weeks after meeting Anthony. She wouldn't say they had hit it off, but they had definitely been on their way to becoming friends.

That day, Alex had been called in for work. It was rare that she and her handler were separated, but it still happened on occasion. Secilia had come down with a bad case of the floo, had an over-115 degree fever, and could barely get out of bed. She had been absolutely miserable, and with no one present to even help her.

Then Anthony had come over, having heard that she was sick, and taken care of her. He'd made her soup, helped her stay hydrated, and fed her medicine, which helped even if it tasted disgusting. He had even stayed by her bedside until she went to sleep before quietly slipping out of her apartment.

From that day on, she had grown closer and closer to Anthony. She shared more things with him, spoke more honestly with him, and began going out to have fun with him. They had eventually discovered a mutual interest in virtual reality laser tag.

After spending so much time with him, it was only natural that she would eventually grow to love him.

Really, it was all Nametech's fault to begin with. They were the ones who had sent her on this mission without any training.

Secilia sighed as she finished drying her hair, set her comb and dryer down, and went over to the clothing rack. She gazed at her underwear. They were a combination of pink and black. Just as Alex had accused, her bra and panties were quite racey. Her panties were nothing more than a thin patch of cloth with a g-string. Meanwhile, her bra was lacy and covered in frills.

It was high-class underwear she had bought several days ago, and while she told herself it was on a whim, the truth was that she did it because Brianna made her feel threatened. The girl was a complete knockout. Secilia was confident in her looks, but not confident enough to say with absolute certainty that she could defeat Brianna in terms of appearance.

After putting on her underwear, she slipped into a bathrobe and left the changing room.

Alex was in the kitchen, cooking. He stood in front of a stove and mixed a variety of ingredients into a pan. It looked like he was creating some kind of omelette, but it was hard to tell.

"Breakfast will be ready soon," Alex called. "Take a seat at the table. I'll have it out in just a bit."

"Has anyone ever told you that you're the weirdest handler ever?" asked Secilia as she sat down at the table, placed her elbows on it, and propped her chin on the butt of her hands.

Alex laughed. "It's not nice to call your brother weird."

"It's not like we're actually related." Secilia closed her eyes and bounced her left leg. "The only reason you can call us siblings is because they sliced our DNA together."

"We still share blood," Alex retorted. "That makes us siblings."

Alex came out of the kitchen a few moments later with two plates. Steam wafted from the plates, and Secilia could smell eggs and chorizo coming from them. The spicy scent of the chorizo made her mouth water, but she tried not to let Alex know how much this smell was driving her crazy.

He set one of the plates in front of her. The omelette was filled with chorizo, cheese, a variety of vegetables, and some type of garnish. She tried not to lean over as she breathed in deeply. Her stomach gurgled.

"Looks like someone is hungry," Alex said with a chuckle.

"Oh, whatever. I didn't have a big dinner last night. Sue me," Secilia snapped with a grumble.

They ate in silence. Secilia could have turned on the TV, but Alex didn't like it when the TV was on while they ate. He said it was bad manners. After breakfast, Secilia cleaned the dishes as Alex sat on the couch and watched the news. She paid only a bit of attention to the newscaster as he talked about how the invasion of rogue demons had finally come to an end. There had apparently been a vampire running around that had changed them all into ghouls. Most of her thoughts were still focused on her own problems, however.

Just as she finished washing the dishes, a loud beeping noise echoed from a device located in the corner of the living room. It didn't look like much. Built like a small pedestal, several glowing blue lines criss-crossed over the entire surface, thrumming with a quiet energy.

"Looks like the boss is calling us," Alex said as he stood up and wandered over to the device. He tapped several buttons on the keyboard embedded into the pedestal. Secilia walked over to him as a small section in the pedestal's top began emitting a bright light. Seconds later, the holographic figure of a man emerged from the pedestal.

The holographic man was very small, no more than a 1/100th scale of his actual size. With graying sideburns, sharp brown eyes, and a trimmed goatee, the man looked very distinguished. He wore a white lab coat that made him appear to be a scientist. Underneath the lab coat was a black shirt, black pants, and boots of the same color.

"Boss," Alex greeted. "It's rare for you to call. Did you need something?"

"Boss" ignored Alex as he turned his attention to Secilia, who straightened her back. This man was just a holographic representation of the real person, so he had no presence, but Secilia still felt a thrill of fear run down her spine at the look in his eyes.

"I hear you failed to seduce the incubus," the man said in a cold voice. *"Furthermore, I just received a report that a War Maiden from Custodes Daemonium became his bondmate."*

"T-that is true," Secilia stuttered. "However, it's not as if having one bondmate will be enough. Anthony will need multiple bondmates. If I can just—"

"That is unacceptable," the man cut her off with a harsh snap. *"Now that the War Maiden has become the incubus's bondmate, there is no way Custodes Daemonium would be willing to share the incubus with us. Damn it. If I had known what they were planning, I would have created countermeasures."*

Alex and Secilia glanced at each other.

"Excuse me, Director Azriel… but are you saying Custodes Daemonium intended to have Brian—their War

Maiden—become Anthony's bondmate all along?" asked Secilia.

Director Azriel scoffed. *"Obviously. Do you think Custodes Daemonium would be stupid enough to send an inexperienced girl to fight against an incubus? She was obviously a sacrificial lamb. Her entire purpose is likely to become a chain that binds the incubus to them. Now that she has become his bondmate, they have a means of controlling him through her."*

Secilia clenched her hands into fists as she listened to Director Azriel. Something throbbed inside of her chest. Her heart beat to an angry staccato rhythm as she thought about how everyone was trying to use Anthony for their own ends. However, beyond her anger was guilt, because she knew that she was no better than Custodes Daemonium or Director Azriel.

"Because you failed to seduce the incubus, your mission has changed," Director Azriel continued. *"You are to kidnap the incubus and smuggle him out of Academy Island. I will be sending a team to infiltrate Academy Island. While capturing him will be left to you, they will help you smuggle him out."*

"You want… me to capture Anthony?" Secilia gawked at Director Azriel.

"That's not a problem, is it? You might have failed to seduce him, but I hear you and he are still quite close. He trusts you. It wouldn't be hard to invite him over and slip a drug into his drink when he's not looking. He might be an incubus, but even he's not immune to drugs and poison." The director's eyes narrowed. *"Or is it that you don't want to do this? Could it be that you've fallen for him? You do know what will happen should you fail, right?"*

Secilia gritted her teeth as her eyes stung with tears. The image of a woman with black hair, pale skin, and brown eyes just like hers appeared within her mind. She clenched her teeth as the vision disappeared. Yes, she knew what would happen if she failed.

"If you don't want Professor Luna to die, then you will do as I say. The support team will arrive within the next two days. Once you make contact with them, the operation will begin. Do not fail me."

The holographic image disappeared, and with it, Secilia's mask finally caved. She fell onto the floor and gritted her teeth as tears poured down her face. Several sobs racked her body, causing her shoulders to shake.

Alex said nothing as she cried. He knew there was nothing he could say to make this situation better.

"I hate that man," Secilia mumbled between her clenched teeth.

"The Boss is definitely not what I'd call a good person," Alex agreed. "If he was a good person, I doubt he'd be so willing to break international laws on cloning." Alex ran a hand through his hair as Secilia sniffled several times, wiped the tears from her eyes, and stood up. "So what are we going to do?"

"What else can we do?" asked Secilia with a resigned sigh. "If I don't do what Director Azriel says, he's going to kill Professor Luna. She's practically my mother. I can't let anything happen to her. Even if…" Secilia clenched her teeth as she struggled against the self-disgust and loathing writhing inside of her. "Even if it means… betraying Anthony."

As she finished speaking, her voice breaking, Secilia glanced out the window, at the myriad of tall buildings filling the skyline. Somewhere within this city, Anthony was likely sleeping with Brianna. She hated how that girl had managed to get Anthony before her, despite how she had known him longer. However, more than her jealousy toward Brianna, Secilia hated herself.

Because she was planning to betray the man she loved.

CHAPTER 1

Brianna awoke with a gasp as a powerful jolt of electricity raced through her body. It wasn't electricity in the sense that she'd been struck by lightning, or the kind that came from sticking your finger in an outlet. This powerful feeling that washed over her in waves was nothing more than pure pleasure.

A shudder traveled through her body, causing the muscles in her thighs to clench, her buttox to flex, and her toes to curl. Sheets of fabric became wedged between her toes as she clenched them, riding out the waves of electric pleasure flowing through her body. She felt her pussy twitch erratically as her juices flowed down her inner thighs, though it was all lapped up by what felt like someone's tongue.

Without conscious thought, she lifted her hips off the bed and ground her vagina against whatever was making her feel such insatiable pleasure. There was something inside of her. She could feel it curling inside of her love canal, caressing her walls with a gentle yet powerful touch that made her mind whiteout from pleasure. She cried out as she came hard.

"Ha… ha… ha…"

Once the moment of utter bliss had passed, Brianna slumped onto the bed, gasping and panting. She blinked several times and stared at the white ceiling. It was the ceiling to her bedroom of her new apartment, which had become familiar to her in the last two weeks she'd lived there. However, the ceiling was not what she was really interested in.

A soft kiss on her inner thigh forced Brianna to lift her tired head. Her neck felt sore, but she ignored it. A pair of bright brown eyes staring at her from between her legs.

"Anthony…" she muttered in a breathless voice.

Still smiling, he kissed her leg once more, then slowly climbed up her body. Brianna bit her lip to stifle her moan as he placed a kiss on the hairless area just above her vagina, then on her stomach. She could feel her abdominals shudder as he planted butterfly kisses all the way up her body until he reached her breasts. He didn't go for her chest, however. After placing one kiss in the middle of her breasts, he crawled up until they were nose to nose.

"Good morning," he said before leaning down and claiming her lips.

Despite how she could taste herself on his lips, Brianna didn't even hesitate to kiss him back. The kiss wasn't passionate. Gentle and soft, loving and tender, Anthony let his lips linger over hers as if reluctant to part. He did eventually. Staring into his eyes, Brianna could not help but feel like she was getting sucked into them, even as her body told her she needed at least another hour of sleep.

"You okay?" he asked, suddenly appearing concerned as if he could sense her feelings.

"I'm fine," she said. "I'm just a little tired."

Despite how she tried to reassure him, Anthony still looked worried. "D-did I wake you too soon? Do you want to sleep more? The alarm went off, but you weren't waking up, so I thought maybe I should wake you. Ah. But then I was watching you sleep, and, I don't know, I just felt this really intense desire to wake you up with an orgasm come over me. Are you sure you're okay?"

Brianna's lips twitched as she listened to Anthony babble and struggled not to laugh. There was something oddly cute about an incubus incessantly worrying over her like a mother hen.

"You don't have to worry. I'm fine," Brianna assured him. Anthony still didn't look convinced, but he nodded and leaned back a little.

"I'm glad you're okay. In that case, I suppose we should get ready for school," he said.

"We probably should." Brianna glanced at the clock, which read 8:50am. That was a lot later than she normally woke up.

As Anthony sat fully up, something large caressed Brianna's pussy lips. She sucked in a breath as the long, hard object rubbed against her clit before becoming firmly sandwiched between her lips. Looking down revealed the culprit... not that she needed to look down to know what it was. Anthony's dick had been firmly imprinted in her body by this point. She could recognize it simply by touch now.

"Er..." Anthony froze for a moment. "This is..."

"You're definitely an incubus," Brianna murmured. Her cheeks were burning. Even though they had sex so much, she still felt embarrassed every single time.

"Ah ha. Ahahaha... ha..."

Anthony rubbed the back of his head and looked sheepishly at her. She turned her head and tried not to stare.

"Anyway… w-we should probably take care of that," she said, stuttering only a little.

"Ah. Are you sure?"

"I-it's not like we haven't had sex plenty of times before," Brianna tried hard not to stutter. She also tried not to blush. She failed at both. "A-anyway, if we don't take care of that, it will cause problems. What if you walk onto the maglev and a cute girl bumps into you? You might lose all sense of reason and attack her right there. What would you do then?"

"I'm an incubus, not a sexual deviant," Anthony said with a morose frown. He perked up a moment later. "Are you sure it's okay?"

"O-of course I'm sure. Stop asking." Brianna was doing her utmost not to squirm as he gazed at her. She was wet. A warmth spread through her body under his stare, causing her to feel flushed. "I also… can't go out like this."

"Like… this?" Anthony tilted his head.

"I mean… I want it… so… um…"

Anthony blinked several times before his eyes cleared. She assumed he was using their connection as bondmates to understand what she meant without her needing to tell him. It was one of the perks that came from having an incubus boyfriend, she guessed.

A smile appeared on his face again as he leaned over, until his mouth was so close to her ear she could feel his warm breath hitting it. A shudder ran through her body. The shuddering intensified when she felt the tip of his cock rub against her pussy lips.

"I'm putting it in now," he whispered, his breathing suddenly turning ragged with desire.

Brianna didn't say anything, couldn't say anything as she felt her own desires for Anthony surge through her, so she just nodded.

She felt her lips being spread open seconds later as something long, hard, and hot entered her pussy. Brianna released a low moan as the intrusion caused her walls to expand to accomodate for it. A moment later and she felt Anthony's hips connect with hers. They were one.

He didn't move, not right away, which allowed her a moment to just bask in the feeling of being filled. When they were connected like this, Brianna felt like she was connected with him in more than just a physical sense, like she could feel his soul melding with hers.

Once Anthony allowed her body time to adjust, he began moving, rocking his hips back and forth with a steady motion that quickly picked up the pace. Brianna heard her voice involuntarily come out. It mixed with the sounds of Anthony's grunts and the slapping of their hips. She cried out his name, cried out incoherent words that made no sense, and just cried out.

Sweat broke out on her body as Anthony made love to her. Her sweat mixed with his and created a slick lubricant. Their bodies rubbed together in a passionate embrace. Her nipples felt extremely sensitive at that moment. Anthony's chest was rubbing against hers, causing her nipples to feel as if electricity was shooting through them.

"Ha… ahn… Ha! Ha!"

Brianna didn't even tell her legs to move as she wrapped them around Anthony's waist, locking them at the heel and pulling him deeper into her burning passage. It was hot. Her body felt like a furnace. His dick felt like it was knocking on the entrance to her womb. She felt so stuffed. It was almost too much.

"Shit, Brianna," Anthony grunted as his face scrunched up in pleasure. "I can't... get over... h-how amazing it feels to... to be inside you."

If Brianna wasn't already blushing, that would have done it. She cried out as he thrust again. Her vagina felt like it was both sucking him in and pushing him out at the same time. The feeling of his dick rubbing against her insides, stirring up her juices, was enough to leave her breathless.

"D-do you really like it?" she asked, panting.

"Mmm. I love it."

Brianna wanted to let him know that made her happy. A warm burst of feelings flowed through her thanks to his words. Yet before she could actually say them, Anthony reached down and pressed his fingers against her clit while still thrusting his dick inside of her. At that moment, she felt something else filling her body. Thick ropes of cum.

Releasing a loud cry, Brianna's mind went white once more as pure ecstasy raced through her body. She barely even realized what she was doing as she pulled Anthony down into a passionate embrace and kissed him, pushing her tongue into his mouth and stirring up saliva between them. She didn't even care that their saliva was flowing into her mouth. She drank the sweet nectar and continued caressing his tongue like she was trying to play tug of war.

The moment soon passed. Once her orgasm ended, Brianna's legs and arms went limp as exhaustion hit her. She stared at Anthony, who was now leaning over her, his breathing heavy and his face coated in sweat. Sighing in content, she pulled him close and closed her eyes. She was so tired...

"Ah! Wait! Don't fall asleep, Bri! We have school! Bri?! Brianna?!"

****

"Are you sure you're okay?" Anthony asked as he stood beside Brianna on the maglev. The magnetic transportation vehicle was such a smooth ride that not even the warm coffee in Brianna's hands were spilled as the vehicle stopped.

A flood of people exited the maglev after the doors opened; while this emptied the place out a bit, it wasn't long before an even greater flood came in. Anthony and Brianna were forced to move off to the side and toward the back as six or seven dozen people stepped into the maglev.

Because they were in such close proximity, practically chest to chest now, Brianna's scent filled Anthony's nose. Her hair was still wet from her rushed shower. She hadn't even had time to do more than comb it. Light droplets of water gave it a glossy sheen.

"I already told you, I'm fine," Brianna said, sounding annoyed.

Anthony recognized he'd probably asked her this question too many times already. He was sure Brianna was bothered by his constant pestering, but he really was worried.

This morning when they were traveling to the maglev station, Brianna had tripped over her own two feet. When they made it to the station, she'd forgotten to insert her ticket into the ticket booth and rammed her knees into the gate. There were still slight bruises on her knees to show for it. She'd also nearly missed the step when getting on the maglev. The girl might have fallen on her face if he hadn't caught her.

Brianna was a War Maiden for Custodes Daemonium. She had been extensively trained in combat and carried a grace that he'd never seen matched by anyone. Even Lilith, who had been well-versed in many forms of combat, did not have this girl's grace. That was why seeing her trip and walk into things worried him.

Since Brianna was getting annoyed, he decided to change topics. "It's your first day of attending a regular high school, right? Are you nervous?"

"Maybe a little," Brianna admitted, her body relaxing as she leaned slightly against him. "Custodes Daemonium does have schools that we attended, but none of them are what I would call normal. Of course, we take all the regular classes a normal high school would, but everyone there is also training to become either a War Maiden, a Magic Warrior, or an Assault Magician. Instead of talking about things normal people talk about, students often discuss the finer points of combat and magic." Brianna paused a little, tilted her head, and sighed. "Of course, there were a few girls who I think talked about normal girl stuff, like what boys they liked and what bands they were following, but I was not a part of that crowd."

"You didn't want to join them?" asked Anthony.

"It's not that I didn't want to." Brianna frowned. "It's that I couldn't."

The maglev once again stopped and numerous people got off while just as many got on. It felt like the amount of space available had shrunk. Anthony and Brianna didn't move from their small little corner.

"Why couldn't you?" he asked.

"Because I was… special," Brianna said with a heavy sigh. "Or something like that. While the other students did get to live a relatively normal life, I had been personally selected by Instructor Noel to become her apprentice. When I wasn't attending classes, I was either receiving personal training from her or traveling with her to experience her job firsthand. I never really had time to be a normal girl."

Anthony carefully studied Brianna's facial expression, which didn't seem to contain any anger or sadness. Through their bond, he could feel that she truly wasn't angry at her circumstances, but he also felt a small sliver of regret inside of this girl.

"Then it sounds like this is a good opportunity to try being normal for a change," Anthony said at last.

Brianna looked startled by his words. She blinked her large green eyes at him, registered his words, and then finally smiled. She nodded once.

"Yes, I suppose it is."

The train stopped again, and this time, it was Anthony's turn to sigh.

"Looks like this is my stop," he said.

"I'll see you when you get home," Brianna told him.

"Yeah. Be careful on your way to school. Don't trip over any feet or run into a gate."

"I-I won't do that!" Brianna snapped, her cheeks flushing a shade of deep scarlet to match her hair. When all Anthony did was look at her knees, still bruised from when she'd slammed them into a gate, the girl turned her head. "Jerk."

Giving the girl a smile and a kiss goodbye, Anthony walked out of the maglev doors.

***

Brianna slumped against the maglev wall as it began moving again. Pressing her head to the glass, she stared out the window, watching the city speed past her.

Anthony's worry wasn't unwarranted, which was why she had put up with his mother hen-like nagging. She was tired. Exhausted even.

Brianna had always been a punctual person. Sure, she had low blood pressure in the morning, but it wasn't like that ever stopped her from waking up at the first rays of morning light. Never in her life had she slept through her alarm clock like she had this morning. To her, this was a sign that she needed to speak with Lucretia Incanscino, and soon.

Her stop didn't arrive until four more stops. When it did, she hefted her music case over her shoulder and proceeded out of the maglev, stepping onto the platform and walking toward the gate. She was fortunate the exit didn't require the use of a ticket.

Having already been to the school once when she registered, it didn't take her more than fifteen minutes to find her way.

Academy Island First National Academy was composed of four large buildings connected via a series of walkways. The buildings were not tall, consisting of only three stories, but what they lacked in height, they made up for in width and length.

As she walked across a bridge separating her school from a small park, she watched the many other students traveling alongside her. Most of them walked in groups. A couple of girls giggled as they traveled past her. A group of boys stared at her as she walked past them, their eyes trailing after her and making her a little uncomfortable, though she knew they likely didn't mean anything by it. There must have been several thousand students.

What really shocked Brianna wasn't how many students there were. It was how many of those students weren't human.

She had grown up in a city controlled by Custodes Daemonium, and while they were not human supremacists, the vast majority of people who lived in the city were humans. Demons generally preferred to live in places ruled by other demons. Academy Island was one of the few exceptions as it had both demons and humans living together in what seemed like perfect harmony.

Out of the corner of her eye, she glanced at a young human boy and a vampire girl as they walked hand in hand. It seemed they were a couple. She didn't know what they were talking about, but the pair were both smiling. A little ways over, two therianthrope boys were chatting amicably with a group of mostly humans. Everywhere she looked, humans were mixed with demons.

The first thing Brianna did after reaching the school was to head for the main office. She walked down the halls filled with people, traveled up three flights of stairs, and reached a basic sliding door. It was made of duranium, as were most doors, so she didn't knock. She pressed a button embedded into the wall next to it, which caused the door to slide open with a soft hiss.

As she stepped into what appeared to be a lobby, Brianna walked up to a desk that blocked off about two-thirds of the room. Beyond the desk were several people sitting at computer stations. A hallway on the other side featured several doors.

"Excuse me?" she said to the woman manning the front desk.

The woman looked up, her longer than normal ears wiggling as she studied Brianna with bright golden eyes. Her features were perfectly symmetrical and were complemented by her glossy black hair. Lush red lips and a full chest further enhanced this woman's allure. Even in a professional business suit, the woman before her contained a sexuality that even Brianna had trouble ignoring.

A succubus. A low-level one, but still a succubus.

"Can I help you?" asked the woman.

"Yes. I'm a new student here. This is my first day," Brianna said. "I was told I should come here before going to my class…"

"Ah." The woman's eyes lit up. "You must be Brianna. Hold on one moment while I get everything you need."

As the woman stood up, walked down the hall, and entered one of the doors, Brianna remained standing where she was. The wait was, fortunately, not long. Seconds after the succubus left, she came back with what appeared to be a tablet of some sort. It wasn't very big. She could probably fit the device in her pocket.

"This is yours." The succubus placed the tablet on the counter in front of Brianna. "This tablet is your student ID, but it's also much more than that. It has a number of apps that you can use, including a map in case you get lost. All of your textbooks are also on this tablet. You can even access our school's library through it."

"Thank you," Brianna said as she picked up the tablet.

"Also, you should know that we do not accept money as payment at this school," the woman continued. "Students pay for everything using merit points. Everyone gets a certain amount of merit points monthly, but you can also earn them by getting good grades, committing to extra curricular activities, and earning achievements. This is another reason you need your student ID. All your merit points are recorded on it, so be sure not to lose it."

"I won't lose it," Brianna said.

"Good." The succubus brightened after explaining everything. "In that case, I recommend heading to your next class. You've already missed first period. You can find out which classroom is yours by accessing your class schedule and selecting the tab titled 'Courses.' Your current password is @cad3my. I recommend you change it when you get the chance."

"Thank you."

After leaving the main office, Brianna turned on her tablet, which opened to a login screen. She entered her student ID, then her password. Her home screen appeared. The first thing she did was click on the settings and change her password from @cad3my to @nth0ny. It was a simple password, but she doubted anyone would figure it out since no one knew about him. After that, she accessed her class schedule application, then selected her second class of the day.

Her second class was advanced magical sciences with Dr. Stromm. When she tapped on the class, a map of the school appeared on the screen. There was a small dot on the map that represented her. A line connected the dot to her classroom. It looked like her class was in the same building as the main office, but it was located on the second floor and on the opposite side.

With just a little trepidation, Brianna began her walk to class.

She hoped her first day went well.

***

Ever since Brianna became his bondmate, the people around Anthony began treating him differently. Men were more aggressive and open about their hatred of him, and women finally began to notice him.

Because he was an incubus, Anthony's body was constantly producing and releasing pheromones that attracted members of the opposite sex and repulsed those of the same sex. As he jotted down notes in Professor Incanscino's class, the result of his pheromones became all the more obvious.

"While S-class Magic Catastrophes are considered untreatable because of the size of the Magic Catastrophe and the amount of power that was used to cause it, Magic Catastrophes that are A-class and below are generally considered treatable depending on what the Magic Catastrophe entails. A good example of this is the Death Knoll Epidemic. A powerful magical disease swept over a small town called Knoll in the Americas, killing around ten thousand people. A group of magicians from the Mages Association managed to find a cure and eradicated the disease using a large-scale magic formula. However, the scale of the magic circle was massive and it took over one thousand magicians to activate it, which just goes to show you how powerful an A-class Magic Catastrophe is. S-class Magic Catastrophes are magnitudes larger and more potent. Thus far, there hasn't been a single person or group who has managed to fix one. Fortunately, S-class Magic Catastrophes are so rare there's only been one in the last fifteen years."

Professor Incanscino stood on her platform and lectured them about Magic Catastrophes, referencing specific Magic Catastrophes that had been solved and highlighting how they were resolved through a combination of science and magic, dubbed magical science for short. While the lecture was interesting, Anthony was well-aware that barely anyone was paying attention.

He turned his head slightly and looked at the young woman sitting next to him. She was staring at him with a dreamy gaze like she was caught in a trance. Even after she realized he had caught her staring, she didn't stop. The smile on her face widened as the red hue spread from her cheeks to the rest of her face and even some of her neck. She batted her eyes at him.

Several seats down, a young man was glaring at him with a look of such loathing it was a wonder the boy's eyes hadn't turned into laser beams and pierced Anthony's heart. The amount of hatred rolling off the other student was palpable. It looked like he was just barely containing himself from leaping over the table and throttling Anthony.

If they were the only people staring at him like this, maybe Anthony could have ignored it, but it seemed as if everyone was doing it. He felt eyes on him from the entire classroom. It was disconcerting.

Professor Incanscino's lecture eventually ended. In his haste to remove the gazes from him, Anthony quickly put away his laptop and slung his bag over his shoulder. He went down the stairs two at a time and traveled to the door. Just before he could leave, however, Professor Incanscino called out to him.

"I'd like a moment of your time, Mr. Amasius."

Anthony struggled against his desire to leave with his desire to stay. He eventually sighed, turned around, and walked over to Professor Incanscino. He climbed up the stairs onto the lecture platform.

The small blonde woman took a step back as he closed the distance, but she didn't give any other indication of being uncomfortable. Her calm expression remained the same as always.

Everyone else left the room. Yet even though the other students were gone, his professor didn't say anything at first.

"You needed something from me?" asked Anthony, deciding that if she wasn't going to start this conversation, he would.

"I need you to get those pheromones under control," Professor Incanscino said at last. "I don't think I need to tell you this, but your very presence is having an adverse effect on people. Even I can feel them affecting me. If you don't do something about it soon, it's going to cause a lot of problems."

"I know." Anthony sighed and ran a hand through his hair. "And I would love to rein these pheromones in, but I don't know how to stop them from leaking out."

"Have you even tried?" asked Professor Incanscino.

"Well, no…" Anthony said at last, feeling a little embarrassed.

"You are an incubus, Anthony. Those powers you have belong to you, so you should instinctively know how to keep them under control." Professor Incanscino wore a patient stare, but Anthony had the most unusual feeling that she was restless. "I suggest you start by closing your eyes and picturing your pheromones disappearing. If it helps, try to visualize your pheromones as a type of pollen that constantly surrounds you. Imagine your body acting like a black hole and sucking the pollen back inside of you. Go on. Try it."

Anthony knew better than to disobey his diminutive professor. Furthermore, he wanted to control this power. He honestly hated all the stares he received from people. The lustful looks from the women and the hateful glares from the men equally annoyed him. If he could get these pheromones under control, he could put a stop to both.

He closed his eyes and did as instructed, visualizing the pheromones his body constantly released as pollen or spores. Once he had the image in his mind, he bit his lip, then changed the mental image of his body into a black hole that sucked all the pollen back in.

At that moment, a strange suction force seemed to emit from his body. Nothing seemed to change on the outside, not visually, but Anthony could feel something entering him. It felt like thousands of small motes of mana were being infused into his body. It was a little like when he and Brianna had sex, and the mana produced from their passionate act entered him, except this was slightly different. It wasn't as pleasurable for one. There was also the fact that he didn't feel more powerful.

"I think that did it," he said, opening his eyes to stare at Professor Incanscino. "How is that?"

"Much better." Professor Incanscino nodded, her blonde ringlets swaying as a very slight smile appeared on her face. "See? I knew you could do it. And now you won't have to deal with the hateful and lustful stares from your peers."

"Thank you for your help, Professor," Anthony said with a smile.

Professor Incanscino waved away his thanks. "You're welcome. Now get out of here. You still have more classes."

"Yes."

Anthony left Professor Incanscino's classroom and made his way to his next class. Just as the professor had said, none of his classmates seemed to sense something was wrong with him. Of course, he still received a few stares, but they were much more manageable.

When the first half of his classes ended, Anthony traveled to Building #2, the shopping center filled with shops and places to eat. He found himself sitting at a table in a small restaurant called Italiano Pizzeria. Eating a personal pizza, he thought about his classes and the reason he was taking them.

Anthony had entered university in order to become a doctor who specialized in Magic Catastrophes. His ultimate goal was to find a way to bring his younger brother out of a coma. However, he was beginning to wonder if any of his classes would help him.

Calvin Amasius had been in a coma for over a year now. He was residing at the Academy Island Hospital for Magical Catastrophes, which was one of the best hospitals to treat Magic Catastrophes and other magical maladies. However, even though the hospital had some of the best minds working there, none of them knew anything about what was happening to him. If the best doctors couldn't heal his brother, then would learning the same things they had learned really help him?

"Someone is looking down," a voice suddenly said.

Anthony looked up to find a dark-haired woman dressed in fashionable clothes standing before him. Her long legs were visible beneath her short skirt, covered in black stockings, and her sleeveless shirt and jacket combo made her look quite sporty. Pink lips that looked more than a little kissable were curled into a delightful expression.

Despite still feeling a little depressed, he was able to push it aside and smile.

"Secilia. I haven't seen you in a while. I was almost afraid you were avoiding me."

"Maybe I was avoiding you," Secilia said as she sat down in the chair across him from.

"Is it because of Brianna?" asked Anthony.

"What do you think?"

"I think it is."

"Then why ask if you already know the answer?"

At the woman's snappish reply, Anthony took the time to study his friend further. He hadn't noticed it at first, but she was wearing a lot more makeup than normal. Secilia was a woman whose natural beauty was such that she didn't really need makeup. The most he'd ever seen her wear was a little eyeliner, some foundation, and lip gloss. Now she looked like she'd packed on several dozen different kinds of makeup.

He considered asking her about it, but given her snappish replies so far, he didn't think that would be a good idea.

"So where have you been the last few days?" he asked instead.

"Just working," Secilia replied. "The company I work part-time for needed me to take part in a large project. We're actually still not done. I was just given some time off because I've been working so hard."

Maybe it was because his powers as an incubus had grown, but he had the distinct feeling that Secilia was not being completely honest with him. Once again, he thought about saying something, and once again he decided not to. Her personal life was hers. He didn't want to be one of those nosy busybodies.

"Sounds tough."

"You don't know the half of it," Secilia groaned as she grabbed a slice of his pizza. "I really can't stand the director. He's a complete sack of shit. If it wasn't for the fact that he's my boss and not someone I can afford to offend, I would have told him to shove his orders up his ass a long time ago."

As Secilia began griping about her boss and how much her work sucked, Anthony wondered if there was anything he could do for her. It sounded like his friend had a lot of pressure and expectations being placed on her. If possible, he would like to alleviate her burden.

Once this thought occurred to him, another thought took its place.

Secilia was a gorgeous young woman, and he had always been attracted to her, but he'd never confessed how he felt because he didn't want to betray Lilith. Now that he'd already taken that final step with Brianna, the chains keeping him from confessing were no longer there. He could tell her how he felt. What's more, if he confessed and she returned his feelings, he could bring up his nature as an incubus and ask if she would be willing to become his bondmate.

He was a little worried. Even if she accepted and agreed to become his bondmate, he would have to tell her about Brianna. He couldn't just bind this woman to him without letting her know what she was getting into. However, at the very least, he wanted to talk with her about this and ask if she'd be willing to accept.

"Hey, Secilia?" he said suddenly when Secilia paused between rants to catch her breath. She had at some point switched from ranting about her boss to complaining about her classes.

"What is it?" she asked.

"Do you want to go on a date with me this weekend?"

"Huh?"

Anthony did not think he would ever forget the flabbergasted expression on Secilia's face as he asked her on a date for the first time ever.

This was going to be one memory he cherished for a long time. A *very* long time.

CHAPTER 2

"Your hair is so gorgeous! I wish my hair was that vibrant!"

"What sort of skin products do you use to maintain such silky smooth skin?"

"Do you have a boyfriend?!"

"Can I be your boyfriend?!"

Brianna did not know what to think as she was bombarded with questions left, right, and center.

She was sitting at her new desk, which was located in the back near the window, but she couldn't move from the desk because all the other students were crowding around her.

It was lunch time now. She should have been hurrying down to the cafeteria so she could grab a bite to eat, but instead she was stuck trying to politely answer the many questions being thrown her way. Of course, some of those questions were downright invasive. On top of trying to maintain her calm facade and be polite, she was also struggling with her desire to cut a few of them down with her Geminius Sword.

"Okay, everyone! Stop harassing the new girl!" a voice suddenly shouted.

Everyone stopped what they were doing and turned to the voice, including Brianna. The person who had spoken was a girl with short brown hair, wolf ears on her head, and a bushy tail sticking out from beneath her skirt. Sharp brown eyes stared at everyone. Despite her wolfish eyes, which looked quite predatory, her face was what Brianna could only describe as cute, like she was looking at a puppy.

For whatever reason, when this girl spoke up, the entire crowd went silent and parted before her like the Red Sea. The wolf girl, a variant of therianthrope known as a werewolf, walked up and held out her hand.

"I'm sorry for the trouble everyone is causing you. It's not often we get new students so late in the year. I'm Hana Ookami. Nice to meet you."

"Brianna. Nice to meet you too."

Brianna reached out and shook the girl's hand. Hana's hand was very warm and rough—not at all what Brianna would have expected from such a cute girl. It felt like she had pads on her hands too.

"Since it's lunch, why don't we go down to the cafeteria?" Hana suggested. "I'll tell you more about the school too."

"Okay," Brianna agreed, partly because she really didn't know what else to do, but also because this girl seemed calmer and more composed than the others. She also wasn't asking Brianna any rude questions.

Brianna stood up from her desk and walked quickly past the other students, following Hana out of the classroom and down the hall.

"Thank you for your help," Brianna said suddenly.

"It's no trouble," Hana replied with an easy-going smile. "Try not to think too harshly of the other students. They are all good people, but I think having such a beautiful new student transfer into their class made them overly excited."

Brianna felt her cheeks burn at being called beautiful. Anthony would often compliment her beauty, but she always felt self-conscious whenever he complimented her, and it seemed these feelings extended to other people as well. Her heart didn't flutter like when he said it. Even so... it was still embarrassing. She guessed she just didn't take compliments very well.

Far bigger than she had expected, the cafeteria was located on the first floor of the main school building. When she and Hana arrived, Brianna could do nothing but gawk as she stared at what must have been thousands of people congregating together, sitting in chairs, laughing, talking, and having a good time with their friends. It was so noisy that she almost wanted to cover her ears.

"Are you not used to seeing so many people?" asked Hana. Brianna could only shake her head. "Was your previous school smaller?"

As Hana directed her toward a large machine with a touch screen, Brianna could only give the other girl a pained smile.

"My school was very small. I don't think it exceeded one hundred people."

"That is small." Hana looked shocked. "What school did you go to?"

"Er..." Brianna hesitated as she wondered what to say since she obviously couldn't tell this girl her school was a special institute operated by Custodes Daemonium. "Um... just a small private school in the Americas."

"Ah, so you're from the Americas." Hana let the machine scan her student ID, then selected one of several meals to choose from. Her student ID beeped again and lit up to show her receipt. "I heard the Americas is pretty chaotic."

"I won't deny that some parts of the Americas are still experiencing a lot of turbulence," Brianna said as Hana stepped aside and allowed her to walk up to the machine. "The Americas is a capitalist nation composed of numerous large-scale corporations. Each corporation controls a specific part of the country. However, they don't much care for the commonwealth beyond what they spend. There are no laws against violence and arms merchants are plentiful, so a lot of gangs have cropped up. This has led to an increase in crime rates. Of course, there are some parts of the Americas that are free of crime, but they're controlled by organizations like Custodes Daemonium. "

"Is that so?" Hana said in a voice that told Brianna she probably didn't care much.

Brianna decided not to focus on the conversation and instead tried to decide on what she should eat. There were a number of different meals to choose from. There was hamburger, pizza, onigiri, curry, various types of salad, pasta —she was astonished at the number of options they had. The school at Custodes Daemonium didn't allow their students to select their meals. All of their food was selected for them based on their personal dietary needs.

Brianna eventually decided to try the curry. When she pressed the button, her screen lit up, displaying the number of merits she now had along with her receipt.

Hana led Brianna to the line, where they waited before getting their food, and then traveled outside of the cafeteria.

Several tables and benches were strewn around the outside. Some of them were full, but it looked like most people preferred eating indoors because there were several tables and benches that were open.

Hana sat at one of those tables, and Brianna followed suit.

"You probably don't know this yet, so I figured I'd tell you a bit about the school," Hana said at last. "This isn't just a high school. We're an escalator school, so we have an elementary, middle, high school, and college. The college campus isn't located here, but the two buildings you see over there belong to the elementary and middle schools respectively. Most of the people in your class have been going to this school since they were six."

"I had no idea," Brianna murmured. "Do you mind if I ask some questions about the school?"

"Feel free," Hana said.

Brianna asked Hana all kinds of questions, from what she could expect from the teachers to whether or not they took any specialized courses.

It seemed that because this school was located on Academy Island, the specialized courses they could take all involved magical engineering, magic theory, and other magic related subjects. There were also advanced science courses that weren't related to magic. However, magic was such an integral part of Academy Island that almost every specialized course dealt with it in some way.

Of course, there were no combat classes. The closest they had to a combat class was gym.

Lunch eventually ended and classes began again. Brianna traveled to her next class with Hana, who fortunately had the same schedule as her. It seemed a lot of students in her class had the same class schedule—the exception being specialized courses such as Robotics and AI Development.

Brianna did her best in each class, answering every question the teachers asked her, but she wondered if maybe she was being too thorough. Everyone stared at her like she'd said something shocking whenever she answered them. Even the teachers looked like they'd been sucker punched. She wondered if maybe explaining trigonometric functions and their relation to advanced magic formulas had been going too far.

Brianna soon found a friend in Hana, who was helpful and did her best to explain everything she needed to know. She was glad to have met someone so knowledgeable. That said, she soon found out that Hana was every bit as nosy as the others. She was just better about hiding it. Out of all the people in their class, she was the only one who hadn't asked her any invasive questions but instead subtly goaded Brianna into talking on her own.

School eventually ended. Brianna walked with Hana to the front gate, chatting with her new friend. However, as they emerged from the gate, Hana stopped walking.

"Is something wrong?" Brianna asked, looking back to find her friend blushing all the way to the roots of her hair as she stared at something in the distance.

The answer did not come from Hana, but from several other girls.

"Hottie at ten o'clock!"

"W-who is that hunk?!"

"I don't know, but… damn. What I wouldn't give to make him mine."

"You are gonna have to get in line."

Brianna looked around to find that, not only was her new friend staring, but several other girls were blushing as they gazed at something as well. It wasn't just girls who were staring either. Boys were glaring hatefully at whatever the girls were staring at.

With a frown, she turned to where all their eyes pointed.

She sucked in a breath.

Anthony was standing not far away. He was leaning against the railing of the bridge that traveled across the street, looking at something on his wristband. She couldn't read the holographic screen that had popped up because she was too far away.

Well, it looked like she now knew why everyone was gawking, but now she couldn't help but wonder what he was doing here.

"Anthony!" she called out.

Several heads turned to her, but she ignored them as Anthony looked up from his holographic screen and smiled at her. She wasn't sure she liked how her knees turned weak when he looked at her with such genuine happiness. Trying to ignore the feeling, she watched as Anthony closed his holographic screen and made his way over to her.

"Hey," he greeted as he reached her, leaned down, and gave her a soft peck on the lips before she could say anything.

His actions caused an uproar. Everyone began chatting all at once. However, so many people were talking at the same time that Brianna couldn't make out what they were saying. Not that it mattered. At that moment, she only had eyes for one person.

"What are you doing here?" she asked.

"You know how when you first started living here, you would always wait for me at the maglev station?" he asked, scratching the back of his head. He looked bashful. She tried to ignore the flutter in her heart as she nodded, and he continued. "Well, I figured I would do the same for you. My classes let out earlier than yours, so I wanted to wait for you and walk home together."

Brianna felt like her chest was going to explode. Her heart was beating so fast. Happiness and embarrassment mixed together to create a truly unusual sensation in her chest.

While she and Anthony were intimate, this was a situation she'd never been in before, so she didn't know what to do. She tried her best to calm down by taking several deep breaths. It didn't really work.

"Are you sure… that's a good idea?" she asked.

When Anthony just looked at her with those bright eyes and that confused face, Brianna almost lost it. How the heck could someone who looked like a male underwear model be so cute? She internally cursed. It was definitely that damn incubus nature of his.

"Ah. You mean…" he trailed off, but she understood.

"Your very presence is already causing problems. Just look around us."

Anthony looked at all the people staring at him, his expression growing even more confused. He furrowed his brow. Looking back at Brianna, he leaned in and whispered in his ear.

"Why is everyone staring at me?"

She gave him an aggrieved look. "Isn't it obvious?"

"But…" He looked even more perplexed now. "I'm controlling my pheromones so they don't leak out, so these people shouldn't be affected by them, right?"

Brianna had not known Anthony was keeping his pheromones from leaking out, but she also couldn't detect them because she was his bondmate. That granted her a form of immunity.

"Even if you're not leaking pheromones, you are still an incubus," she answered.

Anthony looked like he was ten seconds away from pouting. "So I shouldn't come to pick you up anymore?"

The look on Anthony's face made Brianna hesitate to say he should definitely not come to pick her up at school from now on. His expression reminded her of a kicked puppy. It was so pathetic she already wanted to retract her previous statement.

Before she could say anything, however, her new friend grabbed her arm.

"Hey, hey!" Hana tugged on her. "Who is this gorgeous man? How do you know him?"

It seemed that, in the face of a handsome male specimen, even Hana could forget herself.

"Uh…"

Once more, Brianna's mind froze as a new problem occurred to her. How was she supposed to introduce Anthony to her friend? She definitely couldn't tell this girl that she was Anthony's bondmate. Anthony's identity as an incubus was still a closely guarded secret, even if a lot of organizations already knew about him.

"He's, um…"

"I'm her boyfriend," Anthony said, coming to her rescue.

Hana looked from Anthony to Brianna. The look on her face was blank, like she was so astonished that she wasn't even sure what kind of expression she should make. Brianna tried not to squirm at the other girl's stare.

"This is your boyfriend?" Hana finally asked.

"Um… y-yes." Brianna didn't know why she was so embarrassed calling Anthony her boyfriend, but that was exactly what she felt. Supreme embarrassment.

Hana didn't say anything for the longest time, but then she closed her eyes, took a deep breath, and calmed down. When she opened her eyes again, she didn't look as shocked.

"Hello," she greeted Anthony. "I'm Hana Ookami. Brianna and I just met today. I've been showing her around school and helping her get settled in."

"In that case, I owe you my thanks," Anthony said. He smiled. "I was worried Brianna wouldn't be able to fit in. I appreciate you helping her out."

"N-not at all," Hana said, only stuttering a little. "I'm glad I could be of assistance."

Anthony sent Hana one last grateful smile, and Brianna wondered if this man knew what his smiles did to people. He probably didn't. The man didn't even seem to realize that Hana's legs had practically turned into jelly. She knew he was still coming into his own as an incubus, so it was unlikely he fully understood the affects his smile had on members of the opposite sex.

She was going to have to teach him self-awareness.

"Anyway, since school is out, how about we head home?" suggested Anthony as he held out his hand.

Brianna hesitated only for a moment before accepting his hand. She said goodbye to the still weak-kneed Hana, then walked toward the maglev station under the intense stare of numerous men and women.

***

While Anthony said they would be heading home, they didn't actually travel to their apartment complex. They took the maglev to the same stop as their apartment, but after they hopped off, they walked to a park not far from where they lived.

The park didn't have many people present, but there were a few kids playing around. Anthony watched them playing in the sandlot as Brianna led him deeper into the park. There were quite a few trees, though not enough to adequately block everyone's view of them. Brianna eventually stopped when they were what he guessed was somewhere in the middle of the park. He breathed in the scent of grass and tree bark. The soft loam beneath his feet shifted as he adjusted his stance.

"I think this is a good place," she said, setting her music case down and turning to him. "I'm going to create a barrier that will keep people from entering now."

"Okay. I'll keep an eye out and make sure no one runs into us while you're creating it," Anthony said.

"Thank you."

Anthony looked at their surroundings as Brianna opened her music case. The Geminius Sword was located inside, but that wasn't all she had. She reached in and pulled out several flat discs made of stone. When he glanced at them, he could see there was a magic formula on each disc. While he didn't know what they meant, he did know this formula was the cornerstone for the barrier.

There were thirteen discs in total, and Brianna set up each one so they formed a circle, then stepped into the center of the circle and took a deep breath. A strange sensation seemed to fill the air. The hairs on Anthony's neck stood on end as Brianna plunged her Geminius Sword into the ground.

Blue light erupted from around the blade. It quickly turned into thirteen blue lines that traveled from the sword to the discs. As the light hit the discs, each one began glowing brightly before the light they emitted connected to the other discs. Once that happened, a large barrier sprang up around them. It looked like a semi-transparent bubble that emitted a light blue tint.

"I'm really impressed you can create barriers like this," Anthony praised.

Brianna's cheeks turned red. "A barrier like this isn't such a big deal. Any beginner could create one."

"I can't."

"That's because no one taught you. Anyway…" Brianna tried to get her head back on straight. "With the barrier now in place, no one will interrupt us. We can train here to our hearts content."

"Right."

Truth be told, Anthony didn't really want to train, but he knew that he had to if he wanted to be able to protect himself and Brianna. Now that he'd accepted his responsibilities as an incubus, he couldn't afford to languish away. He needed to refine his skills and learn how to control his power.

Standing several yards away from Brianna, Anthony inhaled a slow breath and channeled mana through his body. He could feel a slight tug on his navel as he expended his mana reserves.

The moment his mana began flowing through his body, blue lines appeared on his skin and strength filled his limbs, making him feel dozens of times stronger than he normally felt.

He wasn't the only one who was using physical enhancement magic. Blue lines had also appeared along

Brianna's skin, some of it hidden by her clothes, but the rest visible. They flowed along her arms and legs, disappearing into her skirt, shirt, and socks. However, she soon discarded her shirt and skirt, revealing that underneath her school uniform was her battlesuit.

The battlesuit looked just like a sleeveless and legless black unitard made from leather. It wrapped around her body, conforming to her massive bust, thin waist, and shapely hips. If he looked closely, Anthony could even see her cameltoe. That made it a little hard to concentrate, but he knew now was not the time for that.

"Are you ready?" asked Brianna as she slid her dominant foot forward and raised her hands in what looked like a standard martial arts fighting stance.

"Not particularly." Anthony followed suit, though unlike Brianna with her graceful and obviously well-practiced stance, his was definitely that of a brawler. "But it's not like I have much choice. If I only do things when I'm ready, then I'm afraid nothing would get done."

"That's good enough for me. Here I come!"

Brianna didn't waste time as she rushed towards him, throwing a standard punch the moment she was in range. Anthony raised his arm to block her strike. The power behind her fist was enough to rattle his arm and sent him skidding backwards. Fortunately, they were both using Physical Enhancement. While her strike caused his body to skid across the ground, it didn't hurt like it would have if he wasn't using magic.

Brianna didn't let up after her initial attack was blocked. She took two steps forward and swept her leg up in a powerful kick. Anthony avoided it by leaning back, but then Brianna brought her leg back down just as he was preparing to try and knock her off balance. Her foot grazed his nose. He could have sworn she'd skinned off an epidermal layer of his skin. She had moved her leg so fast he barely had time to realize what was happening, which caused him to stumble backward.

They had barely started fighting, but it was clear to Anthony that Brianna was far better than him. Her movements were smoother, more fluid, and when she struck, she struck hard and without any mercy. It was honestly taking everything he had to keep himself from being defeated.

He raised his arms in a crossguard as Brianna came at him with a punch. However, the punch he expected never came when Brianna opened her fist, grabbed his arm, and pulled him toward her. Now off balance, he had no method of guarding against the woman as she struck him with an open palm to the chest.

A dull thud echoed through the barrier as Anthony stumbled backward, gasping as he raised a hand to his chest. That had actually hurt despite his physical enhancement magic. As he tried to rub the pain out, Brianna stared at him with a stern frown.

"Your reaction time is way too slow," she told him. "Whenever I attack, it always takes you a second to react, and by then, I'm already hitting you with my next attack, meaning all you can do is guard against me. You have to increase your reaction time. Rather than simply guarding against my attacks, plan out how you're going to counter once you've successfully blocked me."

"That's a lot easier said than done," Anthony said. "You attack way faster than anyone I've ever fought against."

"Which is why we're sparring," Brianna said. "If you can successfully fend me off, then you should be able to defeat anyone who doesn't have extensive combat training. I might only be a trainee, but I've fought and defeated plenty of demons in single combat before."

"I understand." Anthony raised his hands in a boxing guard. "In that case, feel free to come at me again."

"That's my plan."

Brianna rushed forward, moving into his guard and launching a sweeping kick that nearly caught him by surprise. He raised his arm and took the attack. It was strong. He nearly stumbled but placed his left foot against the ground and used it to stabilize himself.

Anthony tried to grab ahold of Brianna's leg so he could counter her, but the woman had already retracted her leg. She set it on the ground, then snapped off another kick with the same leg barely a second later. Anthony guarded against that too, but this kick was a mere snapkick, so quick he couldn't counter. As she set her foot back on the ground again, she spun around and Anthony was unable to respond in time as the heel of her right foot crashed into his chest.

He gasped and stumbled back even more. Yet even though her attack had hurt, this time, he managed to grab her leg before she could retract it. With a grunt, he lifted Brianna off the ground and tried to throw her back down. Brianna responded by contorting her body. She placed her hands on the ground, used them to soften her fall then launched a kick at Anthony's face. He was able to avoid it by moving back, but he also had to let go of Brianna's leg.

Rather than let her regain her balance, Anthony went on the attack. He wasn't much of a kicker. He came in with a basic boxing combination that, unfortunately, Brianna managed to avoid with what looked like ease.

"You're telegraphing your attacks," Brianna informed him as she used her palm to redirect his punch. She then lashed out with her other hand, striking him in the torso. The dull thud of the impact echoed around them. "If you telegraph your attacks like this, even a beginner will know when to dodge."

Anthony grunted as he stumbled yet again. He took a deep breath and waded back in so he could continue sparring with her.

"How do I not telegraph my attacks?" he asked as he threw a straight jab at her face. Brianna avoided it by twisting her body to the side and redirecting his attack with her palm.

"The first thing you should do is stop looking at where you're going to attack," she advised as she threw several lightning quick jabs in his direction. He backed away before they could strike. Fortunately, she didn't have a long reach. "Whenever you attack me, you look at where you're planning to attack first. If you have to look at something, look at the area just above the chest. When someone is about to throw a punch, they will normally telegraph it by moving their shoulder."

"The area above the chest. Moving their shoulder to telegraph their attacks. Got it."

Anthony tried to do as she suggested, but he soon realized there was a problem with that. Brianna was currently wearing her skintight battlesuit, and while it seemed this thing had an inbuilt bra to keep her breasts from jumping all over the place, it didn't change the fact that her chest was pretty large.

As an incubus, Anthony had a naturally high libido. Unfortunately, this also meant he was easily distracted by boobs.

He paid for it when she punched him in the nose.

"Crap damn it!" Anthony winced as he touched his nose, which wasn't broken but still hurt. He glared at Brianna with tears in his eyes. "That really hurt."

"Don't be such a baby." Brianna rolled her eyes. "This is nothing. When I was being trained by Custodes Daemonium, it wasn't all that unusual for me to have my bones broken."

"Ugh… they sound like brutal people." He sighed and straightened out before adopting a fighting stance again. "Okay. Let's do this again."

Brianna smiled. "I'm glad you're so determined. Let's keep sparring."

Anthony was not sure how long they fought for, but by the time he was done, his body felt like a giant bruise. Brianna hadn't gone easy on him at all.

He limped his way into Brianna's apartment, groaning as he leaned down to remove his shoes. The door shut behind him and a soft beep of the lock activating issued from the door. Brianna removed her shoes more easily than he did his, then stepped further into her living room, once more dressed in her school uniform.

"I have some healing cream," she told him. "You should take off your shirt and sit on the couch while I get it."

"Yeah. Okay."

Anthony did as she suggested. Meanwhile, Brianna went into her hallway and wandered into the bathroom. As he sank onto the soft mattress of the sofa, he leaned forward and tried not to wince. Most of the damage done was to his front, but Brianna had slipped around him with her insane speed and gotten a few punches into his back. She had also been fond of knocking him to the ground with leg sweeps.

Brianna came out with a small canister, which she set on the coffee table. A light green cream was inside.

She knelt before Anthony, scooped some cream onto her fingers, and dabbed it onto his chest. It stung at first. Anthony released a soft hiss as Brianna's mere touch caused pain, but then she began rubbing the cream into his skin, and a cold numbness swept across his body. He sighed in relief.

"This healing cream sure is something," he muttered.

"It's made by Custodes Daemonium," Brianna said. "It uses a unique blend of herbs that have been genetically modified with magic to enhance their healing properties. You can only get these herbs at our headquarters too. No one else knows how to grow them."

"That so? I guess an international organization like Custodes Daemonium would have all the good stuff."

As Brianna continued applying the cream, Anthony looked down at her breasts, which were still completely covered but also completely visible. His mouth felt a little dry. As he continued to stare, his pants grew tight as his dick became hard.

Brianna didn't fail to notice.

"So even this turns you on?" she asked, her cheeks growing red.

"I-I can't help it," he muttered, looking away.

She sighed. "I guess... being easily turned on is not something you can help."

"Why do I feel like you just insulted me?"

"I-I didn't. Please don't misunderstand. I didn't mean that as an insult."

"Relax. I'm just teasing."

"T-that's kind of mean..."

Brianna paused for a moment as though considering something, then reached behind her back and undid the zipper of her battlesuit. She slid the suit off her shoulders and peeled it down until her breasts were visible. When Anthony saw her large tits with their light pink nipples, he couldn't stop his dick from growing even harder, until it was literally pushing against his pants.

"You really are horny," Brianna muttered.

"S-sorry about that."

"I'm not… complaining or anything, though it is going to cause a problem if we continue like this."

"What?"

"Nothing."

Brianna reached out and grabbed the zipper to Anthony's pants. She unzipped them and undid the buttons, then helped him shimmy out of them, pulling them and his boxers down until they were hanging around his knees.

His dick now free, Anthony felt a slight chill as the cool air hit his burning cock, but the feeling only lasted for a moment before Brianna leaned down and took him into her mouth. He groaned at the warm and wet sensations traveling through his cock.

Brianna couldn't take all of him into her mouth. Removing his dick, she leaned down further and pressed her tongue against his shaft, lathering it in saliva. Anthony gritted his teeth as his breathing grew heavy. The feeling of her small, soft tongue running against his dick was unbelievable. He wanted to cum right then and there.

However, Brianna leaned back after thoroughly coating his dick in her saliva. He was about to ask why she stopped, but then she grabbed each of her breasts and leaned forward again, this time engulfing his dick in her tits.

"I… I've never… um… I mean, I read about this in an online catalog," Brianna tried to explain as she began rubbing his dick with her breasts. Her face was so red it matched her hair. Her green eyes trembled as she looked up at him, and it was such an unbelievably sexy sight that Anthony had to bite his lip to control himself.

"You don't... even realize how sexy you look... right now," he said through gritted teeth and heavy breathing.

"Do you... like this?" asked Brianna.

"It feels amazing."

"T-thank goodness. I was... a little worried. Then... I'm going to continue."

"P-please do."

Brianna began moving more vigorously, and the sensation of her smooth skin rubbing against him created a feeling that was different from anything he'd felt before but was altogether pleasant. The closest he could think of to this was a handjob. At the same time, this was infinitely more pleasant than any handjob.

Of course, when he said handjob, he was just talking about masturbation. No woman had ever jerked him off before.

Anthony could tell his end was coming. He tried to warn Brianna about it, but his entire body seemed to contract before he could. Brianna let out a surprised shout as thick ropes of cum shot from his dick and got all over her neck, chest, and some of her face.

Anthony slumped back as his muscles relaxed. While he was breathing heavily, Brianna looked down at the cum on her body, and began rubbing it into her skin. She also raised her fingers, now covered in his cum, to her mouth. As she began sucking his cum from her fingers, Anthony felt his dick swelling once more.

"You really are an incubus," Brianna said.

"What's that supposed to mean?" asked Anthony.

Brianna shook her head. "It means nothing. It's just an observation."

Anthony still felt like she was backhand insulting him, but he knew that was just his own thoughts. He could feel Brianna's emotions through their bond.

Reaching for her hands, Anthony pulled Brianna onto the couch and pushed her down until she was lying on her back. Now situated between her legs, his dick was nestled against her lush pussy lips, still covered by her battlesuit.

"Since you've done such a great job pleasing me, I'd like to return the favor," he said.

Brianna looked away as if unable to return his gaze. She nodded once, which was all the confirmation Anthony needed.

It wasn't long before Brianna's cries and moans were echoing through the apartment.

CHAPTER 3

Anthony was a little worried that Brianna might not be sleeping well.

He sat in the maglev as it swiftly traveled along the railing, mindful of the woman using his shoulder as a pillow. Brianna was fast asleep. When he glanced in her direction, he found himself partially mesmerized by her long eyelashes, thin eyebrows, and the way her hair fell about her gorgeous face like scintillating flames wavering in the wind.

The fact that her breasts were pressing into his arm was just a bonus.

There weren't many people on the maglev, a fact that he was grateful for. It meant he could concentrate on controlling his mana properly.

His pheromones were the result of his incredibly strong mana. Like a succubus, when Anthony released his mana without restraint, it created a strong magnetic force that both attracted and repelled.

Of course, he called it a 'magnetic force,' but magnetism had nothing to do with it unless he was talking about animal magnetism. The pheromones he released subconsciously was simply his mana, which contained a very strong intent—that being to attract women and repulse men. Only by controlling his mana and keeping it safely locked away could he stop men and women from reacting to him every time he walked around in public.

It was not long before the maglev stopped, the magnetic clamps locked the maglev down, and the doors opened.

"We've arrived," Anthony said to Brianna.

Brianna might have been sleeping, but it seemed she had been expecting to get off soon. She woke up with a soft groan. As she removed her head from his shoulder, Anthony grabbed her hand, stood up, and gently tugged her along. Brianna followed without complaint. She blinked several times as though ridding the blurriness from her eyes.

"Are you okay?" asked Anthony. Brianna smiled at him, but she didn't say anything. "Bri?"

"I'm… fine, but *we* have a bit of a problem," Brianna said.

The way she emphasized "we" did make him worry a bit, but he decided he would learn what she meant sooner rather than later.

"Is that why we're going to see Professor Incanscino?" he asked.

"Yes," Brianna answered him.

The station they had gotten off at was the one next to his university, the Institution of Magical Sciences. All five buildings loomed over them, visible even from a distance. Of course, they weren't the largest buildings present, but at somewhere around ten stories tall, they were still fairly big.

Anthony and Brianna traveled into building One, entered the elevator in the main lobby, and went all the way to the top floor.

The entrance to the top floor differed from everything else. It looked older, more refined, like something he would have expected to see from the Baroque period or a vampire noble's mansion. Columns decorated the walls along with expensive artwork. While the walk wasn't long until they reached the double doors made from expensive wood, Anthony felt a minor headache. Even now, seeing his professor's ostentatious decorations left him exhausted.

Anthony reached out to knock on the door, but just before he could, the door swung open as if pulled back invisible levers. Brianna shared a look with him before they both walked in.

Professor Incanscino was sitting behind her desk, which looked far too big for such a tiny woman.

Her office also seconded as a living room. A pair of couches sat off to the side with a coffee table in their center, and there was a fireplace several yards behind the couch facing them, though it wasn't a real fireplace but a holographic one.

Most of this room was made of windows, meaning there was a great view of Academy Island's skyline. It was mid-morning right now, so the sun was already fairly high up. It looked like the many buildings off in the distance were being outlined by brilliant rays of sunshine.

"I knew you two would be coming in some time today," Professor Incanscino said. However, it didn't come from the "professor" sitting behind her desk, who continued to diligently work on what he believed was grading reports.

Anthony and Brianna both turned to the two couches. Sitting on one of them was none other than his diminutive professor, whose blonde hair had been articulately styled into ringlets. She was drinking from an expensive tea set, though he knew she wasn't drinking tea. Professor Incanscino only drank black coffee. Dressed in her usual pink and white lolita outfit, her body framed by the light, the doll-like beauty appeared so picturesque that Anthony couldn't help but feel his breath stolen from him.

He didn't show it though.

"You were expecting us?" Anthony asked.

"Of course," Professor Incanscino said as she idly sipped her coffee. "I knew it would only be a matter of time before you two came here."

"And how far into the future did you have to look to know we'd be here?" asked Brianna.

Professor Incanscino smiled at them, but she didn't answer the question and instead gestured for the pair to sit down.

They had no reason to refuse her offer. Anthony might not know what was going on, but he knew Brianna would get to the reason they were here soon.

Anthony sat on the couch with Brianna on his right, though he became just a little startled when Brianna released a slight yawn and leaned into him. Why was she so tired? He'd noticed it before with little things like how she had missed her alarm clock, or how she'd accidentally gotten toothpaste in her eye when they were brushing their teeth this morning. However, he couldn't figure out the reason for it.

"Looks like you two have been having fun these past few days." Professor Incanscino observed Brianna's behavior with a mirthless chuckle. "I see you've gotten the full incubus treatment."

"What is that supposed to mean?" Anthony asked.

"It means Brianna's body is finally experiencing what I like to call orgasmic exhaustion."

"The heck kind of name is that?" asked Anthony.

"Brianna, I believe you should tell him what's going on," Professor Incanscino said. "It wouldn't have as much of an impact if it came from me."

"I-I suppose I should," Brianna muttered with a bitter sigh.

"Tell me what? Is there something I need to know?"

Anthony looked between Professor Incanscino and Brianna, but while the professor just wore a wide smirk, Brianna looked almost pained as she straightened her spine and turned to me.

"Anthony… I don't think I can keep going on like this," she said seriously.

"W-what do you mean? Like this? I'm not sure I understand."

"I… I didn't want to say anything because I thought I could handle it, but I… I mean we… that is…" Brianna lost her confidence midway through whatever speech she'd been planning to make. Stuttering several times, her cheeks turned bright red before she coughed into her hand and continued. "We're having too much sex. My body is… um… I'm afraid we can't continue like this."

Anthony thought he felt something break inside of him. He stared at Brianna in shock, fear, and even a little horror. Her words made it feel like his insides were being shredded apart, mauled by a vicious beast.

"Does that mean… I mean, do you not want to have sex anymore?"

The very thought made him pale. Anthony liked sex. No, he loved having sex, but sex was about a lot more than just pleasure for him. He literally couldn't live without it. As an incubus, his body replenished its reserves of mana through sex.

Of course, sex wasn't his only means of restoring mana. Holding hands, kissing, and being intimate could also accomplish this goal, but sex was what gave him the most mana.

He had noticed that he'd been having sex with Brianna quite often. It wasn't all that unusual for them to have sex two or even three times a day. They generally had it first thing in the morning, when they got home, and just before going to bed. Brianna had never once said anything or asked him to stop, so he assumed she was okay with it. However, what if he was merely projecting his feelings onto her? What... what if she didn't actually like having sex with him?!

"Anthony, whatever you're thinking, I demand you stop it," Professor Incanscino cut into Anthony's internal worrying like a sword cleaving through flesh. "Brianna isn't saying she doesn't enjoy having sex with you, or that she wants to stop. Are you saying that, Brianna?"

"No! Of course not!" Brianna suddenly looked like she was on the verge of panic as she waved her arms back and forth. "T-that's not what I'm saying at all. I really like having sex with you! Er... what I mean is, I enjoy being intimate... with you, so, um, it's not that I don't want to have sex. It's just that I don't think my body can take having it so much."

"Then... you do like having sex with me?" Anthony asked uncertainly but with rising hope. Brianna's cheeks were flushed an intense shade of scarlet, but she nevertheless nodded even as she tried to make herself smaller. Anthony placed a hand against his chest and sighed in relief. "Thank mana."

"You really should be more clear with him," Professor Incanscino said to Brianna.

"That's why I came here," Brianna interjected. "I figured you could explain this better than I could."

"Yes, I can indeed explain this better than you," Professor Incanscino said. "You were right to come here."

"Explain? Explain what?" asked Anthony, now looking confused again.

Professor Incanscino released a weary sigh like his question exhausted her. She set the cup down on a small plate, clasped her hands together, and placed them on her left knee, which she had thrown over her right leg. The act served to draw his eyes to her thigh, hidden by the thick fabric of her dress. He took a deep breath and willed himself to calm down.

If his professor noticed his actions, she didn't let onto it as she said, "Anthony, have you even tried finding another woman to join your harem yet?"

Anthony froze. Professor Incanscino looked like she wanted to smack him.

"I mentioned it before, but one women will never be enough to satisfy an incubus," the diminutive blonde woman began. "While having sex with an incubus does not drain the vitality or life force of a woman, it is impossible for any creature, be they human or demon, to keep up with your race. Brianna has only been your bondmate for about one week, and while her mana is capped, her body is exhausted and unable to maintain its energy."

As he listened, Anthony felt a frown growing on his face. He glanced at Brianna, who looked away, then turned back to Professor Incanscino.

"I guess that explains why she's been making little mistakes in our daily life." He ran a hand through his hair and

sighed. "You are right. I haven't really been trying to find another woman to join my harem, but it's not like finding a person I'd want for a bondmate is easy, you know. If I have to build a harem, I don't want just anyone to join."

"That is a fair point," Professor Incanscino admitted. "However, you're going to have to sooner or later. Brianna is the one who will suffer the most if you don't."

"What do you think about all this?" Anthon turned to the redhead.

"M-me?" Brianna stuttered when he looked at her, then looked down at her hands as she clutched her jeans. "I… knew what I was getting into when I decided to become your bondmate. I knew you'd have to find other women to bond with, so I don't really mind not being your one and only."

"Are you really okay with that?" asked Anthony.

"Yes." Brianna took a deep breath, looked at him, and smiled. "We've already been over this once, but I accepted that I would not be the only woman you are with the moment I decided to become your bondmate. I do not have a problem with it, though I would like it if you consulted with me before adding a woman to your harem. I'd at least like to make sure they meet my approval."

"I understand." Anthony nodded as he placed a hand over Brianna's. "I'll never bond with a woman who hasn't met your approval."

"Thank you," Brianna murmured.

Professor Incanscino watched the two with a complicated expression. Half-amused, half-longing, the look on her face was something Anthony had never seen before.

"In any case, I do know one woman who I think we can add, someone who will meet your approval," Anthony continued.

"You do?" Brianna looked curious when he suddenly mentioned having a potential bondmate.

Anthony nodded. "You've actually met her before. It was the day Professor Incanscino asked us to come to school in order to test my new abilities."

"You mean Secilia," Professor Incanscino said, placing her left leg on the ground and crossing her right leg over it. "She's definitely a good option. Secilia doesn't have any combat experience, but the girl is a mechanical genius with an incredible knack for building complex equipment and hacking. That suit you tried on the first time you sparred with the combat drones were made by her. She is also the one who created the algorithm for the combat drones themselves. You could definitely do worse."

Brianna thought about everything the professor said for a moment before eventually nodding her head. "Okay. I think she is also a good choice. You should approach her soon."

"I will," Anthony said. "Actually, I plan on meeting with her this weekend. I can bring this matter up to her then."

Anthony didn't realize his words were the wrong thing to say until after they had already left his mouth. The temperature suddenly dropped, causing him to shiver as he looked at Brianna, whose face had slowly gone emotionless. Her deadpan stare made him wish he could hide behind his professor.

"I see. You brought her up because you already had plans with her."

"Er…"

"It seems you like to work fast. You didn't even consult with me before asking her on a date."

"That's…"

"Relax." Brianna smiled as the temperature returned to normal. "I'm just kidding."

"Are you?" asked Anthony.

"Yes."

Anthony stared at Brianna, who slowly looked away, unable to maintain eye contact.

***

Anthony stood at the entrance to Santa Clara Central Park—an old park that had been left untouched since before the San Andreas Fault caused a large section of the state once known as California to split off. The park had a large man made pond, an Olympic swimming pool, a recreation center, and even a baseball field. If he looked through the trees, he could see families gathered there.

He tapped on his wristwatch. A holograph screen suddenly appeared over it. This screen was just a clock. It was currently 11:45pm. His date should be arriving soon.

Taking several deep breaths, Anthony tried to steady himself. He was nervous. This was actually the first time Anthony had ever romantically pursued someone. Lilith had chosen him, not the other way around, and he had been on his deathbed when Brianna made the choice to become his bondmate of her own volition. This time, whether or not Secilia became his bondmate would be up to him.

"It looks like someone is deep in thought," someone suddenly said in an amused voice.

Anthony smiled as he turned around. "More like trying to steady my nerves." He paused when he caught a glimpse of the woman who had appeared behind him. "You look… really, really good."

"Do I?" Secilia twirled a long strand of dark hair between her fingers and gave him a coquettish smile.

The shirt she wore possessed no shoulders, allowing for a tantalizing glimpse of both her shoulders and collar bone, but it also possessed a frilly section just below that, which kind of looked like a shoulder cape. Her shirt was a light pink. Meanwhile, she wore jean shorts that showed off a healthy amount of leg. Finishing the outfit were a pair of heeled sandals with white bows on the front.

"You do," Anthony breathed out a sigh of admiration.

Secilia did blush a little, but most of her face was taken up by her smile. "Well, thanks. I'm glad you appreciate the effort I put into looking good for you."

"So you were trying to look good for me?" Anthony teased.

"Obviously." Secilia rolled her eyes. "You asked me out on a date, remember? What woman would go on a date without making sure she looked her best? I'll tell you. None."

"You bring up a good point." Anthony was actually certain there was at least one girl who wouldn't care about such things, but Brianna was something of a special case, and he didn't want to bring up another woman while he was on a date with Secilia.

"I hope you have a plan for our date," Secilia said.

"I have thought of a few things we can do," Anthony admitted. "First, you haven't had breakfast or lunch, right?"

As if to answer his question, Secilia's stomach let out a slight gurgle, causing the woman's cheeks to finally turn red. He grinned. It seemed not even she was immune to being embarrassed over some issues.

"Let's find a place to eat first," he suggested.

"I guess that's fine," Secilia said, locking her arm around his as she regained her composure. "But it had better be someplace nice. I don't want to eat at one of those junkie fast-food chains."

"Well, there goes all my ideas. I guess that means we won't have lunch."

"Don't make me smack you."

"Relax. I know of a few places."

"Not fast-food places, I hope."

"…"

"You really are asking me to smack you, aren't you?"

***

Brianna glared at the dozen war machines surrounding her. All of them looked fairly human, with two legs, two arms, a torso, and a head, but that was where the similarities ended. Made entirely of a bright, silvery metal that gleamed in the blue light of the barrier, these machines had no face. It was just a plate of slightly curved metal.

Channeling mana through her body, Brianna could feel strength flowing through her as she spun her Geminius Sword around in her hand before spreading her feet wide and adopting a defensive stance.

She did not move from her position. When dealing with multiple opponents, it was better to let them come to you.

On some unspoken signal, two of the combat drones charged forward at the same time. The one in front of her sent a probing attack, a straight thrust of its sword, which Brianna redirected with a simple twist of her wrists. Sparks flew along her blade as she forced the simple broadsword over her head, around her body, and into the floor. Then she twisted her body to avoid the attack coming at her from behind. The combat drone behind her had also tried to impale her. It would have impaled its own comrade instead, but both drones had high combat capabilities and logic processing. They were able to move away from each other in time.

Three more combat drones came at her, this time from the left, right, and behind. Brianna decided not to wait for them to reach her. She went after the first one, slamming her sword into it with an overhand slash. Sparks scattered everywhere as her attack struck. However, because she was not using the Gemiunius Sword's key feature, its ability to use spatial magic to severe molecules, her attack didn't actually do any real damage. It still knocked the drone back.

That was one less drone to deal with.

Brianna spun on the balls of her feet, swinging her blade around to parry an attack from the drone on her left, then shifting her grip and maneuvering the blade to counter the drone on her right. Blocking both attacks caused her arms to shake. However, while taking two attacks from powerful machines would have caused most people's arms to go numb, Brianna barely felt it thanks to Physical Enhancement.

She didn't know how long she sparred with these combat drones. Her body moved without conscious thought, attacking, defending, and counter attacking until her body was covered in sweat and her breathing was ragged.

Because she wasn't using the Geminius Sword's magic, she couldn't deal any killing blows to the combat drones. That said, thanks to her physical enhancement magic, several did end up getting dented, and one even had cracks running through its faceplate by the time she was finished.

"At least you didn't outright destroy any drones this time." Lucretia Incanscino waved her hand as she fixed the damaged drones by turning back their time to before they had been damaged. She continued speaking as she did. "I suppose I should be thankful for the little things."

"I remember how you complained about Anthony and I destroying them last time." Brianna walked over to where Professor Incanscino was standing. "I figured I'd show you some courtesy by not getting too rough. Besides, using the Geminius Sword's primary function would have defeated the purpose of coming here."

"Oh? Does that mean you're feeling better?" asked Lucretia Incanscino.

"I was never feeling bad to begin with," Brianna insisted. "I just wanted to get some practice in."

"If saying you don't feel worried and jealous makes you feel better, then we'll go with that." Lucretia shrugged her slender shoulders. "However, you should know that while you can put on a facade, Anthony is likely to see right through it. He might not know exactly what is bothering you, but he can feel when you are agitated through the bond. Since you can't hide your feelings, it is better to be honest—at least with him."

"I'll keep that in mind."

Brianna felt a little miffed by Lucretia's words, though she knew the woman was just speaking the truth. She'd already seen Anthony's ability to read her mood at work. He might not always know what she was thinking, but he always knew when she was happy, sad, angry, or any other number of emotions. If he felt her emotions were unstable but didn't know why, he would simply ask about them.

"I guess I am a little jealous," Brianna admitted after a few moments. "I am Anthony's bondmate, yet he and I have not gone out on a single date. Meanwhile, a girl he hasn't bonded with is getting to go on a date with him. I know this will probably end with Secilia becoming his bondmate, and I am okay with that, but I dislike the fact that she got to go on a date with him first."

"Be sure to let Anthony know that," Lucretia said. "He might know what you are feeling at any given time, but he will never know why unless you tell him. Just like with any relationship, you need to communicate with him."

"I will."

"Still, I am a little surprised," Lucretia continued.

"Surprised? What's so surprising?" asked Brianna.

"I'm surprised that you didn't decide to spy on his date with Secilia," Lucretia said.

"Do you think I'm so petty and incapable that I'd spy on Anthony?" When all Lucretia did was stare at her, Brianna looked away, grabbed her left arm, and awkwardly held it. "I already know how this is going to end, so there is no need for me to spy on them."

"Ah. Yes, that does make sense."

"Besides, I have a familiar following Anthony to make sure nothing happens," Brianna admitted. "It will let me know if Anthony is in danger."

"And you're sure you aren't using it to spy on him from a distance?" asked Lucretia.

"Of course I am sure!" Brianna snapped. Her cheeks felt like someone had lit bonfires on them. "While there are some familiar's that allow you to share senses like sight, hearing, smell, and touch, the one I'm using is just a basic paper familiar. It's only purpose is to let me know if something happens to Anthony. I can't actually see what he is doing."

"Okay. Okay. There's no need to get so upset," Lucretia said.

"I'm not upset."

Brianna felt more weary from this conversation than she did from sparring those combat drones. However, now she also felt a little curious. She studied the small woman and her doll-like appearance, which didn't go unnoticed by the woman in question.

"Something on your mind?" asked Lucretia.

"I was just thinking... you seem to know an awful lot about relationships," Brianna began. "Have you been in a lot of them?"

With something of a mirthless smile, Lucretia shook her head. "I haven't. If you must know, I have only been in a relationship with one person my entire life, and it was a very long time ago."

"Oh." Brianna paused. "May I know how long ago this was?"

"You may not."

"Does that mean it was a *really* long time ago?"

"... Ask me another question like that, and I'll turn back time so much you'll have to wear diapers."

"Yes, ma'am. Sorry, ma'am."

* * *

While eating out was no longer popular thanks to the change in social structure, that didn't no one ever went to restaurants to eat, or that some restaurants didn't flourish.

Society in this day and age thrived on people working late into the night. Because it wasn't unusual for someone to work ten or even twelve hours a day, a lot of people no longer ate at home. While this meant most people ate takeout or something simple at the convenience stores that had cropped up, some companies made it a point to take their employees out to dinner.

Because of this, a number of prominent restaurants had cropped up, all of them 3-star and above. While the restaurants were expensive, it was a point of pride for an employer to be able to pay for his entire staff to eat there. Being able to pay for an extravagant meal was like a symbol of status among companies. The better the restaurant they could afford, the better they were likely to pay and treat their employees.

Something like that.

Anthony did not know too much about the work force beyond the basics, but he did know it was thanks to these social changes that he and Secilia were not looked down on when they entered the 4-star restaurant called Caffe Boa.

It was an Italian restaurant, though calling the food they served Italian might have been misleading since Italy no longer existed. In fact, all of Europe had been dismantled and was now known as the European Federation, which was ruled by the three Vampire Warlords. Only a few small countries like Britannia had been able to keep their autonomy.

Well, he guessed it was two Vampire Warlords now, since Cane was no longer around.

After entering the restaurant and letting the hostess know they were eating for two, he and Secilia were shown to a small table set near the back. It offered them a grand view of the inside, and because there was a large window on their right, they were also able to see the street outside, though all that meant was they could watch passing traffic.

"You're lucky I know so many good places to eat," Secilia sighed as she leaned back in her chair.

"I am very grateful to you, Madame Secilia. Your wisdom and knowledge is boundless indeed."

"I don't need your sarcasm," Secilia replied as she idly looked at the drink menu. "Anyway, I'm still surprised you don't know a single restaurant. Do you not go out?"

"Not really, no," Anthony answered as he followed her lead.

"What about with that girl?" Secilia asked. "The one who lives next to you?"

Anthony paused for a moment, then sighed. "We haven't gone out on a date yet."

"So I'm the first person you've taken on a date?"

"Yes."

For whatever reason, Anthony's one word answer made Secilia smirk like she'd just won a round trip across the world.

The table they were sitting at was small, just big enough for two people, which meant they were sitting closer together than he was used to. Several times during their conversation, Anthony accidentally bumped his foot against hers.

"Are you trying to play footsie with me?" asked Secilia.

"If I was, then I would have taken off my shoes," Anthony answered.

"Hmph."

Anthony was very glad he'd managed to reign in his incubus pheromones. Nobody was really paying much attention to them. Aside from the appreciative looks of the hostess and the waitress who came by to take their order, nobody stared at him like he was something to be lusted after or hated.

After taking a look around the restaurant, he looked back at Secilia and felt a sudden chill run down his spine. She didn't seem to have noticed that he was watching her. Now completely unguarded, Anthony saw what appeared to be anguish on her face.

"Secilia, are you okay?" he asked.

"What?" Secilia blinked several times, coming back to herself, then smiled. "Of course I am. Why wouldn't I be okay?"

"No reason, I guess," Anthony said carefully as he thought about what he should say next. He frowned, then reached out and placed a hand over hers, startling the girl. "You know, if there is anything you'd ever like to get off your chest, you can feel free to tell me."

Secilia looked shocked for a moment. Her lips trembled like she might cry, but then she sniffled once and her smile turned gentle but also pained, like she was keeping something trapped inside of her.

"Thank you, Anthony. That means a lot to me."

Anthony nodded as he retracted his hand.

Their meals and drinks arrived half an hour after they ordered, and even though they were eating, the two kept up light conversation. They mostly traded insults and bantered. However, that was par for the course with them, and Anthony enjoyed Secilia's sharp wit. After they ate, they languidly sipped at their drinks (vodka and tonic for Anthony; a martini for Secilia) before paying for their meal and leaving.

"So, where to now?" asked Secilia as they walked down the street.

"Well, we have the whole day ahead of us," Anthony began. "I was thinking we could go to the aquarium first, then the amusement park, and then maybe we could see a movie."

"That's... kind of a full day, isn't it?" Secilia actually looked taken aback. "Do we really need to do all that?"

"Well, I guess not," Anthony admitted. "Sorry. I guess I got a little overexcited. I've always thought about what I wanted to do on a first date, but since there's so much I'd like to try, I couldn't think of just one thing."

"So you figured hitting up every dating cliche was a good idea?" asked a now amused Secilia.

Anthony responded with a shrug.

Since they couldn't do everything on his list, they decided to hit up the aquarium, which was closer to their current location than anything else.

The aquarium was indoors and several stories tall. It not only had about four stories above ground, but six more stories underground.

Each story was dedicated to certain types of fish. All the ones above ground were for fish that could be found simply from swimming around the shallow waters and reefs, while the ones below ground were dedicated to the deep sea creatures like the angler fish. Aside from the large tank in the very center of the building, which traveled from the top to the bottom, there were numerous smaller tanks that featured other types of fish.

"It's been a long time since I've been to the aquarium," Secilia said as they walked around the large centerpiece. There were all kinds of fish swimming inside of it, including sharks. "I don't think I've been to one since elementary school."

"I've never been to an aquarium before," Anthony admitted. "I've never had the chance."

"Well, you're here now. Come on. Let's look around."

Secilia grabbed Anthony's hand and dragged him through the aquarium. They looked at all kinds of different creatures, many of which Anthony had never seen before. He wasn't well-versed in aquatic creatures. In fact, apart from which fish he liked to eat, Anthony admittedly knew nothing about the ocean.

"Hey! Look at these ones! They're kissing!"

The fish Secilia found inside of one particular tank were indeed kissing. Both fish were a light, whitish pink color and had what appeared to be really large lips, which they were continuously bumping against each other.

"Maybe they're lovers," Secilia said.

As the woman pressed her hands against the glass, Anthony caught sight of a small holographic display next to the tank. It contained information about the fish in question. He read it out loud.

"Kissing gourami. The name is derived from how the fish appear to kiss; however, this act of 'kissing' is actually believed to be a territorial dispute between two males." Anthony paused to look at Secilia, who was now staring at him, and then the fish tank. "Looks like those are both men."

"Huh? So these fish are into BL? Good to know. I've lost interest with this. Let's find another fish."

Anthony couldn't help but chuckle as the woman dragged him off.

They traveled through most of the aquarium, going all the way to the top, then down to the bottom. Anthony had never learned more about fish than he did on this day. He would probably forget most of it since he didn't particularly care about the ocean, but it was nice seeing the way Secilia's face lit up, especially when they saw the dolphin exhibit.

Several hours passed, and by the time they were leaving, the sun had already begun to set.

Anthony glanced at the sky. The different hues of red and pink painted a lovely scene. However, he wasn't thinking about how pretty this picture was. His thoughts were on Secilia and what he should do now.

The reason he had invited her out was to ask if she'd become his bondmate, but he had no idea how to start such a conversation. It wasn't like he could just come out, tell her that he's an incubus, and ask her to mate with him. No sane person would believe him. He needed to be delicate about this.

Maybe he should invite her to his apartment?

"Say… do you want to come over to my place?" Secilia suddenly asked before he could suggest she come over to his apartment. When he looked at her, the woman had carefully concealed her facial expression behind a poker face as she twirled her hair. "My brother isn't over right now, so it'll be just the two of us."

"Oh. Um, sure. I don't mind coming over to your place," Anthony said.

"Great." Secilia smiled at him, but it wasn't a true smile. Anthony could not help but think something was wrong, though his date began dragging him off before he could say anything.

They took a maglev to the stop closest to Secilia's apartment, then walked the rest of the way. Her complex looked a lot like his. Apartment complexes generally didn't look much different from each other. Most of them were created based on the same generic blueprint. This was done to keep the city from looking chaotic, though it also meant individuality had been thrown by the wayside in favor of order and functionality.

Secilia's apartment was on the second floor. After she unlocked the door with her wristwatch, she gestured for him to follow her.

"Come on in. Don't forget to take off your shoes."

"What kind of heathen do you take me for?"

"The kind who doesn't take off his shoes when entering someone else's apartment, obviously."

"Wow. Your confidence in my etiquette is awe-inspiring."

He walked through the door, which Secilia closed behind him, and looked around her apartment as he slipped out of his shoes.

The apartment didn't look much different from his own. The kitchen and living room were separated by a wall, unlike his place, but aside from that and the difference in furniture, the differences were miniscule. Oh. And it was also about two or three times larger than his place.

"Feel free to sit down. Can I get you something to drink?" asked Secilia.

"Um… water is fine, thanks," Anthony said.

Anthony wandered into the living room and sat down on the couch, which spanned most of the wall. On the other side of the room was a holographic TV. He thought about turning it on, but he couldn't find the remote, so he just sat there until Secilia came out of the kitchen with two glasses of water. She offered one to him.

"Thank you," Anthony said as he took a drink.

"You're welcome." Secilia sat next to him and drank from her own glass.

They sat there in silence for a few moments. Anthony felt a tightness in his chest and tension in the air. He struggled with himself, wondering what he should say, but he knew that the longer he remained silent, the harder it would be to say what he needed to. Taking a deep breath, Anthony mustered up his courage to speak.

"Hey, I wanted to tell you something important," Anthony said at last.

"Something important?" Secilia appeared curious. "What is it?"

"I'm… I'm not human," he finally said. "I'm what's called an incubus. That's like the male version of a succubus."

"I know what an incubus is, Anthony. At least, I know about all the legends and stories people tell about them. So, you're basically a man who can't live without having a lot of sex? Like a manwhore?" asked Secilia.

"I'm being serious here." Anthony frowned. "Look, I know it's unbelievable, but I really am an incubus. You remember how I looked all emaciated before? That was because I had been starving myself. I refused to have sex with a woman for any reason because I didn't want to betray the woman who saved me and my brother when I was younger. I didn't realize how stupid I was being until recently. The reason I look so different now is because I have a bondmate."

"Bondmate? That's what succubi call the men in their harem, right?" asked Secilia as she stared into her glass. "I guess it would make sense to call the woman you bind to you by the same name." She paused, biting her lip, then continued. "Your current bondmate… it's that girl, right? Brianna?"

"That's right." Anthony sighed. "Brianna is my bondmate. However… as you've probably guessed, just having one bondmate isn't enough. Just like a succubus, I need several bondmates to survive, and I was wondering… I mean, you don't have to, but I wanted to know if…" Anthony stopped talking as his voice stalled, but then he gathered his courage once more. He had already come this far. He couldn't stop now. "If you would become my bondmate."

Anthony looked at Secilia, who was no longer looking at her glass but at him instead. Her eyes were a little wide. Her lips trembled. He nearly panicked when he saw tears in her eyes.

"Secilia, what's wrong? Why are you crying? Did I say something wrong? If I did, I'll apologize!"

"You didn't say anything wrong." Secilia wiped the tears from her eyes, her lips trembling like she didn't know whether to smile or grit her teeth. "I was just thinking about how I wished you had said this sooner."

Anthony was about to say that at least he was saying it now instead of later, but before he could open his mouth, a sudden bout of drowsiness slammed into him. He blinked several times as the muscles in his body seemed to relax. His vision faded for a moment. When it returned, Secilia was gently laying him on the couch. He looked into her tearfilled eyes and struggled to keep them open.

"S… Secilia…" he muttered.

"I'm sorry," Secilia gasped out that apology, hiccuping several times as crystal clear liquid ran down her cheeks. She leaned down until their foreheads were touching. Water splashed against his face as she continued to cry. "I am… so sorry. I didn't want for this to happen. I'm sorry."

Anthony was struggling to retain his consciousness now. His mind addled and fading fast, he couldn't figure out what was happening. What was going on? Why was Secilia crying? Why was he so tired?

He fought for several more seconds, but then, with an exhausted sigh, his body and mind finally gave out.

The last thing he saw was Secilia crying over him.

CHAPTER 4

Secilia continued to sob even after Anthony was rendered unconscious. She had lost most of the strength in her legs, so her forehead was pressed to his. Even though they were so close, she couldn't see his face because her vision was blurred with tears.

The apartment door opened not long after the deed was done, though Secilia didn't raise her head or turn around. She already knew who she would find.

"You know, you really should be more cautious," Alex said behind her. "Had I not been watching you from the shadows, your actions just now would have alerted Anthony's War Maiden friend."

"What?"

Secilia sniffled several times and wiped her eyes with the back of her hand, though this did little to stop the tears from flowing down her face.

She turned around to look at Alex. Nothing seemed different about him at first, except for the serious expression on his face, but then she noticed he was holding several sheets of paper. Secilia had no idea what they were. However, she noticed there were some strange patterns drawn on them.

"Is that a magic formula?" she asked.

"The War Maiden's familiar," Alex confirmed. "I dispatched it before it could send a signal to her, but we should definitely hurry. I don't doubt the War Maiden sensed something when I destroyed her familiar."

"What… should I do?" asked Secilia.

"For now? Nothing. Leave everything else to me."

Secilia nodded and glanced down at Anthony, lying unconscious on her couch. She bit her lower lip hard enough to draw blood before reluctantly stepping away from him.

Alex went into a storage space in the small hallway and came back with a large suitcase, one big enough to fit a human inside. He set the suitcase down, then picked up Anthony and placed him inside. Of course, the suitcase wasn't fully human-sized. To fit Anthony inside of it, he had to make sure the man's legs were curled into his chest and his arms were folded, but he was eventually able to close and seal the suitcase. Once he did, several glowing blue vein-like lines began running across the suitcase's surface.

"Nametech's technology sure is something," Alex muttered with a bitter smile. "I'm not sure how it works, but this suitcase can somehow stop a person's time, putting them in a form of suspended animation. It should be enough to keep Anthony sealed until he's at the boss's main lab." Secilia said nothing as she stared bitterly at the suitcase like it was the cause for all her problems, leading Alex to continue. "I don't think we'll be able to return to Academy Island after this."

"That's fine," Secilia mumbled quietly. "There's nothing here for me anyway."

Alex scratched the back of his head. "I guess not. Anyway, the team the boss sent should be at the airport. Let's go."

Since they were short on time—Brianna would not doubt be arriving soon just like Alex had said—they grabbed the suitcase, took an elevator to the first floor, and made their way out of the apartment complex. They wouldn't be coming back, but it didn't matter. This place was just a temporary residence for them to sleep in while they worked as undercover agents.

No one paid any attention to them as they walked through the busy streets. No one could have possibly known about what had just happened.

Secilia took one last look at the building that had been her home for the past year, wiped her eyes again, and then hurried to catch up with Alex.

They had a plane to catch.

***

Brianna's entire body went stiff as her connection with her familiar was abruptly severed.

Because she wasn't paying attention, she completely missed the combat drone's next attack, and a surprised and pained scream tore from her lips as a hard fist slammed into her face without mercy.

She was sent sprawling to the ground. Fortunately, she still had Physical Enhancement activated, which kept her from getting too injured. The stinging sensation where the fist had struck her was also quickly fading and the whiteness blocking her vision disappeared. All of that was secondary to the panic racing through her chest.

"What's wrong?" asked Lucretia as she suspended the combat drones' operations. All the machines that had been surrounding Brianna suddenly shut down.

"My familiar was destroyed," Brianna said as she stood to her feet. She looked in the direction she had last felt her familiar and bit her lip. "Something must have happened."

Lucretia frowned as though pondering the situation for a moment before nodding. "In that case, we should head to wherever your familiar was last. It was watching Anthony, right? We need to make sure nothing has happened to him."

"Yes," Brianna agreed.

With a somewhat weary sigh, Lucretia closed her eyes, spread out her hands, and began generating a large amount of mana. Brianna felt a strange surge travel through her body like an electric pulse. A pair of incredibly complex magic formulas appeared on each of Lucretia's palms, which she brought together to form an even larger and more complex magic formula. Moments after the formula had appeared it vanished. Brianna wondered what that was about, but then, to her astonishment, Lucretia's body began separating—no, it was more like another Lucretia was walking out of her body.

Cell division is the process by which a parent cell divides into two or more daughter cells. This was something she had learned in her biology class several years ago. What she was seeing now vaguely reminded her of that, except instead of one large cell dividing into two cells, it was one person becoming two.

"Is this… time magic?" asked Brianna.

"It is," Lucretia confirmed. "This is the me from six hour ago. She can only last for six hours, but she will take my place for today. Now, let's not remain here. We should hurry up and find Anthony."

"You're right."

At the mention of Anthony, Brianna's heart began pounding in her chest. She didn't know what had happened, who had destroyed her familiar, but it had been tasked with watching Anthony. If something happened to it, then it was most likely because someone was targeting him.

They left the school and went to the nearest maglev station. The moment they arrived, Brianna needed a moment to determine which maglev they should take. She knew the general direction of her familiar's last known location, but she didn't know how to get there. She spent nearly five minutes looking at the holographic screen that showed the various routes and calculating which one would take her to that location.

"It's this one." Lucretia pointed at one of the routes.

"What?" Brianna asked.

"Anthony went on a date with Secilia, right?" Lucretia didn't give her a chance to answer as she shrugged. "That means he probably went to her apartment after the date concluded. I suspect she might be somehow involved with this, so the most logical conclusion is that your familiar vanished somewhere around her apartment complex."

Brianna checked the route Lucretia had pointed at and tried to determine if that really was the location she'd last felt her familiar. After staring at it for a moment, she determined that Lucretia was right. It was hard to tell since she only had a vague sense of direction. However, when correlating her sense of direction with the route, she could tell that it was indeed in the same direction she'd sensed her familiar just before it had been destroyed.

"Let's go," Brianna said as she turned on her heel and walked further into the maglev station.

There were a lot of people at the station, though that was only natural since it was the middle of the day and a weekend.

Careful not to let her music case hit anyone, Brianna slipped around a group of men walking in the opposite direction as her, walked past a gaggle of girls of varying species (she saw humans, vampires, therianthropes, and even a dryad in that group), and moved toward the correct maglev platform. Lucretia followed behind her, walking as if she knew exactly what was going to happen before it happened. Her movements were so fluid and graceful that even Brianna found herself envious.

That was the Time Witch for you.

They arrived just in time to hop on the next maglev. As the door shut behind them, Brianna found a place in the corner of their car to unobtrusively stand. Lucretia followed her.

While she didn't receive as many stares this time as she did when Anthony was present, the two of them cut an unusual enough figure that quite a few people glanced in their direction. She couldn't rightly blame them. One of them was dressed in a skimpy battlesuit that almost resembled a one-piece swimsuit, while the other was wearing pink and white gothic lolita clothing. Sure, there were vampires, therianthropes, dryads, nymphs, and even a few elementals on the train, but those were fairly common races on Academy Island.

Brianna crossed her arms and began tapping her index finger against her forearm as she waited for the maglev to reach its destination.

"You are worried," Lucretia observed with a placid expression. "You should relax. We don't know if anything has happened to Anthony yet. Worrying like this is just going to make you too high strung to help your bondmate should he need you."

"That's very easy for you to say." Brianna scowled. "Your bondmate isn't the one in danger."

"This is true. I cannot say I've been in quite the same position as you before either." Lucretia paused here to look at the people surrounding them. She frowned, then turned back to Brianna. "However, while I have not been in this position before, I can say with certainty that you should calm down. If Anthony really is in danger, you will need to have a clear head. You won't be able to help him if anxiety is clouding your judgment."

"I… yes, you are right."

Brianna sighed, closed her eyes, and took several deep breaths. All War Maidens were taught basic meditation techniques, to help them keep a clear head while out on missions. She was no different. Instructor Noel had often told her the same thing Lucretia had just now. That was why she capitulated so easily and began meditating while the maglev continued moving.

The moment the maglev stopped at their destination, however, Brianna snapped her eyes open and rushed out the door before the crowd could beat her. She didn't even pay attention to whether Lucretia was following her. The single-minded determination to discover what happened to her familiar and Anthony kept her moving and even caused her to activate Farsight as she left the station and began making her way toward her destination.

A feeling of unease permeated her the closer she got to where she last felt her familiar. She eventually stopped in front of a building that wasn't too dissimilar to her own apartment complex. She looked up. This building was the location where she'd last felt her familiar. Without hesitation, she walked inside.

The lobby, like the building itself, looked almost like a carbon copy of her own complex, but Brianna paid no attention to its aesthetics as she traveled to the elevator. She walked in and pressed the button for the second floor. Before the elevator door could close, Lucretia stuck out her hand, forcing it to open for her, and walked inside.

"I don't appreciate how you left me in the dust like that," Lucretia said as the door closed and the elevator began moving.

"Sorry," Brianna muttered.

"Your concern for Anthony is admirable," Lucretia said with a sigh. "I suppose it's not surprising. Incubus give their entire selves over to their bondmates, granting them eternal love and loyalty in exchange for mana. However, it's not as if this is a two-way road. Bonding yourself to an incubus creates an empathic connection. You might not be able to feel it like he can, but the love he has for you is continuously pouring into you. Every time he touches you, every time he kisses you, every time you have sex, it is like you're being filled with more than just mana and sperm. It's not something you can remain unaffected by."

While Brianna blushed at Lucretia's sperm comment, the rest of her was taken aback by the woman's words. She seemed to know so much about incubus. This infamous woman whose strength was on par with the top demons in the world had once said she was basing her knowledge on what she knew of succubus, but Brianna had to wonder if that was really true. She spoke as if she had experienced what Brianna was currently experiencing first hand.

The idea was ridiculous, of course. The last incubus had existed around 500 years ago. Even if this woman was the infamous Time Witch, there was no way she could have lived for that long. Magicians were still human and possessed a human lifespan.

When they reached the second floor, Brianna walked out and began traveling down the long hallway, following the vague feelings left from her familiar, until she was eventually standing in front of a door.

It looked the same as all the other doors. Like most complexes, this one used sliding doors that could be locked using a person's wristwatch.

The door was locked, which meant she wouldn't be able to open it. Doors like this used a key app that created a unique code for that specific door. It was impossible to open unless you had the correct keycode to unlock it.

There were some hackers who could create the keycodes needed to open doors like this, but Brianna didn't know the first thing about hacking.

She set her music case on the floor, undid the latch, and flipped it open. The Geminius Sword lay resting inside. Brianna grabbed the sword and pulled it out, activating its basic functions to extend the blades, then set herself in a wide stance as she glared at the metal object obstructing her.

She was just about to slice the door clean open.

"Wait."

She was stopped by Lucretia.

"There is no need to break the door down. That will just cause problems," the small woman said.

"Then what should I do?" asked Brianna. "How can I open this door?"

"You don't need to do anything." Lucretia stepped in front of Brianna and pushed her away. "I will open the door. Just stand back."

Brianna frowned, but she knew better than to argue. She stepped back as Lucretia stood before the door, created another magic formula on her palm as she accessed her mana, and placed the formula on the door.

A clock appeared within the magic circle. It looked like one of those old-fashioned clocks that used roman numerals to tell time. Currently, the hour hand was on the V and the minute hand was on the IV, but even as she watched, both hands began moving backwards. The minute hand moved faster than the hour hand. It also moved more. By her estimation, the minute hand moved back by about half an hour. Then the door slid open.

"It looks like it hasn't been that long since someone opened this door," Lucretia said as she walked inside.

Brianna followed the woman. What she found upon entering was a standard living space. The living room and kitchen were separated by a wall, but there was no door leading into the kitchen, which looked a little bigger than the one in Anthony's apartment. The living room was clean. There was a couch, a coffee table, and a holographic TV. On the opposite side from the entrance was a sliding glass panel that led to a balcony.

"It doesn't look like anyone is here," Brianna said.

"No, but someone was definitely here half an hour ago," Lucretia said.

"Anthony and Secilia?" asked Brianna.

"Probably." Lucretia shrugged. "I haven't checked her registry, but this is definitely Secilia's apartment."

"Let's look around and see if we can find anything," Brianna said at last, although she wasn't sure if she should expect to find anything or not.

Brianna and Lucretia searched the apartment for nearly fifteen minutes, but they found nothing. Anthony wasn't there. Secilia wasn't there. There was also no evidence or signs of a struggle. Nothing looked out of place. In short, they had nothing.

As the realization that she didn't know what happened to Anthony and could no longer track him set in, Brianna sank to her knees and pressed her hands against the floor. Her heart felt like it was being constricted. An icy hand had clutched her heart in its unfeeling grasp and was slowly squeezing it into a pulp. She had never felt this helpless before.

"I was afraid this would happen," Lucretia sighed. "Hold on a moment. Let me see if I can reconstruct the events that happened here before we arrived."

"Re… construct?" Brianna looked up and stared at Lucretia as the small woman walked into the middle of the room. "What do you mean?"

"The ability to manipulate time has many uses," Lucretia explained. "I generally use it for small things like grading papers these days. I also occasionally have to use large-scale time magic when helping out the Academy Island Private Security Forces. Aside from being able to turn back time, I can also grasp the many threads of time and use magic to reconstruct events that happened in the past. It's a lot like being able to watch a recording, which helps with criminal investigations. We won't be able to interact with anything, but we can at least see what happened."

Brianna was pretty astonished by what she was hearing. What this woman was suggesting was theoretically possible, but she had never heard of anyone who was able to do it.

Spells required mana, and the harder and more complex a spell was, the more mana it required. Large scale spells that affected entire cities, for example, generally required several hundred or even several thousand magicians to cast magic at the same time because one magician just didn't have enough mana for it. Even attempting to cast such a large spell would kill someone.

Time magic was particularly complex. It was one of the most complicated magic branches in the entire world, right up there with spatial magic. Even simple spells that manipulated time required a vast amount of mana. That Lucretia could do something like reconstruct an event in time so they could view it meant she had more mana at her disposal than several dozen magicians.

It was no wonder she was hailed as the strongest living magician of all time.

Brianna could feel the sudden surge of mana emanating from Lucretia. It sent a shiver down her spine.

A magic formula suddenly appeared underneath the woman, more complicated than anything she had ever seen before. Brianna knew only a little about magic. She could use basic skills like Physical Enhancement and Farsight, but most of her knowledge was related to combat. Even the spatial magic she used was something she could use because of the Geminius Sword. She didn't actually understand how it worked.

As the magic formula appeared, something strange happened to the light inside the room. The shadows shifted, changing positions as if the sun was lowering in the opposite direction it should be. She looked outside, but nothing seemed different, which meant whatever was happening only affected this small room. Just as this thought occurred to her, the door opened and two people walked in backwards. One of them, the man, was pulling a large suitcase behind him.

She recognized the two people. They were Alex and Secilia, the half-sibling duo whom she'd met only once before.

The two continued moving backwards, but the speed they were moving at increased as Lucretia pushed more mana into her magic circle, which began spinning at a rate so fast Brianna had to look away for fear of getting dizzy. She watched the two. Her eyes felt like they were about to bulge out of their sockets as she saw the man set the case down and open it up, revealing an unconscious man inside.

"Anthony!" she shouted in shock as she took a single step forward.

"D-don't move!" Lucretia shouted, causing her to freeze. "Time magic is very delicate. If you move, it will create ripples that I will have to factor in while casting. That will make this a lot more difficult than it needs to be. Just stand still and watch."

Brianna gnashed her teeth together as a feeling of helplessness washed over her, but she knew there was nothing she could do right now. Even if she did go over to them. What she was seeing right now was nothing more than a reconstruction of what happened at some point in the past. She couldn't change anything.

And so Brianna watched as time reversed itself, then watched as time slowed down and began playing in regular motion. There was no sound. It seemed Lucretia couldn't replicate sound, so they were forced to merely watch what was happening. Brianna could fortunately read lips. So she was able to read the lips of Anthony and Secilia as they sat on the couch and sipped some water while talking.

It looked like Anthony was telling Secilia about his status as an incubus. He talked about how he and Brianna were bondmates, how he needed a total of seven bondmates to unlock his power, and asked her if she would be willing to become his bondmate.

Secilia's response was shocking.

Brianna didn't know how to feel as the dark-haired beauty broke down in tears as she watched Anthony grow weaker. She felt a surge of red hot anger race through her at the realization that Anthony's drink had been drugged. At the same time, the girl was bawling her eyes out as she pressed her forehead to his and apologized over and over.

It was at this point that Alex came into the room. He had the slips of paper that composed her familiar in hand, meaning he was likely the one who had destroyed it. After they spoke some more, Alex lifted Anthony, set him in the suitcase, and then the two of them left the apartment. Once the door shut behind them, the memory ended.

Lucretia gasped as she fell to the floor.

"L-Lucretia!" Brianna squawked as she ran over to the woman, who was kneeling on the floor and gasping. Her shoulders heaved, sweat covered her forehead, and her body was shaking as if she'd exerted too much strength and exhausted herself. Brianna didn't know what to do.

"I'm… I'm all right," Lucretia said, though she certainly didn't look it. Her face was drawn and pale. "I'm okay. I just… need a moment to rest. Reconstructing a moment in time like that takes a lot of mana. The further back I have to go, the more mana it takes. It also requires a huge amount of focus, so the mental strain is a lot greater than simpler spells like the one that lets me create time clones."

Brianna nodded several times at the woman's words, but she didn't say anything. There wasn't much she could say. All of this was beyond her.

The shaking of Lucretia's body eventually stopped and the woman was able to sit down on the floor. She closed her eyes and took deep breaths like she was meditating. Brianna quietly remained beside her, even though she was also impatient to look for Anthony. It took a few minutes, but Lucretia's complexion soon improved.

"Okay." Lucretia opened her eyes and stood up. Brianna followed suit. "We should go now."

"Where are we going?" asked Brianna.

Lucretia looked at her with a hard glint in her eyes. "We're going to the Academy Island Private Security Forces' main headquarters. We'll need their help if we want to find out where Anthony was taken."

****

"… do this…"

"… Already… too late…"

Voices penetrated the foggy haze surrounding Anthony's mind as he came to. He didn't know where he was. He couldn't even see. He tried to think, but even that was hard. It felt like his mind had been bound in chains, making it impossible to concentrate on anything.

As he became a little more awake, Anthony became more aware of his surroundings. There was no breeze and the air tasted sterilized, meaning he was indoors and the location was something like a hospital. He wasn't wearing anything except a pair of boxers. While the air reminded him of a hospital, the bed that he was lying on was hard and uncomfortable, and his arms and legs were strapped to it, preventing him from moving. If he could have used Physical Enhancement, he could have broken free. His mind, sadly, was unable to focus his mana.

"It looks like he is waking up," a male voice said.

Anthony slowly opened his eyes, but he was forced to shut them again when a bright light penetrated them. He tried not to groan in pain. Blinking several times, he opened his eyes more slowly, allowing them time to adjust.

The room he found himself in was definitely some type of laboratory. All kinds of equipment littered the room. A lot of it was medical equipment he recognized like the vitals monitoring unit attached to this bed, but there was also a lot that he didn't recognize.

Two people were in this room aside from himself—a man and a woman.

The man looked like he was in his forties or fifties, with black hair that had graying sideburns, brown eyes, and a trimmed goatee flecked with gray. He wore a white lab coat over a black button-up shirt and black pants. His face was lined with a few wrinkles. Anthony could tell from the way his wrinkles were set that this man frowned a lot.

He looked past the man to study the woman. His eyes almost widened when he saw the dark-haired beauty with hair tied into a ponytail, perfectly unblemished skin, and long legs clad in black stockings and a skirt. Like the man, she wore a white lab coat. Unlike the man, her countenance appeared much kinder. What really struck him wasn't just her beautiful appearance, however, but the fact that she looked nearly identical to Secilia.

"Who…?"—Anthony tried to ask—"who are you people?" but the words wouldn't come out. His mouth felt so numb.

"It seems the drugs are still affecting him," the man observed. "Hmph. You don't need to know who we are. A guinea pig has no use for such knowledge. All you need to know is that from now on, you belong to me."

Anthony wanted to be angry at this man, wanted to break out of these bindings and pound this asshat into the ground, but all he could muster up was a feeble feeling of resistance. He was still so tired. It was probably because of the drugs this man was talking about.

Thinking about how he'd been drugged made Anthony remember the last thing he saw before passing out. Secilia's crying face. It was easy to deduce that she was the one who had drugged him, but he didn't know why. Why would she do such a thing? He looked back at the woman again, the one who looked so much like Secilia. Was she the reason?

"Director Azrael! You need to see reason!" the woman said. Her voice was imploring. "What you have just done violates international law! You kidnapped a citizen of Academy Island—an incubus at that! Do you really think they won't notice what happened?!"

"Shut up, woman!" The one called Director Azrael whirled on her. "You do not get to talk back to me! You might be the most brilliant mind in cloning technology, but do not forget that I own you! If you do not want those two cherished children of yours to die, then you will stop talking back to me and do as I say!"

Anthony couldn't even begin to follow along with this conversation. He didn't know what was happening. However, the look on the woman's face told him enough; he could tell this man was forcing her to act against her will.

The woman's lips trembled, but she said nothing. Director Azrael snorted, turned around, and walked over to Anthony, who tried to struggle out of his restraints. Unfortunately, the drugs were still affecting his mind. He couldn't concentrate enough to call upon his mana, so he couldn't use Physical Enhancement.

"The drugs didn't last nearly as long as I expected," the director said. "It's only been a few minutes since we brought you out of that suitcase, and yet you are already beginning to show signs of resisting us. You have an amazing constitution. I'll be looking forward to seeing how that incredible physique of yours can benefit me."

Anthony opened his mouth to say something, but he couldn't get a single word in before the man grabbed an injector filled with green liquid and jabbed into his neck. A short and sharp burst of pain was quickly followed by a feeling of numbness. His limbs relaxed as he closed his eyes and felt darkness engulf him again.

CHAPTER 5

The Academy Island Private Security Forces was a task force created by the Academy Island Board of Directors for the sole purpose of protecting its citizens from internal and external threats. Outfitted with some of the most advanced weapons in human history, Brianna had once heard a rumor that their equipment was at least twenty years ahead of everyone else, thanks in no small part to the numerous research and development companies that made this island their base of operations.

As she walked down the narrow hallway filled with glass windows, she began to understand that the rumors were not exaggerated.

She watched as a group of soldiers marched past her. They were wearing what, at first glance, appeared to be standard kevlar vests. Only someone who'd been trained in mana sensing or was naturally sensitive to fluctuations in mana would have noticed the blue veins running through their armor. Their armor was enhanced with mana just like her battlesuit. Not only was the armor enhanced, but their guns also had the magic formulas burnished into them, though she had no idea what they did.

"It looks like they are panicking over something," Brianna observed.

"Of course." Lucretia turned just her head to look at Brianna as she continued to walk down the corridor. "The incubus they were letting live here was kidnapped by an unknown group. You of all people should know how serious this situation is."

Brianna did indeed know how serious this situation was, but she hadn't expected everyone else to know about it too.

"They don't," Lucretian continued as if she could read her mind. "The rank and file are not actually aware that the person kidnapped was an incubus. They just know someone of incredible importance has been kidnapped, which is why they've been ordered to mobilize all available forces."

"Oh. So I see," Brianna said for lack of anything better to say. However, as they turned another corner and moved out of the way so several soldiers could march past, her curiosity got the better of her. "By the way, what position do you hold among the Academy Island Private Security Forces?"

"My rank?" Lucretia stopped in front of a door and waved her wristwatch over a scanner, which emitted a soft beep before the door slid open. She turned her head once more to look at Brianna as she answered. "I'm technically not a member of the Private Security Forces. I'm more like a contractor who occasionally does part-time work for them. But. Hm. If you had to give me a rank, I suppose it would be 'Commander'."

With those shocking words, she walked through the door, forcing Brianna to follow her.

The room on the other side reminded Brianna of a command room. A large table with a holographic display showcasing an entire map of Academy Island lay in the center. There were numerous tables situated against the wall. Each one featured a monitor displaying some kind of information, from camera feed to what appeared to be flight records and even a list of names. Not only was it large, but there were nearly a dozen people inside. All of them looked like they were busy jabbering to each other.

The moment Lucretia entered the room, however, all of them stopped what they were doing and saluted.

"Ma'am!"

"At ease," Lucretia said with an arid wave of her hand as she walked further into the room. "We don't have time to stand on ceremony, so I think we can avoid formalities right now. Give me a sitrep, if you would."

"Ma'am!"

Everyone snapped off another salute.

Lucretia sighed.

Brianna was quite shocked to see how everyone treated this woman. She, of course, understood who Lucretia really was, but she didn't think the infamous Time Witch would hold much power among a group of private military forces. Fear? Yes. Definitely. Power? No.

While Brianna was trying to get her head on straight, a beefy man dressed in military fatigues with more muscle than she'd know what to do with walked over to them. He had a buzzed head of brown hair and several scars on his face. With his massive physique, he cut an imposing figure.

"Captain Dennison, what do you have for me?" asked Lucretia, who looked positively ridiculous standing next to the man. It was like looking at a rabbit standing beside a bear.

"Ma'am." Captain Dennison didn't salute, but he did give her a respectful nod as he handed the woman a tablet. "After you contacted us, we did our best to track down the people you described. We found out they left exactly two hours ago via a private jet that was located on the Nametech landing strip in Los Diavolos Airport."

"Nametech, huh? Figures they would be the ones who caused such a large disturbance." Lucretia clicked her tongue as she looked at the information on the tablet. "Come to think of it, they also had a hand in the vampire incident not long ago. While I don't think they were the reason for the rogue demon attacks, I had always been curious about how that vampire managed to acquire so many rogue demons. There's no way they could have all been smuggled into the city without our knowledge."

Curious, Brianna leaned over to see what it displayed too. It looked like a video feed. Brianna narrowed her eyes when she saw Alex and Secilia walk up the extending stairs of a private jet alongside what looked like several therianthropes. Alex was carrying the same suitcase that she remembered Anthony being stuffed into.

Red hot anger filled her veins.

While she was becoming a boiling pot of rage, Captain Dennison stared at Lucretia with a disconcerted frown.

"You believe Nametech was somehow responsible for the appearance of those rogue demons?" he asked.

"If my guess is correct, then those demons weren't rogue at all," Lucretia announced. While Captain Dennison stared at her in confusion, Lucretia issued several commands. "I want you to mobilize several squads, one for each Nametech facility. Have them perform an inspection of every one of them."

"That would be in violation of Academy Island laws, Ma'am," Captain Dennison pointed out. "You know we are not allowed to conduct a search of any lab or research facility. The entire reason we are able to have so many outstanding companies base their operations here is because we provide them with a place to conduct their research without meddling in their affairs."

"Those laws only apply when it does not concern the safety of our citizens," Lucretia corrected. "While it isn't concrete proof, we currently have enough evidence to place them under suspicion, which means we can perform a search without a warrant."

"Ma'am." Captain Dennison saluted again.

"I also want you to have someone track that private jet," Lucretia continued. "Find out where it went. I don't care what means you have to use to find it. Just make sure you do."

Giving Lucretia yet another salute, Captain Dennison moved off and began barking orders at several other soldiers, commanding them to gather up squadrons and get their intelligence division to track the jet Anthony was being smuggled in.

While they did that, Lucretia closed her eyes and took several deep breaths.

"That boy... I swear, he is so much trouble," she muttered.

"Have you known Anthony long, Lucretia?" asked Brianna.

"Long enough," Lucretia responded. "I knew him because of my association with Lilith, though I never paid much attention to him when he was a part of her harem. To me, he was just that cute kid who would sometimes talk to me when I was around. That said, he was Lilith's favorite. She always spoiled the boy rotten. That's probably why he can't do anything for himself and needs someone to push him along."

Despite the situation, Brianna's lips trembled as she fought against smiling. She didn't know why, but listening to Lucretia gripe about Anthony made her want to laugh.

However, the situation once more settled on her seconds later, and a frown soon marred her face.

"What should I do?" she asked.

"For now? Nothing. There is nothing you can do." Lucretia shrugged. "All you can do for the moment is get some rest and let these people do their job. Once we have the destination of that jet, you and I will be busy, so it is important to rest while you can."

Brianna wasn't sure she liked the idea of resting when Anthony was in danger, but she also knew Lucretia was right. She couldn't do anything. She wasn't an intelligence analyst, didn't know how to use all the equipment surrounding them, and was really only good for fighting. It was hard to accept, but she was basically useless right now.

With a heavy heart, Brianna found a place to unobtrusively stand while everyone else worked.

And she hated it.

***

Luna did not let Director Azrael or anyone else know about how her heart trembled.

She stood inside of a large research room—the same room Anthony was in.

The man in question was still lying on the bed, completely unconscious, his body being constantly fed drugs through an IV drip to keep him that way.

Luna tried not to bite her lip in sorrow as she paid attention to the monitor showing Anthony's bio information. It contained a map of his body, several diagrams that showcased info such as his heart rate, biorhythms, and even his mana.

"This boy has quite a bit of power," she murmured.

The diagram showcasing his mana was quite something. It didn't match a Vampire Warlord, the Beast King, one of the four Succubus Queens, or the famous Kyuubi of Kyoto, but it was on par with data she'd gained on vampire nobles. He still only had one bondmate. From what she understood, an incubus gained more power when they had more bondmates, so he hadn't reached his full potential yet. That was impressive enough.

Of course, the chances of him reaching his full potential now were slim.

After monitoring his vitals for a little longer, Luna left the room and traveled down a long corridor, until she reached Director Azrael's office.

The director was sitting behind his desk as he read through reports. He stopped the moment she entered, however.

"How's the test subject?" asked Director Azrael.

Luna walked further into the room, which was not large. It didn't have any decorations. Aside from the large window behind the desk, this room was unfeeling and empty. The only object inside was the desk and the holographic computer the director was using.

"His condition is stable and I was able to acquire the DNA samples you requested. However…"

"However?" asked Azrael with a raised eyebrow.

"It looks like his mana levels are dropping," Luna continued, taking a deep breath. "It isn't a large drop. I suspect since his body is at rest, he's not using that much mana to maintain his existence. However, it is significant enough that your test subject will likely die prematurely before our research can achieve any results."

"Then we'll just create some clones he can fuck," Director Azrael said, his tone uncaring. "We can create as many clones as needed. We'll have them fuck him until their life is expended, then replace them once they die. We can do this as many times as we need to get the results I want."

Luna did everything in her power to hide her disgust at this man. It was not easy. Ever since this man had taken over Nametech, he had committed one heinous act after another in the name of profit. He had even taken all her research on cloning and began using it to create clones whose only purpose was to be disposed of so their limbs could be used as prosthetics.

She carefully kept her feelings hidden as the door into the office slid open.

"Shall I prepare clones for this purpose then?" she asked. "We will need to reconfigure them, so it might take awhile."

"Go ahead and do so. I can't have our test subject dying on me," Director Azrael instructed, though his eyes narrowed. "You are being awfully cooperative. Are you not going to tell me I'm in the wrong?"

"What's the point? You won't listen to me anyway."

It was a simple parting shot, one that wouldn't affect anything, but it was all she could do right now.

She turned around and noticed Alex walking over to them. He smiled at her as she walked past. Just as their paths crossed, he placed his hand behind his back, and she slipped a small disc into it. The disc disappeared into his back pocket moments later. Hopefully, Director Azrael would not notice.

***

"You called for me, sir?" Alex said as he stood before Director Azrael. The sound of the door closing as Luna walked out reached his ears.

"I did. Give me your report on Anthony Amasius and the War Maiden," Director Azrael said. He didn't give any explanations for why he wanted that information, but Alex didn't expect one. This man never told his subordinates anything.

Alex nodded and began talking. "The War Maiden is called Brianna. She is, to the best of my knowledge, still a trainee. From what I've observed, she has an incredible talent for using Farsight, but her ability to use physical enhancement magic was lacking until she became Anthony's bondmate."

"So I was right," Director Azrael mumbled. "Those damn people at Custodes Daemonium were trying to chain the incubus to their organization." He paused his thoughts and refocused his attention on Alex. "And how strong is this War Maiden?"

"That I am unsure of," Alex answered honestly. "We have not had the chance to see her go all out. However, she is incredibly talented at wielding the Geminius Sword and has perfected her use of Physical Enhancement thanks to her bond with Anthony. I suspect she might be capable of fighting against vampire nobles on even footing. She might even be a match for Alexandra Sil'yazhelyy."

"So you think she is capable of defeating the Beast Princess of Russia?" he asked.

"It's just a guess." Alex shrugged. "In either event, she won't be the real problem. If you're thinking about the people who are likely going to try and rescue Anthony, then the one you should really be worried about is Lucretia Incanscino."

Alex knew it was probably wrong to feel vindicated, but he felt a small sprinkling of joy when he saw Director Azrael's face turn pale.

"The infamous Time Witch? Why would she care about what happens to this incubus?" asked the man.

"Did you not read my reports?" Alex asked, trying to keep the mocking tone out of his voice. "Lucretia Incanscino is a professor at our university. Not only does she teach there, but it seems as though she is Anthony's benefactor. I believe I sent a report near the beginning of last year stating that it was under her authority and power that Anthony was allowed to live on Academy Island like a normal person."

No such report actually existed, but Director Azrael was the kind of person who rarely ever read reports thoroughly. He skimmed over them with a quick glance. There was no way he could know Alex was bullshitting.

Of course, the director could have easily discovered this information himself, but the man never cared to look into anything unless he felt it could make him more money. His insatiable greed was the driving force behind his existence.

"Is there any way for her to track your flight's route?" asked the director.

"I don't know. Probably."

The man gritted his teeth. "In that case, I suppose we will have to abandon this base. Tell your… sister to get her things packed. I'll have someone else secure the test subject."

"Yes, sir."

Alex didn't remain in the office for long. After the dismissal, he traveled to the shared room he and his "sister" were staying at.

The door opened for him, and he took a look around as he stepped inside, frowning only a little at how barren this place was. He liked his old apartment because it had so many great decorations. This place was empty and felt impersonal.

Secilia was sitting on one of two cots. Her back was against the wall, knees drawn up to her chest as she hugged them, and eyes staring blankly at the wall on the opposite side. She didn't even respond when he entered the room. Alex could only sigh at the dead look in her eyes.

"Hey, I have something for you."

Alex tossed the disc Luna had given him onto the cot. Secilia blinked several times before her eyes went from the wall to the disc. After a moment of staring, she reached out and picked it up, turning it about in her hands.

"This is… a holographic recording?" she murmured questioningly and looked at Alex.

He shrugged. "It's from Luna."

That was all the information Secilia needed. Her eyes brightened a little as she held the disc on her palm and activated it.

A soft glow emitted from the projector inside before a holographic image appeared hovering over the disc, it was a one hundredth scale image of a woman who looked like an older version of Secilia. Luna. The woman looked at Secilia with a smile, though they both knew she wasn't actually smiling at her since this was just a recording.

"Before I say anything else, I wanted to apologize for not being able to tell you this in person. Director Azrael is still wary and won't allow me to see you." That was how Luna began. However, she quickly shifted gears. "By this point in time, I highly suspect the Academy Island Private Security Forces will be mobilizing to reclaim Anthony Amasius. Director Azrael is a cautious man. He will likely begin trying to relocate us and Anthony to another one of his bases. That will be our chance to rescue Anthony and escape. However, we will need Anthony's help if we want to make it out of this. I want you to grab the antidote for the drug that's keeping him under. It's kept in a stored locker located inside of research lab number two. You know which one that is. With your talent at magical engineering, computer science, and hacking, you should be able to hack into the locker and secure the antidote. After we all board the transport that will take us to our next location, you should find a chance to administer the antidote to him, and then we can make our escape."

Secilia's eyes never left the woman's face. Her eyes had brightened with every sentence that passed Luna's mouth. Alex shifted uncomfortably as he watched.

"There are so many things I want to tell you." Luna's eyes grew moist. "I wish I could be there to tell you all this in person. I wish I had been able to have a larger hand in raising you. I wish Azrael had not forced us apart. However, wishes never get us anywhere. We will always have to take matters into our own hands. For now, I want you to focus on rescuing Anthony. Once we are safe, I hope we can become a family again like we were before that man ruined our lives. Goodbye for now, and good luck."

The holographic recording ended and the image vanished. Secilia continued staring at the flat disc in her hand. Alex, who shifted from foot to foot as he waited for Secilia to talk, waited for several minutes before deciding to speak when it became clear that she wouldn't.

"What should we do?" he asked.

"Of course we're going to get that antidote," Secilia said at last, crawling off the bed and standing up. "We have to save Mother, and I still need to make amends to Anthony. Even if… even if he hates me after what I did, I at least want to do one last thing for him."

Alex nodded. "In that case, you will need to act fast. I have to prepare the transportation, so you'll need to get the antidote without me. Research lab two is probably going to be guarded. Do you think you will be able to get past them?"

"Don't worry about that," Secilia said. "I might not be able to fight, but I do have a plan."

***

Brianna had been leaning against the wall as Lucretia commanded the numerous members of the Academy Island Private Security Forces. She had to admit that she was impressed with how the Time Witch ordered them around. Lucretia was such a small woman. The idea of someone so tiny commanding a private militia seemed ridiculous, but not a single person present disputed her orders.

At the same time, Brianna couldn't help but feel useless. There was nothing she could do right now, so she'd been left to stand around and wait until Lucretia had a use for her, but it seemed like that would be awhile.

"Lucretia, ma'am." One of the officers at the communication station called over to the woman.

"What is it?" asked Lucretia.

"The battalions we sent to search the Nametech headquarters have fallen under attack. They are currently experiencing heavy resistance and haven't been able to enter."

"Hmph. The fact that Nametech is resisting us only adds more proof that they are doing something illegal. If they weren't, why would they bother attacking our forces?" Lucretia crossed her arms. "Tell our forces they have been authorized to use C-grade equipment and lethal force if necessary, though I would prefer to do this without any loss of life. Is there anything else to report?"

"Yes, ma'am," the officer continued. "It seems all the people putting up a fight against our forces are rogue demons."

"They aren't rogue demons," Lucretia said. "If my guess is right, those demons are actually clones."

"C-clones, ma'am?!" The young man seemed startled.

"Yes. It looks like those rumors about Nametech practicing cloning are more than just rumors," Lucretia said.

The two weren't bothering to keep their conversation quiet, so everyone could hear what was being said, including Brianna.

She was pretty shocked to learn that Nametech was practicing cloning, one of the four biggest magical felonies someone could commit. That such a large company practiced something so ghastly horrified her. Of course, this was the same company that had kidnapped Anthony, so she knew these people weren't saints of any sort.

After the conversation ended, another communications officer called out to Lucretia.

"Ma'am, we've managed to track the Nametech private jet."

"Oh?" Lucretia gestured for Brianna to come closer, then walked to the communication station. Brianna followed her, stopping just behind Lucretia as the woman stared at the monitor. "Show me."

"Yes, ma'am."

The woman manipulated the display screen, which revealed a map of Academy Island. A small dot appeared on the map.

"This is the private jet that Secilia and Alex took off in, and this—" The woman manipulated the screen again, causing the view to zoom out and reveal more than just Academy Island. "—is the route they took. Unfortunately, our satellite feed cut out here. I suspect there is a magic jammer located somewhere in this region."

A small line traveled from the dot on the screen into the Americas. It continued moving across the Americas before stopping in a mountainous region. Brianna recognized the area.

"Those are the Rocky Mountains," she said. "I hear it used to be the site of several national parks, but during the Age of Rebellion, numerous factions fought there and it's now become a wasteland. No one should live there anymore."

"Which makes it the perfect secret base for a company like Nametech." Lucretia nodded several times as she spoke. "They can experiment to their heart's content and no one would know. Okay. I want you to prepare a private jet for me. Brianna and I will travel to the Rocky Mountains, secure Anthony, take down Nametech, and come back."

Brianna brightened when she heard Lucretia say she was going on the operation to rescue Anthony. She hated not being able to do anything.

Yet just before Brianna could give the woman an affirmative, someone else spoke up.

"I can't let you leave."

A holographic screen suddenly appeared over the table that had originally contained a map of Academy Island. The face on the screen was that of an old man with many wrinkles. His shock white hair was slicked back, revealing a couple of sunspots. However, while this man looked incredibly old, his dark eyes were sharp like a blade. Even though she was only seeing him through a display, Brianna sensed how dangerous this man was.

Lucretia stepped forward and glared at the man as she flicked a blonde ringlet over her shoulder.

"Do you really think you can stop me from leaving if I want to, Felton?" she asked. "Do not forget our agreement. You are not in control of what I do. If I wish to leave, I will, and if you wish to stop me, then I'll simply destroy you."

"Hmph. I'm well aware of your power," the man called Felton said. "I'm not stopping you because I wish to stop you. Do not forget the reason you came to Academy Island. If you leave, you will be outside of our jurisdiction. I don't think I need to tell you what will happen should Cael discover you've left."

Brianna shifted at the mention of another top-class magician ranked among the strongest humans alive. She looked at Lucretia, who was now frowning like she wanted to tell this man that she didn't care.

A moment of silence passed in the room. It seemed as if everyone was holding their breath.

"Who is this man?" Brianna asked no one in particular.

Captain Dennison answered her. "That's Feltonis, our commander-in-chief. He's in charge of the Academy Island Private Security Forces."

Brianna nodded in gratitude at the information. She knew who Felton was, but she had never seen his face before now.

"You do bring up a good point," Lucretia said at last, sighing. "If I left, that foolish man would surely sense my presence and come running. I cannot afford to deal with him right now. Fine. I'll remain here."

"A wise choice," Felton said.

Lucretia glared at Felton like she was staring at a worm, but then she huffed and turned to Brianna, who suddenly felt her spine go ramrod straight.

"Since it looks like I cannot go and rescue Anthony, I will select a team to travel with you." Lucretia paused for a moment. "You should be strong enough now that you can use Anthony's physical enhancement magic in conjunction with Farsight and the Geminius Sword. However, I suggest you use caution. You will probably be going up against genetically modified clones. I have no idea what sort of abilities they might have."

That did indeed sound quite dangerous. Despite that, however, Brianna did not shy away from the task being laid out to her. Anthony was in danger. Her lover, her friend, the person she had come to cherish was in trouble. There was no way she could stand idly by and let him be taken from her.

"Don't worry," she said, feeling a surge of determination rush through her. "It doesn't matter what I'm up against. I will rescue Anthony and bring him back."

***

Secilia parted ways with Alex immediately after listening to Luna's message, traveling all the way to research lab number two.

Nametech's main headquarters, or rather, the secret base where they did their primary research, was located underground. Because it was underground, much of the space consisted of long tunnels that led to vast rooms. Secilia passed through a number of cloning facilities, which were just large rooms about the size of a football field, filled to the brim with cloning tanks. Inside each tank was a person. There were humans, vampires, therianthropes, and even succubus.

It took a bit of time to reach research lab number two, which was in a remote location far removed from the rest of the base.

Secilia, her back pressed against the wall, took out a small handheld mirror and used it to look around the corner. Through the mirror's reflection, she saw two therianthropes standing guard. They were both of the cheetah variety, meaning they were incredibly fast. There was, of course, no way she could defeat these two in a fight. Heck, she couldn't even defeat another human in a fight. She didn't know the first thing about combat.

Which meant she needed to get creative.

Secilia backtracked a bit and stepped into a room that looked like a storage closet. She turned on the lights and looked around before finding what she wanted—a small panel that she could access after removing the cover with a multipurpose tool she had stowed in a pouch at her hip. Removing the panel revealed a number of pipes, wires, levers, and circuitry.

She reached back into her pouch and pulled out a cable, one end of which she attached to her wristwatch and the other was plugged into the circuit board. A holographic display appeared above her wristwatch. It asked for a password, but she used a hacking program she had created for just this purpose. The program quickly demolished the security. Once she hacked into the powerlines, she accessed the nearest cloning room, selected one of the vampire tanks, and activated it with orders to kill the two therianthrope clones guarding research lab number two.

Once the orders were given, Secilia detached the cable, stashed it back in her pouch, and put the access panel back in place.

She waited for several minutes before moving again. This time, when she reached research lab number two, the two therianthropes were lying in pools of their own blood. Standing over them was a vampire with pale skin, blood-red eyes, black hair, and blood dripping from his fangs. He looked at her as she walked up to him, but he didn't say anything. She didn't think he could say anything.

"Guard this room," she ordered.

The vampire clone nodded and Secilia walked into research lab number two.

She walked past a lot of unused equipment. There were a number of medical tables and a variety of outdated machines, including an older version of the cloning tank. This room wasn't used much anymore, which made it great to store a variety of items inside.

At the very back of the room were a series of lockers, the kind that required a keycode to open. Secilia once again used her device to hack into the lockers, opened each one, and looked inside. Each one contained different medicine. Some of it was simple over the counter stuff that anyone could buy, but there were also numerous illegal drugs, including drugs that enhanced a person's physical strength at the cost of making their muscles atrophy faster. Secilia found the antidote in the fourth locker she checked.

She had just grabbed the antidote when a loud roar echoed from beyond the door. This was followed by the sound of something slamming into the wall, followed by a terrifying crunching noise. Secilia replaced the antidote bottle with a similar-looking bottle, closed the lockers, activated the locking mechanism, and stowed the antidote inside of a hidden compartment on her right stiletto heel.

Just as she set her foot down, the door to the room was torn open and a lion therianthrope marched in the room. Behind the therianthrope were three people. Director Azrael was the first to enter after the therianthrope. One of the other two people was bound with advanced stun cuffs. Luna. The last person was holding a gun to her back and forcing her to move along. Alex.

"I should have known you two would try something,but I had not realized you would be this daring" Director Azrael said.

"W-what's going on?!" Secilia shouted. "Alex! What is the meaning of this?!"

"Did you really think he wouldn't tell me of your plans?" asked Director Azrael. "I never trusted the two of you. Why do you think I made Alex your keeper while you were living on Academy Island? He's been keeping an eye on you and reporting everything you do back to me."

"No…" Secilia took a step back, until her back was pressed against the lockers. "Alex… why?"

"You know me, Sis," he called her "sis" in a mocking voice. "I don't want to be on the losing side, so I will do whatever I think is necessary to win."

"Grab that defective product," Director Azrael ordered the lion therianthrope.

"P-please don't hurt her!" Lucretia shouted as she struggled against the stun cuffs. She wasn't able to get them off, however, and instead she was electrocuted for resisting. "If you dare hurt her, I'll bite off my own tongue!"

"That would be unfortunate," Director Azrael admitted. "I still need your expertise for now." He looked at the therianthrope that was now looming over Secilia. "Don't kill her, but don't be gentle either."

In a moment of panic, Secilia tried to scramble away from the therianthrope, but the massive creature grabbed her face before she could. It's hand was so big her entire face was covered. She grabbed its thick forearms and struggled to pry its grip from her face, but the therianthrope was so much stronger than her. It lifted her off the ground and slammed her into the lockers.

Pain exploded in her head before everything turned dark.

CHAPTER 6

As Secilia's body went limp, Alex clenched his hands into fists. He looked at Luna, who was biting her lip. She shared a glance with him. Then she looked away.

He sighed.

The lion therianthrope lifted the unconscious girl under his arm and walked back over to Director Azrael. Her arms and legs swayed from side to side and her hair swished around. She was completely dead to the world.

"Hmph." Director Azrael snorted. "What a fool. Did she really think I wouldn't know what she was trying to do?" No one said anything. The director turned around. "Let's hurry up. We cannot afford to stay here any longer."

With the director leading the way, Alex, Luna, and the lion therianthrope exited from research lab number two and walked back the way they had come. As they walked, Director Azrael began speaking to Alex.

"Have you secured the test subject?"

"Yes, Director. He's already onboard the maglev."

"Good. In that case, we have no reason to remain here. We're abandoning this lab."

"Sir."

Luna said nothing as Alex spoke with the director. Her face was set in an emotionless mask, but Alex knew that was a facade. This woman had just watched someone who was like a daughter to her get her head smashed into a locker.

The platform they walked to was large—about the size of a football field—but there was only one maglev, and it only went in one direction. This maglev was used for emergency escapes. Essentially, it was built for the very reason they were using it now.

All of the cargo had already been loaded onto it. Most of the handling was done by the clones wandering around the exterior. Several large machines were in the process of loading up the cloning tanks. Even now, the gates on the far side were open and a large number of lifts with several cloning tanks were being transported to the maglev.

Director Azrael turned to the lion therianthrope. "Put the girl in a holding cell."

The lion therianthrope didn't say anything, but that was because he was programmed to be mute. He heeded the director's orders without a second thought. Alex watched and clenched his teeth behind his closed mouth as the lion therianthrope disappeared.

"Her too." Director Azrael pointed to Luna. "Put her in a holding cell as well. I don't want her trying anything."

"Yes, sir," Alex said.

Keeping a firm grip on Luna and the gun on her back, Alex led the woman into the maglev and directed her toward the holding cells. He was mindful of the security cameras located all over the maglev.

The holding cells were close to the back. They looked similar to jail cells. Each one had a small cot and nothing else.

The cots also didn't look like they would be comfortable to sleep on. Secilia was still unconscious, lying on the cot in the jail cell to his left. The cell had already been activated. Several large beams of plasma kept anyone from going into or out of the cell.

The lion therianthrope was present, standing guard near the door. Alex eyed him for a moment. However, there was nothing he could do about this man.

Alex directed Luna into the cell across from Secilia. Before shoving her into the cell, he placed something in her hand, then pushed. The woman stumbled into the cell. The plasma bars activated seconds later. As they did, Luna whirled around and glared at him.

"Be sure not to cause any trouble," Alex said. "I'd hate for anything to happen to you." Turning, he looked at the lion therianthrope. "Come on. Director Azrael is waiting for us."

The lion therianthrope didn't say anything, but he did follow Alex out the door.

***

Luna watched as the door closed behind Alex. She waited for a moment to see if he and the leonid would come back. When it looked like neither Alex nor the leonid were going to return, she moved over to the cot and sat down.

Because she was right across from Secilia, Luna had a perfect view of the unconscious girl. Her heart clenched seeing her like this.

Luna took several deep breaths. Once she felt sufficiently calm, she looked down at the object in her hand. It was just a small sheet of paper. However, what was written on the paper was important.

It said: *Anthony is being kept in the back of the train. Wait until my signal to act. You'll know it when it happens.*

She closed her hand around the message, leaned back against the wall, and waited for the moment she could act.

***

Maglev—derived from magnetic levitation—was a system of train transportation that used two sets of magnets, one set to repel and push the train up off the track, then another set to move the "floating train" ahead at great speed by taking advantage of the lack of friction. Because of this very reason, maglevs were able to compete favorably with airplanes in terms of speed. The fastest maglev to date traveled in excess of four hundred miles per hour.

It took around one hour to get all of the equipment onboard, but once that was done, Director Azrael ordered his clones to get the transportation moving.

Alex was given more or less free reign to move about the maglev. He'd proven himself when he betrayed Secilia and Luna to the director, and there wasn't any need for him to hang around Director Azrael anyway. The man had that big leonid for a bodyguard, and in any event, Alex was not very strong.

Leonid was the name of the therianthrope that looked like a lion. Out of all the therianthropes, they were physically one of the strongest. With something like that guarding him, Director Azrael would not need to worry about someone hurting him unless he was attacked by someone whose powers were on par with a vampire noble.

There were a total of forty-two compartments to this maglev. The one in the middle was the suite where Director

Azrael was staying in. Near the back were the storage compartments, which also included the holding cells and the compartment where Anthony had been stashed away. Alex was heading to the front, which was where the control room and operating center was located.

Only one clone was inside of the control center when he arrived, a young woman with black cat ears and a back tail—a therianthrope known as a pantherian. She was monitoring the board that operated the maglev's main system. Perhaps it was because she didn't expect anyone hostile to be on the maglev, or maybe it was because she had been programmed only to operate the system, but she didn't turn around.

Alex hesitated for only a moment before raising the gun in his hand and pulling the trigger. He looked away as blood splattered all over the console. A loud thump echoed around the room as the woman's head slumped against the controls.

Despite the urge he felt to vomit, Alex didn't stop as he went over to another control station, which controlled the holding cell, doors, lights, and other features inside of the train. The first thing he did was lock down all the doors in the first half of the train. After that, he unlocked all the doors in the back, then turned off the power for the holding cells.

"Secilia and Luna should be able to get out now," he muttered. "Now I just need to do the last part here."

Alex grimaced as he went over to the control station that operated the maglev's movements. The overpowering stench of blood threatened to once again make him vomit. His bullet had gone clean through the pantherian clone, and now blood was oozing all over the console.

He tried to keep calm as he removed the woman from the seat and set her against the wall. Alex tried not to look at the glassy eyes staring at him as he stood back up, sat down in the seat, and looked at the control panel.

It was a very good thing he was in the engineering department at the Institution of Magical Sciences. They had worked with maglev's once or twice in the past, and he had first hand practice controlling their operating systems, so even though this OS was slightly different from the one he had worked on, it was close enough that he was able to figure it out quickly.

There were two notable types of maglev technology: electromagnetic suspension and electrodynamic suspension.

With electromagnetic suspension systems, the train levitated above a steel rail while electromagnets, attached to the train, were oriented toward the rail from below. The system was typically arranged with a series of C-shaped arms, with the upper portion of the arm attached to the vehicle, and the lower inside edge containing the magnets. The rail was then situated inside of the C, between the upper and lower edges.

In electrodynamic suspension, both the guideway and the train exerted a magnetic field, and the train was levitated by the repulsive and attractive force between these magnetic fields. Some configurations made it so the train could be levitated only by repulsive force. The magnetic field for this system was produced either by superconducting magnets (known as JR-Malev) or by an array of permanent magnets. The repulsive and attractive force in the track was created by an induced magnetic field in wires or other conducting strips in the track.

This one used an electrodynamic suspension, which meant it was dynamically stable. However, it also meant this train had wheels, since the current induced in the coils and the resultant magnetic flux was not large enough to levitate the train at slow speeds.

Alex operated the controls and slowed the train down before forcing it to come to a stop. He watched through the windows as the scenery that had been previously blurring by at upwards of 300 miles per hour came to a stop.

The area outside the maglev was rugged, a dramatic landscape with layers of rock formations, steep canyons, and towering spires. It looked like the terrain would be hard to move through and very easy to get lost in. Alex thought that was a good thing. If it was easy to get lost in, then it would be easy to lose any pursuers in too.

But just before Alex could sigh in relief, the door to the maglev's control room dented inward as something powerful slammed into it. Alex only had a second to stand up before a claw punctured a hole through the door and tore it open.

Two people entered the room. The first was the leonid, and the second was Director Azrael. While the therianthrope wore the same expression as always, the director's lips were drawn into a thin line and his eyes were narrowed. He looked angry.

"When you betrayed Secilia and Luna, I thought for sure I could trust you," the director said. "That was my mistake. I should have realized any clone that hasn't been personally programmed by me could never be trusted."

Alex almost scoffed at the comment. This man never trusted anyone that he hadn't personally tinkered around with. All the clones that had been created since Director Azrael took over were programmed with absolute obedience to the director. It was a wonder that vampire, Frederic Bloodstone or whatever, had been able to control them at all, but he guessed even clones were susceptible to a vampire's power once turned.

"Yes, you really should have realized I'd never obey a prick like you," Alex as he reached for the gun at his side.

"I consider this a lesson well-learned." Director Azrael narrowed his eyes. "Kill him."

Alex reached for the gun and pulled it out of his holster. His aim was not at the therianthrope but the control panel. He was able to pull the trigger exactly two times, the bullets penetrating the control panel and causing sparks to fly. Then the leonid was on top of him.

The floor and walls became painted with blood.

***

Secilia felt like her head was being split open as her consciousness returned. She couldn't remember what happened. Her head throbbed like she'd gone out drinking with some girlfriends all night, but she didn't think that was what had happened because none of her friends drank.

Opening her eyes, she blinked several times as her blurry vision sharpened. The gray ceiling above her was not one that she was familiar with.

"Secilia, I'm so glad you're awake," someone said to her left.

Turning her head, Secilia found plasma beams traveling horizontally across a small space. There were sixteen in total. It looked like this place was a holding cell or a prison of some kind. On the other side of her cell was another cell, and this one contained a woman she was very familiar with.

"Mom...?"

Secilia sat up, though doing so made her head pound even more. She shifted until her legs were dangling over the side of her cot, leaned forward, and placed her head in her hands. Had she ever felt this bad before? She couldn't remember if she had or not.

"How are you feeling?" asked Luna.

"Awful," Secilia replied immediately. "I feel like someone cracked my skull open. What happened?"

"You were knocked unconscious by a therianthrope under Azrael's control. It slammed your head into a locker," Luna said.

"Is that what happened? I certainly feel like I might have a concussion."

As she sat there and tried to regain her bearings, Secilia's memories began slowly returning. She remembered traveling to research lab number two, sicking a clone on two other clones, getting the antidote for the drug keeping Anthony under, and then being captured. As she recalled that last part, Secilia remembered everything.

She looked up at Luna.

"Alex?! Did he—?!"

"He should be getting ready to shut down the holding cell and stop the maglev from moving," Luna answered. "We'll have to be ready for when that happens."

"So he didn't join Director Azrael?" Secilia sucked in a deep breath before releasing it all in one go. Her body felt like it was sagging. "That's good. When I saw him holding a gun to your back, I thought for sure he had joined... but that's impossible. He hates that man even more than I do."

"I'm sorry for not telling you about this part of the plan," Luna said softly. "I wanted everything to be convincing. Azrael is a cunning man. If you had given him even a small reason to be suspicious, I'm afraid this plan would never even get off the ground."

"I get that," Secilia said. "Don't worry. I understand. So long as we can save Anthony, I don't really care about how we have to go about it."

"You must really care for that man," Luna said with a wistful smile.

"I do." Secilia returned the woman's smile with one of her own. "I didn't think much of him when we first met. He was just this skinny kid who wore really baggy clothes and didn't seem like much, but he's very smart and dedicated, and he's always looking out for others. He's also got quite the tongue. It's rare to find someone so capable of keeping up with me in a game of wits and words."

"He sounds like a great man," Luna said. "Once we make it out of here, you will have to introduce me to him properly."

"I… maybe…" Secilia's lips trembled as she thought about the last time she'd spoken to Anthony. She clasped her hands together and clenched them hard. "After what I did to him, I'm not… really sure he'll want to have anything to do with me."

Secilia had betrayed Anthony. She'd brought him to her apartment, drugged his drink, and smuggled him to a secret base where the man in charge planned on performing numerous inhumane experiments on him. If their positions had been reversed, Secilia wouldn't forgive him. She couldn't expect him to forgive her.

"You may be right," Luna admitted. Perhaps she realized that offering words of comfort right now would not help. "However, even if he decides to never trust you again, I think you should at least explain the situation to him and apologize properly."

"I will," Secilia said.

At that very moment, the plasma beams to their holding cells fizzled out.

"It looks like Alex has succeeded." Luna stood up and moved over to Secilia, holding out her hand. "Come on. Let's go rescue the man you love."

Secilia stared at the hand, which looked so much like her own. Of course they did. Their hands were identical. Luna's hand was a little larger, had a few more wrinkles, and didn't possess the calluses that Secilia's did, but they were definitely the same hand.

"Yes. Let's."

Secilia placed her hand in Luna's and allowed the older woman to pull her up. Her head throbbed painfully the moment she stood. While her legs felt wobbly, Secilia still tried her best to shunt aside the pain as Luna rushed out of the cell, pulling her along for the ride.

"W-where is Anthony being kept? Do you know?" asked Secilia as they raced out of this compartment and into the next one.

"He's being kept in the very back!" Luna answered.

The compartment immediately after the one they exited was a storage room. Boxes were stacked on top of each other on either side. Each box was an advanced storage unit, which used a fusion of technology and time magic to keep anything locked inside in a form of stasis. Secilia remembered making these several years ago. That was before Azrael had taken over as director.

After the storage compartment came one containing cloning tanks, though all of them were empty. It looked like Azrael had disposed of all the clones inside each tank. He couldn't have done anything else. Clones required the nutrients found in the special liquid contained within each tank, but in order for the liquid to be constantly pumped into the tanks, they needed to be hooked up to an advanced system. These were just tanks. The system itself was too big to take with them.

They passed through two compartments worth of cloning tanks before reaching the end. This last compartment appeared small thanks to all the medical equipment stashed inside. What caught Secilia's immediate attention was the large portable bed. It was the kind that could be removed and attached to a variety of different pedestals. This one looked like it was currently attached to a pedestal that was embedded into the floor of this compartment.

Anthony was lying on this bed. Metal locks around his arms and legs kept him bound in place. His eyes were closed and his breathing was so slow she almost thought he was dead.

Secilia rushed up to Anthony's bed and yanked the IV drip filling his bloodstream with drugs from his arm. Then she accessed the bed's operation system, undoing the locks, which opened with a soft click. Once his limbs were free, Secilia lifted her leg and opened the small compartment on her heel. She pulled out a small cylinder containing a glowing green liquid. The cylinder was one of those emergency syringes. She placed the syringe against Anthony's neck and pressed the top button with her thumb, narrowing her eyes as the contents disappeared into Anthony's body.

She threw away the syringe and leaned forward on baited breath, watching Anthony for any signs of waking up. It took a moment. However, when Anthony's eyes finally opened, Secilia could have cried in relief.

"Anthony! Anthony, you're awake!"

"Secilia?" Anthony sounded groggy. His voice was throaty like he wasn't fully awake. He blinked several times as his eyes focused on her. "What... happened? Where... where are... we?"

"I'll tell you later," Secilia said as she helped him sit up. "First, we need to get out of here. It's dangerous."

Anthony needed several seconds to fully wake up. He'd been constantly pumped full of drugs for almost 24 hours.

Incubus had an incredible immunity to magic and drugs, but it took time to build up resistance, and Anthony's body had been pumped full of a drug that was powerful enough to knock even a therianthrope out for several days.

While Secilia patiently waited for Anthony to recover enough to move, Luna went over to the back and unlocked the door. A blast of warm air rushed into the compartment. After looking outside, she came back over to them.

"We should escape from the maglev once you can move," she said.

Anthony gave her a blank look. "Who are you? Why do you look like Secilia?"

"My name is Luna," she answered. "I'm a professor who specializes in biology and cloning. I suppose you could say I am Secilia's mother."

"Oh." Anthony blinked several times. It seemed he still wasn't fully awake. "Well, nice to meet you."

Luna gave him an amused smile. "Were our circumstances not so dire, it would be very nice to meet you too."

Before anything else could be said, the door to the compartment was torn apart, and a loud roar resounded from the other side as a massive therianthrope covered in fur stormed in. It was the leonid. He glared at them with blood red eyes. Another roared emerged from him as he opened his mouth, revealing sharp teeth. The fur on his back, arms, and legs bristled as he rushed forward with the obvious intent to cause harm.

Anthony must have recovered or perhaps he was stronger than Secilia gave him credit for. He leapt from the bed, blue lines appearing all over his body. They looked a lot like the circuits of a super computer's motherboard. He rushed forward and slammed into the leicenthrope, meeting the creature's attacks head on.

The leonid raised a massive hand and brought it down, claws out as though to tear Anthony's flesh from his bones. To Secilia's great surprise, Anthony did not back down, instead lifting his right hand and catching the attack with his palm. With a grunt, the man thrust his hand up, forcing the leonid's clawed hand away, then took two steps forward and slammed his other fist into the leonid's stomach.

While the attack was precise and powerful enough that Secilia could actually hear the thud of flesh meeting flesh, it didn't seem to do much. The leonid barely reacted to being hit. In fact, it didn't even seem to notice it.

Roaring again, the leonid tried to attack Anthony with several more claw swipes, but the man was like lightning. He moved left, right, ducked, and dodged from side to side. Occasionally, an attack would come in too fast, but then he would just block it with his hands or forearms.

For a moment, Secilia was stunned as Anthony fought the leonid barehanded. Therianthropes were physically the most powerful demons in existence. They could punch a hole clean through walls made from composite materials like duralloy and adamantite. Their bodies were so powerful and durable that normal bullets bounced right off them.

Leonids were a particularly powerful breed of therianthrope. Other types like werewolves, pantherians, and nekomatas were ants compared to leonids. Yet here was Anthony, a young man who had barely come into his incubus powers, who was still dealing with a drug running through his body, and he was fighting one of these therianthrope barehanded.

If the situation were not so dire, she would have found it ridiculous.

While Anthony became locked in combat against the leonid, Director Azrael appeared from behind the massive monstrosity and looked at Secilia and Luna.

"I'm beginning to regret letting you two live," he said. "I kept you both alive because I have a need for that brilliant mind of yours, Professor. However, it seems you are going to insist on spurning the small measure of kindness I have shown you."

As the man spoke, the leonid tried to hit Anthony with a double claw attack, but the young man slammed his hands into the creature's paws. Now with their hands locked, the two pushed against each other. Their muscles strained. The glowing lines flowing across Anthony's body brightened.

"Kindness?" Luna scoffed. "You did not show us any kindness. You killed my husband and threatened to kill Secilia and Alex if I didn't do as you ordered. You kept me imprisoned and used my children as bargaining chips to force me into working for you. You wouldn't know kindness if it smacked you in the face."

"I kept you and those creations of yours alive," Director Azrael said.

"Because you needed me!"

"I'm not going to argue semantics with you. It doesn't matter now anyway." Director Azrael raised his hand, revealing that he was holding a gun, which he pointed at Luna. "Since you have become far more trouble than you're worth, I'm going to dispose of you both. It will be difficult finding someone to replace you, but I'm sure it won't be impossible. There are many brilliant minds out there, after all."

Secilia and Luna froze as the man pointed a gun at them. Neither of them were combatants, and they didn't have any supernatural abilities that would let them survive a bullet. They were just normal people.

Director Azrael kept the gun pointed at Luna, but then he smiled and aimed it at Secilia.

"NO!" Luna shouted as she pushed Secilia out of the way.

Seclia fell to the ground, hitting the metal grating hard enough that pain shot up her tailbone and through her spine. At that exact moment, Director Azrael pulled the trigger. The sound of a gunshot echoed in the small compartment. Secilia felt as if she was watching everything in slow motion as Luna flew into her like she'd been struck by something hard. Her body slumped against Secilia, face on her chest.

"M-Mom?" Secilia said.

She looked down at the woman on her chest, who wasn't even an inch. It wasn't until nearly a second later that she felt something dripping onto her chest, staining her shirt.

Secilia shifted again and took the woman into her arms. As Luna's head rolled back, Secilia saw that her mother had a bullet hole traveling straight through her head. Blood leaked from the wound. Luna's eyes were open, but they were completely glassy and sightless. The last expression on her face was one of desperation.

"No, no, no, no! Mom!"

A cry tore from Secilia's lips as she realized her mother was dead. She was dead. She wasn't coming back. Even if she wanted to reject what happened, reject this terrible reality, she couldn't, not when she was seeing her dead mother with her own eyes.

It felt like a hole had opened in her chest. She couldn't help but remember all the times she and her mother had shared before Director Azrael had taken over the company. She recalled listening to her mother read her bedtime stories, the times her mom had taught her about technology, the times her mom got angry at her for tinkering with her machines, or that time she hacked into the central database and implanted a painting program into the moving equipment. All of it flowed into her mind. At the same time, it felt like all the joy and happiness from these memories was being sucked into a quantum black hole.

As tears poured from her eyes, Director Azrael lifted the run and aimed it at her. Secilia was too distraught to even notice.

***

Anthony still wasn't exactly sure of anything. He didn't know where he was, how he'd gotten there, or what he'd been doing before finding himself in this place. His mind felt like it had been trapped within a dark fog. A smoky haze. The drug that he'd been pumped full of was still inside of his body.

Despite this, when the therianthrope charged into the compartment and attacked them, Anthony had activated Physical Enhancement and met the attack headon.

Thanks to his magically enhanced body, he was able to fight this beast on even terms. It helped that the compartment was narrow and the leonid was so big. Thanks to that, his opponent had a very limited range of motion, while he could move about much more freely.

He dodged around most of the attacks that came his way. A lot of the therianthrope's attacks were very straightforward. It didn't throw any punches. It came at him with wide claw swipes and sometimes tried to impale him, but all of those attacks were easy to spot and therefore easy to dodge.

Anthony had also been sparring with Brianna a lot. She was far better at combat than this giant cat.

While he was battling against the leonid, Anthony still kept an eye on Secilia and the woman who looked like an older version of her, so he saw when Director Azrael tried to shoot Secilia. He would have helped her, but the leonid made it impossible for him to move away. The gun went off as Luna pushed Secilia out of the way. Unlike the girl now lying on the ground, he'd seen how the bullet blasted a hole straight through the woman's head.

As Secilia cried over her mother, the man in the lab coat aimed the gun at her, and Anthony knew he had to act.

Leaping back, he channeled as much mana into his left leg as he dared. Raising it, he slammed it into the floor and unleashed all the stored up mana in a single burst. The entire floor split open and the train shook. The man was knocked off balance. He still pulled the trigger, but his shot went wide. The leonid that Anthony had been fighting also suffered when the floor collapsed underneath him.

Anthony didn't wait to see the true results of his attack. Spinning around, he darted over to the crying Secilia and her dead mother, lifted them both into his arms, and raced toward the open door in the back. Gunshots echoed around him as the lab coat wearing man tried to shoot them. However, his aim was off. He probably didn't have proper training. That headshot of his had likely been a case of luck and not actual skill. Anthony didn't even bother looking back as he leapt out of the train, onto the tracks, and then turned around and darted toward a canyon several dozen yards away.

The canyon was large and rugged, spanning what appeared to be dozens of miles in all directions. He had no idea where this was. It didn't matter, however. He raced through the complex maze of mountainous cliffs, pumping mana into his legs so he could move faster, so he could go further. He ran and ran and ran. Only after the sun began going down did he stop.

He set Secilia and Luna on the ground. While Secilia sat up, the woman merely slumped and lay unmoving on her stomach.

"M-Mom..." Secilia's anguished whisper tore at Anthony as the dark-haired beauty crawled over to her mother. She rolled the woman onto her back. More tears spilled from her eyes as she found a sightless gaze staring back at her. "Please... Mom. You have to be alive. You can't... you can't be dead. You can't... leave me... please...!"

Anthony didn't know what to do or say, so he stood back and did nothing as Secilia collapsed into Luna's chest and began wailing.

CHAPTER 7

Anthony let Secilia cry for as long as he could, but he understood they couldn't remain there. That doctor in the lab coat and the lion therianthrope were still a threat. He was sure they would begin searching for the two of them very soon.

He placed a hand on Secilia's shoulder. The girl turned her head and looked at him, her eyes red and swollen, her cheeks stained with tears.

"Anthony…"

"Come on," he said in a soft voice. "We need to keep moving. Otherwise, that director guy will find us."

"But… Mom…"

"We'll take her with us." Anthony looked at Secilia's mother, at her glassy eyes and still chest, then fixed his gaze on Secilia again. "We won't be able to keep her body since it will start to decompose, but we… we can at least find a good spot to bury her."

At his words, Secilia looked like she might start crying again. Yet as she stared into his eyes, she settled down and eventually nodded.

"Okay…"

With her agreement, Anthony lifted Luna into his arms. She wasn't light. However, she also wasn't heavy. It was a little hard to carry her because she was dead weight, but his strength had grown since accepting Brianna as a bondmate.

"Let's keep heading deeper into the canyon," Anthony suggested.

"Okay," Secilia agreed readily enough.

He glanced at her again, at her dull eyes and worn face, at the way her shoulders had slumped. She looked like one of those people who had given up hope. It was like she had reached the end and no longer had anything to live for.

He wished he could do something for her, but he didn't know what he could do.

They set off at a slow pace. Anthony wasn't worried about Director Azrael or the leonid finding him right now. It would take them some time before they could begin searching. This mountainous canyon was also quite large, so it would take them a while to search everywhere, and while leonid's did have a good sense of smell, it wasn't as good as other therianthropes. It would be harder to track them by scent.

It didn't look like there were any trees in this canyon, but there were several areas that contained really tall grass. They stayed clear of those spots and continued traveling through the canyons. As he looked up, Anthony noticed the sky had grown dark. The sun had almost disappeared below the mountain. It would be hard to continue traveling in this rugged terrain once that happened.

"We should find a cave or something to rest in," Anthony said. "We also need to find a spot to… to bury your mom."

"Y-yeah." Secilia looked like she was barely holding herself together. He worried she might break down, but there was nothing he could do right now.

They eventually found a cave after walking for what felt like an hour but was probably less time than either of them realized. It was not a large cave. He would have said it was about the size of his bedroom back home, but that was enough for them to rest in.

"I don't think we're going to find any firewood or anything," he said after a moment. "We won't be able to start a fire to keep warm or cook food… not that we have any food to cook."

Now that he was more aware of their situation, Anthony was realizing how ill-equipped they were. He was no survivalist. Even so, he knew at least a little about surviving in the wilds. Back when he and Calvin had to fend for themselves, he would often hunt for food rather than rely on stealing from others. It was easier that way.

"What should we do?" asked Secilia.

"Let's… let's bury your mom first," Anthony said at last.

Secilia nodded but didn't say anything. He was sure she did that because she'd start crying if she spoke too much.

Anthony set Luna's body on the ground and searched around for a soft patch of dirt. Most of this area appeared to be made of densely packed dirt and rocks, so it took longer than he would have liked. The stars had already appeared in the night sky by the time he began digging.

He used Physical Enhancement to dig the hole with his bare hands, which also helped protect his hands from being torn apart. He didn't know how wide the hole needed to be.

That being the case, he widened it out until it was at least two yards long and one yard wide… or thereabouts. He was guesstimating.

While he worked, Secilia watched him with a complex expression. She couldn't help him dig. Not only did they not have the tools for that, but Secilia didn't have any special powers. She was just a regular human.

"I think that's big enough." Anthony stood up and stepped back to study the large hole he had dug in the ground. After a moment, he turned to Secilia. "I'm going to put your mother in now. Is that okay?"

Secilia opened her mouth to say something, but then she abruptly closed it. She looked at her mother's body, bit her lip, then looked back at him. She didn't answer him in words. After nodding at him to proceed, she turned away as if she didn't want to see what was going to happen.

Anthony sighed and lifted Luna again before gently lowering her into the hole. He began moving the dirt again, covering the hole until it was nothing but a large mound. Once he was done, he tried to clap the dust off his hands as he stood up and moved to stand beside Secilia.

"Are you okay?" he asked. Secilia shook her head, still not speaking. With a frown, Anthony grabbed her hand and began pulling her along. "Come on. Let's get into the cave. I'm not sure what kind of animals come out here at night, but at the very least, we should find a place to hide from that director guy. He might have a means of tracking us via satellite."

Secilia didn't resist as Anthony pulled her along behind him. They entered the cave and sat down. Secilia brought her knees up to her chest and hugged them. Her actions and the expression on her face made her seem extremely fragile, like a glass figurine that would shatter at the slightest touch.

Neither of them said anything for the longest time; Anthony didn't know what to say and Secilia didn't seem like she was even capable of talking. He worried that his friend might be in shock.

After several moments of silence passed, Secilia finally spoke.

"I'm sorry," she said, her voice a croaking whisper.

"Are you sorry because you kidnapped me?" asked Anthony. "Or is it something else?"

"I'm sorry for that and everything else," Secilia admitted. "I never wanted to hurt you. I never wanted to drag you into my problems. I can't… ever apologize enough."

Anthony said nothing as he leaned against the wall and crossed his arms, attempting to ward off the night's chill, but also trying to keep his hormones in check. He wasn't sure how long he'd gone without sex, but it must have been awhile. His body was acting up. It was telling him he would need mana soon. Fortunately, he still had at least half his mana left, so he wouldn't run out for at least another day or two, depending on how much he used.

"I'm sure you've already realized it," Secilia suddenly continued, "But I work for Nametech. On the surface, they are a company that creates advanced prosthetics, but that's only on the surface. In truth, Nametech is a company that practices cloning. The prosthetics they make are created with cloning technology. They make a clone of the person who needs the prosthetic, use advanced growth technology to accelerate the clone's growth, then kill the clone and remove the limb needed. The limb is then attached using bonding magic that bonds flesh, muscles, bones, and even nerves at the molecular level."

"That explains how you knew so much about Nametech," Anthony said at last. "It also explains where all those rogue demons Frederic Bloodstone used were coming from. They weren't rogue demons at all. They were clones that he had discovered and took control of."

"Yes," Secilia said. "We're not sure how he discovered what we were doing, but he attacked the warehouse where several of our clones were stored, activated them, and had them begin running amok in the city to mask his movements." She paused as another thought occurred to her. "He might have also somehow found out about Director Azrael's interest in you and attacked for that reason. I heard he tried to steal your powers."

"As if such a thing is even possible." Anthony released a dry laugh at the idea that a vampire could steal an incubus power. "I think I already know the answer, but I'd like to hear it from you. Were you sent by Nametech to seduce me?"

Secilia's lips trembled as she nodded. "I don't know how Director Azrael discovered your existence. Someone must have told him, but I have no idea who. Anyway, he sent me to Academy Island to find and seduce you. I was supposed to become your bondmate, then take you back to his base in the Rocky Mountains." A mirthless smile appeared on her lips. "I failed, of course. When we first met, you always kept your distance, and I was never what you'd call a seductress. I don't even know the first thing about seducing someone."

Anthony nodded. "Back then, I was afraid that if I bonded with someone, I would forget about Lilith, so I always did my best to never get too close to anyone."

"It showed." Secilia raised her head to look at him and smiled, though it wasn't what he would have called a happy smile. Her eyes were swollen and puffy too. "In any case, after constantly seeing you day after day and becoming your friend, I began to really like you—no." She shook her head. "I fell in love with you. However, I knew that if we became bondmates, I would have no choice but to take you back to Director Azrael. I didn't want that. I didn't want you to be used in that man's twisted experiments. That's why I never tried to force the issue. I thought so long as no one became your bondmate, I could delay this issue indefinitely."

"And then Brianna became my bondmate," Anthony said.

"Yes," Secilia agreed with a grimace.

Anthony could not begin to imagine how this girl felt. She had befriended him, fallen for him, but she tried her best to never get any closer because she was afraid of what she would be forced to do if she did. She spent all that time trying to protect him from the person controlling her from the shadows, only to end up failing because he had bonded with Brianna.

The cold night air caused him to shiver, but he ignored the chill in favor of continuing their conversation.

"Is the reason you kidnapped me because Director Azrael was holding your mother hostage?" he asked at last.

"Luna isn't my real mother," Secilia admitted, a wry and mirthless smile appearing on her face. "I'm actually a clone. I was created using Luna's DNA about twenty-one years ago. Unlike the other clones that received growth hormones to accelerate their growth, I was allowed to grow naturally." She hugged her knees tighter. "Luna was… very kind to me. While I was just a clone, she treated me like her own daughter. She'd teach me about the world, tuck me into bed and tell me bedtime stories, and even tried to make food… though she wasn't very good at it. She couldn't cook to save her life."

As Anthony listened to her talk, a thought occurred to him.

"Then doesn't that mean Alex isn't your real brother?"

"Alex is still technically my half-brother." Secilia shrugged. "He's also a clone, though he's younger than me by about ten years. He was made using the DNA from Luna and another doctor named Callaway. He was Luna's husband in case you're curious. Since I was made from just Luna's DNA, I'm what you'd call a complete clone. Alex is more like a baby that was grown in an artificial womb, though he was still made using cloning technology." She hesitated again before telling him a secret. "Mom… Luna is barren. She can't conceive children. I think she dabbled in cloning because she wanted to have kids."

"Makes sense." Anthony grew quiet for a moment, and Secilia didn't talk either, allowing him time to think and absorb what she told him. Finally, he asked a question. "What about Director Azrael? How did he come into the picture?"

Secilia set her chin on her knees and didn't talk for a moment. Anthony thought maybe she didn't want to talk about that man, which he wouldn't have blamed her for, considering what happened, but she did begin speaking after a while.

"Director Azrael was originally Mom's student," she said at last. "However, unlike Luna and Callaway, who only wanted to have children they could raise and believed cloning technology could improve humanity's quality of living, Director Azrael was only interested in making money. Despite being Mom's student, he would often argue with her over how she used cloning, saying she didn't understand how the real world worked, or that she and her husband were naive fools. And maybe they were. After all, Director Azrael did end up killing Callaway and then took me and Alex hostage. He forced Mom to become his subordinate to protect us and forced us to follow his orders to protect Mom. Maybe if we hadn't been so stupid, none of this would have happened."

There was an old saying about how hindsight was always 20/20. It was impossible to know what would happen in the future. Maybe you would choose one path, only to realize later on that it was a mistake, but it wasn't like you could know you were making a mistake at the time you made that choice.

"I don't think you or your mom were stupid," Anthony said at last. "No one could have known what Director Azrael would do."

"Maybe not, but there were signs." Secilia shook her head as though to deny his words. "We should have realized he was evil once he began spouting nonsense about how we should be using cloning technology to turn a profit."

Anthony couldn't say anything to dispute that.

As they sat there in the darkness of the cave, with only sparse amounts of moonlight to illuminate the interior, Anthony thought about everything he had learned. Secilia had suffered so much. He had no idea she had gone through so much pain. If he could, he wanted to help her, to ease the pain in her heart, even if only a little.

The problem was that he didn't know how he could do that.

***

It took several hours to get an airplane ready to leave. Brianna didn't know what sort of preparations had gone into getting everything ready, but Lucretia did introduce her to the team she'd be traveling with. They were a mixed bunch of humans and demons. There were two human men, a vampire woman, and two therianthropes—one man and one woman who looked and argued like siblings.

She didn't know any of them beyond their names, and they would probably never see each other again after this mission, so she didn't bother remembering every little thing about them. Even if she was inclined to remember, her mind was so focused on rescuing Anthony that she couldn't think about anything else.

The airplane they rode in was a smaller stealth plane. The interior was large enough to seat their entire team, but it didn't have much more room than that.

Much like the rest of the world, airplanes now incorporated a variety of flight and wind magic into their creation. There was magic to reduce wind resistance, increase thrust and propulsion, and protect the aircraft's exterior. Since the one they were on was a stealth craft, it also had magic that reduced the reflection/emissions of radar, infrared, visible light, radio frequency spectrum, and audio. This particular aircraft was experimental, according to Lucretia, but it was also the most advanced aircraft in the Academy Island Private Security Forces's arsenal.

As she sat on the long bench that spanned most of the aircraft, her Geminius Sword on her lap, she tried to ignore the conversation from her "teammates."

"I can't believe we're being sent into the middle of nowhere just to rescue a couple of college brats," a black man with massive muscles and a buzzed head mumbled as he crossed his arms. Brianna thought his name was Abe.

"I hear one of them is Commander Lucretia's student or something," the therianthrope woman said. She was a tigress therianthrope. Her hair and ears were primarily orange with black and white stripes. A long tiger tail extended from the black unitard she wore underneath her armor.

"So we're being used for a personal request?" asked the other therianthrope. He had the same hair and striped pattern as the woman. "Well, I guess that's fine. It means the commander will owe us one, doesn't it?"

"Hmph. I don't care if she owes us." Abe did not look at all pleased. "You know that woman as well as I do. It doesn't matter if we help her by rescuing one of her students. That frigid bitch is as cold as ice. She'll never let us cash in on a favor."

"You don't know that," said the vampire. Like the rest of her species, she had glowing red eyes and sharp fangs. Skin as white as snow, like freshly fallen powder, made her appear almost ethereal. Her hair was blonde and tied into a bun behind her head. "In either event, I'm more interested in knowing why this student of hers was kidnapped. There has to be something special about him, doesn't there?"

"Who knows?" Abe shrugged.

"She might know." The other human man, who had tanned skin and a trimmed goatee, pointed at Brianna. "She seems close to Lucretia, and she's a War Maiden. I can't imagine her not knowing."

At those words, everyone turned to look at Brianna, who suddenly felt a chill run down her spine as she was put in the spotlight. While their stares made her a bit nervous, she knew showing fear would only invite them to pressure her. That was why she sent all of them a glare.

"Everything about the people we are rescuing is confidential. I can't tell you anything."

"Che." Abe scoffed. "Figures."

"Well, whatever. Just don't get in our way when we arrive at our destination," the tan man said.

Brianna said nothing to that, and the squadron of elite men and women eventually ignored her and went back to their own conversation.

The ride was incredibly smooth, so smooth Brianna couldn't even tell they were flying. It didn't take long before they arrived at their destination. An announcement was made over the speakers by the pilot.

Because there were no windows in this aircraft, Brianna couldn't see anything, but she felt the atmospheric shifts in the aircraft as it descended. It wasn't long after that the aircraft set down on something with a loud noise. The engines whined a moment before cutting out. Then the ramp near the back lowered.

"Okay, people! Let's move!" Abe stood up from his seat, grabbed a black rifle with glowing blue lines and magic formulas covering the surface, and held it at the ready. "Remember to be cautious. We don't know what sort of dangers we might run into."

"Yes, sir!" everyone but Brianna said.

Brianna followed the group down the boarding ramp and into what looked like a docking bay. She immediately spotted the private jet sitting several yards away. It was the same one that Secilia and Alex had smuggled Anthony in.

The squadron traveled across the docking bay far more slowly than she would have liked, though she said nothing because she understood they were just being cautious. Once it was determined that no enemies were present, the group moved to the doorway at the end of the room. It was a large double-door made of composite alloys. It was locked. However, the vampire lady pulled a chord from the vambrace around her left wrist, inserted it into a small slot after removing an access panel on the wall, and hacked into the door.

"Let's keep going," Abe said as the door opened. "Keep an eye out for suspicious activity."

No one said anything, but they did proceed into the hallway with more caution than before.

The place they were in looked like a combination of maze, underground bunker, and research lab. There were numerous rooms that contained all kinds of medical and research equipment. Some of the items were ones Brianna knew from sight like the medical tanks and bio scanners, but there were a lot of devices she had never seen before.

Of all the objects they found, it was the cloning facilities that got their attention.

"Holy fucking shit," Abe said as he and his squadron gazed upon a large room that was clearly designed for mass producing clones.

"You ever seen anything like this?" asked the therianthrope woman.

The other therianthrope shook his head. "Never."

There were a lot of cloning tanks arrayed in rows, so many Brianna couldn't count them all. Floating within those tanks were people. Just a cursory glance revealed humans, therianthrope, vampires, succubus, and several other demons like dryads and nymphs. The fact that such a large-scale cloning operation existed was shocking.

Abe took a deep breath. "We should move on. We're not here to gawk."

Brianna remained silent as they searched the rest of the underground base, but while they did find a lot more experiments related to cloning, including some paper files that must have been forgotten at some point, they could not find Anthony or the people responsible for kidnapping him. That said, they did eventually find the empty maglev station.

"It looks like whoever owns this place has already left," the vampire said as she accessed a control panel near the tracks. "It says here that a maglev left this station exactly five hours ago. Whoever is in charge here probably realized Academy Island would send a task force to retrieve the target and decided to leave before that could happen."

It was already dark outside. Through the exit where the maglev had left, the velvet sky with its array of stars became quite clear.

"Damn. It looks like this mission is becoming a pain in the ass." Abe groaned, but then he straightened and issued orders. "Okay, everyone. Back to the aircraft. We're gonna leave this base behind and follow these tracks. With luck, they will lead us to our target."

As the group headed back the way they had come, Brianna took one last look at tracks before following after them.

She hoped Anthony was okay.

✳✳✳

Anthony woke up when the urge to pee hit him. He opened his eyes and blinked when he couldn't see. Blinking didn't help, which he realized was because it was too dark.

That was when he remembered where he was. He and Secilia were inside of a cave, hiding from a leonid and Director Azrael of Nametech.

Climbing to his feet, Anthony walked with caution toward the exit. It was hard to move since he couldn't see. He didn't want to accidentally trip on something, or even worse, step on Secilia, whom he could only just make out as a black lump on the ground.

After finally making it outside, he looked at the sky, which was filled with stars and the moon. It was brighter out here than it was in the cave. With the light from celestial bodies to illuminate his path, Anthony wandered around to one side of the mountain their cave was located in and relieved himself.

As he was making his way back, a sound caught his attention. A low growling noise seemed to echo around him. The sound caused him to glance around. He couldn't find anything at first, so he began walking again, but then the noise came back, louder this time. Anthony paused and cocked his head to the side, listening. That noise sounded like it was coming from above him.

Anthony looked up—only to see a massive lump of flesh and fur descending toward him! With a startled yelp, he activated Physical Enhancement and jumped back. The creature that tried to pounce on him crashed into the ground, shattering the earth and kicking up a layer of dust.

"Oh, hell," Anthony muttered as the creature finally stood to its full height.

The beast before him was the same leonid that he had been fighting back in the maglev. It's golden brown fur bristled as it growled at him. The thick mane of darker hair descending from its head was also bristling and looked sharper than before. Anthony didn't know what that meant, but he did notice the blood red eyes this therianthrope had. It reminded him of a few holographic videos he'd seen of people who'd overdosed on drugs.

With a loud roar that shook the nearby mountains, the leonid raced toward him and swung his clawed left hand. Anthony leapt back. The hand slammed into the ground with a loud crashing sound before gouging out chunks of earth. If Anthony had been hit with that, it would have surely split him open and crushed his bones.

Anthony knew he couldn't let his enemy set the pace. After landing back on the ground, he bent his knees and pushed off. The ground beneath his feet cracked as he raced toward the lion therianthrope, which roared again and swung another meaty paw. Anthony ducked. He could feel the wind rushing over his head as he slid along the ground. As he came up, he tucked his right fist into his torso and thrust it forward, slamming his fist into the lion therianthrope's stomach.

With Physical Enhancement activated, Anthony's strength was impressive. Professor Incanscino had once told him that he was probably about as strong as most therianthrope when he used it. Despite that strength, however, his attack didn't seem to do much. The leonid was lifted into the air and sent back, but he landed on the ground, skidded for several yards, and then burst forward like a predator pouncing on his prey.

Anthony gnashed his teeth together as he leaned back to avoid another claw swipe. His eyes felt like they were going crossed when the paw passed close to his face.

Rather than come back up, he fell backward, rolled along the ground, and skipped to his feet several yards away. His therianthrope enemy roared as he charged forward. This time, when the beast raised his hand to attack, Anthony stepped forward and raised his arm. He grunted when his forearm caught the beast's forearm, effectively blocking the attack. While he would have liked to launch a counter, the leonid attacked with his other paw before Anthony could make a move, forcing him to duck and scramble backwards.

It was just like their last battle. This leonid was incredibly powerful, enough that Anthony's physical enhancement magic was only able to put him on even terms with him. Unfortunately, while Anthony could fight this demon evenly, he still had a very distinct disadvantage.

He would eventually run out of mana.

Anthony needed to do something, needed to somehow end this fight before his mana ran dry, but he didn't know what to do. He didn't have any weapons that would help him take care of this enemy.

Just as he was wondering how he was going to take care of this therianthrope, Secilia ran out of the cave in a hurry, her eyes wide in panic.

"Anthony! What was that loud noise… just… oh…"

At the sound of Secilia's voice, the leonid turned its attention from Anthony to her. His eyes narrowed as he glared at the woman, who had suddenly frozen solid as if she'd been turned into a block of ice.

"Secilia! Run! Quickly!"

Secilia looked like she was about to do just that, but then the leonid roared and charged at her before she could dash off. The creature was quick, far quicker than some human who had never exercised and couldn't use physical enhancement magic, so it was on Secilia before she could move. Secilia tripped and fell to the ground as the creature bore down on her.

Anthony cursed as he pumped as much mana into his limbs as he could without making them explode and charged. His mad dash brought him right to the therianthrope. He shoulder slammed the creature. While he might not be strong enough to truly injure his opponent, he was at least strong enough to lift the blasted beast off his feet and send him crashing into the mountainside.

The mountain shook as the rocky surface cracked around the therianthrope's body. Despite how such a powerful attack looked like it should have hurt, the leonid didn't seem to have experienced any pain as it pried itself from the mountain and squared off against Anthony again.

Anthony was prepared to once more deal with this near indomitable opponent, even though he knew he was just wasting mana, but then a loud whine echoed through the valley. Anthony, Secilia, and even the leonid looked up as a black aircraft flew past them. It was a stealth craft. Anthony didn't know the make or model, but Secilia did.

"That's the AZ-32 Loki!" she exclaimed.

"The what?" asked Anthony.

"It's the latest stealthcraft used by the Academy Island Private Security Forces!" Secilia's eyes were on the aircraft as it came back around and began circling them. The low whine caused Anthony's teeth to vibrate. "It's engines can run completely silently and it has a max speed of 1,200 miles per hour. It's the most advanced modern stealth craft in existence. Only two have currently been made."

"That speed seems kind of excessive," Anthony muttered. "There isn't a pilot alive who could put up with those G-forces… well, maybe a therianthrope could, but I doubt it could maneuver a craft going that fast."

Secilia shrugged as though to say she wasn't sure why anyone would make such a fast-moving aircraft either.

While they were having their conversation, the leonid finally turned its attention back to them. It released a loud growl as it prepared to charge. Anthony grimaced as he moved in front of Secilia to protect her.

Yet just before the leonid could attempt to re-initiate combat between them, the stealthcraft swooped even lower. A boarding ramp opened on the bottom. A figure, dressed in a skintight black battlesuit that had glowing blue lines traveling across it, leapt out and landed lightly on the ground.

"Brianna?!" Anthony shouted in shock.

"Leave this to me!" Brianna said back as she raced toward the therianthrope, spinning her Geminius Sword like it was lighter than a feather.

The leonid roared at this new challenger and charged, but Brianna was far quicker. She moved to the left, avoiding an overhand swing that crashed into the ground, then swung her sword, which cleaved through the therianthrope's arm in a spray of blood. The arm fell to the ground with a meaty thump.

The leonid didn't seem to notice his arm being severed. He swung at Brianna again with his remaining hand, but she dodged and removed that as well. Once both hands had been removed, she dashed forward and swung the double-bladed weapon with an incredible swiftness that left only blurs in its wake. More blood sprayed from the leonid's body as his legs were removed and he fell to the ground.

While the leonid didn't seem to feel any pain, he still growled in what sounded like pain as he tried to climb back up despite missing all of his limbs. Brianna turned back toward it, walked up to it, and stabbed it through the back.

Her blade must have pierced his heart. The therianthrope stopped moving a moment later.

Having watched the entire battle, which had only taken a few minutes to conclude, Anthony could only think of one thing to say.

"I really need to get myself a weapon."

Secilia looked at him like he'd said something weird. All Anthony could do was shrug.

CHAPTER 8

The moment the battle had concluded and the lion leicenthrope lay defeated, Brianna turned toward Anthony.

A lot of emotions ran through him. He felt gratitude and a little bit of hurt pride. He, of course, wished he had been able to defeat the therianthrope himself, but he also understood that without a weapon, the most he could expect in that battle was a stalemate.

Beyond gratitude, the primary emotion he felt was definitely joy; he was so incredibly happy to see Brianna that he wasn't quite sure how he was containing himself. Anthony wanted to run up to her, lift her into his arms, kiss her until she was breathless, and then take her in that cave he'd been sleeping in. He was certain the only thing stopping him was his situational awareness.

He wasn't sure if now was the best time to do that.

"Anthony," Brianna muttered his name before she dropped her Geminius Sword and dashed forward.

Anthony barely had a moment to realize what she was doing before she pounced. It was probably a good thing he'd grown stronger and his reflexes had become sharper. He was able to catch the girl as she slammed into him. Even so, he still grunted and staggered back as Brianna wrapped her arms around his neck and hugged him for all he was worth.

"I was so worried about you," Brianna croaked out in a hoarse voice. Her tone contained so much emotion that Anthony found himself a little overwhelmed. "I… when you vanished… I didn't know what to do. I should have been there. I shouldn't have let you go off on your own. I'm sorry. I'm so sorry."

Hearing her apologizing over and over caused something inside of him to squirm. It was an uncomfortable feeling, but he tried to put it aside and focus on the girl in his arms.

"It's okay." He hugged her back, relishing in the feeling of her thin waist in his arms. "None of this is your fault. You couldn't have known what would happen."

"I should have been more vigilant," Brianna refuted. "I shouldn't have let you out of my sight. I promise, this will never happen again."

Anthony wondered if maybe the bond worked both ways between them. Brianna was displaying a lot more emotion than he thought she would have. This redhead could be extremely adorable and acted embarrassed on many occasions, but she'd never struck him as the type to act like this. Perhaps she really had just been that worried about him? It was a nice thought.

"Um…"

While Brianna and Anthony had become embroiled in their own little world, Secilia stood uncertainly behind him. He hadn't forgotten about her, of course, but he'd been so happy to see Brianna again that he'd let his emotions get the better of him. Brianna, too, had finally noticed the presence of Secilia.

The redhead got off Anthony and looked at Secilia with a glare so fierce the other woman took a step back. Anthony could tell Brianna was angry. Not only did her glare look like it could kill, but her emotions were running hot through their bond. Red anger. Black hate. They were like poisonous serpents coiled around his mind.

"You… you kidnapped Anthony…" Brianna clenched her hands into fists and took a step forward. "Anthony… took you out on a date because he wanted to ask if you would become his. He wanted you to become his bondmate… and you betrayed him."

Secilia flinched as tears gathered in her eyes. Her lips trembled as she took a step back and placed a hand on her chest, eyes darting to and fro as if looking for a place to run.

Before she could bolt off, and before Brianna could berate her anymore, Anthony stepped between them.

"That's quite enough," Anthony said, looking at Brianna. "I don't blame you for being angry, but you don't know the full story yet. I know it's hard, and I'm extremely grateful to you for being so angry on my behalf, but please, at least hear her out before you accuse her of betrayal."

"Anthony…" For just a moment, pain flashed through both Brianna's eyes and the bond. He felt an acute sensation in his chest like he was being stabbed. It disappeared after a moment as the War Maiden took a deep, calming breath and backed down. "Very well. It sounds like there is a lot more going on than someone simply betraying the man who loves her."

Secilia flinched, but Anthony merely offered a pained grin since that seemed like the best concession he could ask for.

Brianna did not seem like the type to hold a grudge. However, he also knew he didn't know everything there was to know about this woman. She hadn't been his bondmate for that long, barely two weeks in fact, which meant there were plenty they still didn't know about each other.

"Thank you. Anyway, we should get going."

Brianna agreed. "We should definitely leave. Lucretia is waiting for you back on Academy Island."

At that moment, the low whine of an engine resounded around them as the stealth craft slowly set down. The boarding ramp was still extended. When Anthony looked over, he saw several people standing on the boarding ramp and looking in their direction. He didn't recognize any of them, but they were wearing the uniforms of the Academy Island Private Security Forces.

Brianna went over to her Geminius Sword and picked it up. She spun it around in her hands several times as though testing to see if the battle had damaged it. During that time, Anthony looked at Secilia.

"I'm sorry about what she said."

"It's okay." Secilia smiled, but it was filled with self-deprecation and made his chest ache. "I know I deserve it. Your bondmate… she isn't wrong."

Anthony shook his head. He didn't agree with her at all, but now wasn't the time to get into that conversation. It could wait until after they were back on Academy Island.

***

The stealth aircraft, aside from being one of the latest marvels in stealth technology, was also one of the fastest. Despite being on in what could be termed as the mid-east of the Americas, it only took four hours to reach Academy Island.

Of course, four hours in a plane with a group of people he didn't know was a little awkward. The squadron from the Academy Island Private Security Forces kept looking at him like he was an oddity. To make matters worse, the two girls sitting with him were tense.

Secilia looked like she was trying to make herself smaller, shrinking her shoulders as she slouched into the bench, eyes darting to and fro. She reminded him of a mouse that had been trapped by a cat. On the other hand, Brianna had a cold look on her face, like she was upset with something.

Anthony leaned over and whispered in the redhead's ear. "Are you angry at me?"

Brianna blinked, eyes widening as she turned to him, though she must not have realized how close their faces were until she turned. She leaned back a little.

"Of course I'm not angry at you. Why would I be?"

"I don't know." Anthony leaned back and shrugged. "You seemed angry, so I thought you might be."

"I'm not." It was like his words had a magical effect. Brianna relaxed her shoulders, the tension easing, before she reached over and grabbed his arm, hugging it to her chest. "I am more upset at myself than anything else. I know you do not blame me for what happened, but I still feel this wouldn't have happened if I had been more vigilant."

There were many things that Anthony could have said to that. He could have told her to stop blaming herself, could have told her that none of this was her fault, but he knew Brianna better than that. Words wouldn't help.

With that thought in mind, Anthony slid his arm out of her grasp and moved it around her shoulder, pulling the girl close. Brianna squeaked a little as she found her face pressed to his chest. However, after the shock had passed, she took a deep breath and closed her eyes.

"You're not being fair," she muttered.

"Life isn't fair," Anthony fired back.

Brianna said nothing as she scooted her body closer.

While Anthony acted like he and Brianna were the only people present, he wasn't unaware of the others. The squadron of Private Security Force soldiers were staring at him and Brianna with a combination of fascination, jealousy, and anger. The two human men were definitely expressing jealousy. It looked like they were trying to bore a hole through his head with their eyes. On the other hand, the female vampire and therianthrope were staring at him like he was a rare animal that had just been put into a zoo.

However, the reaction he noticed the most was Secilia.

The girl sitting on his left was staring at him and Brianna with longing and pain. Her eyes wavered as she gnawed incessantly at her lower lip. The hurt in her eyes made Anthony want to hold her too, but he didn't know if that was appropriate. She was not his bondmate. What's more, regardless of whether she had a valid reason for doing so, she *had* kidnapped him. That was an indisputable fact. Given that, he wasn't sure what Brianna would do if he were to comfort Secilia. Their situation might take a turn for the worst.

"Che," the man with tanned skin spat as he continued glaring at me. "Some men have all the luck."

As if his quiet mutter was all they needed, the others began speaking in hushed whispers that weren't nearly as soft as they seemed to think they were.

"What do you think is going on there?" asked the vampire woman as she spoke with the therianthrope.

"Not sure," her female therianthrope companion said. "But it is odd, isn't it? That girl is a War Maiden, right? I didn't think they were allowed to form relationships. Actually, what is this girl even doing on Academy Island anyway?"

"It's a question for the ages."

"Those two are probably fucking," the black man said. "Look at how close they are. Damn normies. They think they can act like a couple in front of us? Not on my damn watch."

While Brianna stiffened and looked like she was going to pull away, Anthony tightened his grip around her shoulder and tried to ignore the peanut gallery. They were annoying. However, it wasn't like he hadn't dealt with worse.

The aircraft eventually set down. The landing was lighter than he'd expected. Anthony barely even felt it.

Before he, Brianna, and Secilia could unstrap their crash webbing, the Academy Island Private Security Force squadron stood up and made for the boarding ramp. The black man, who Anthony learned from Brianna was called Abe, activated the ramp, lowering it to the floor so he and his squad could step out.

"We already did what we came here to do. No sense in sticking around to watch these two act so nauseatingly sweet with each other," were his parting words.

"I don't think I like that man," Anthony said as the squadron left.

"You aren't the only one," Secilia muttered, though she clammed up when Brianna leaned forward to look at her.

Anthony noticed this and sighed. "Come on. Let's get out of here."

After undoing the crash webbing, Anthony, Brianna, and Secilia emerged from the aircraft to find themselves in a large docking bay. This aircraft wasn't the only one present, though it was the only one of its kind. Anthony didn't know what the others were. They looked like fighter craft. Of course, he was only judging by the general shape and the weapons on their hulls.

"That's a Mach 4 Phantom!" Secilia exclaimed as she looked at one sleek craft in particular. Her eyes were sparkling like a pair of stars. "That's currently the fastest fighter jet ever made. It's capable of traveling at the speed of sound while still retaining full maneuverability. I hear only a few powerful therianthrope can pilot it. The gravitational forces exerted on the body when it's going top speed can turn a human into a pancake."

"You sure know a lot about our technology," a voice said from several feet away.

"Professor Incanscino," Anthony greeted with surprise.

The woman who had spoken was, of course, the diminutive blond professor. The woman looked extremely out of place standing in the middle of a military docking bay with her blonde hair styled in ringlets, cute face that made her seem like a child, and pink and white lolita outfit. The stark contrast between her clothing and appearance and that of everyone else was so great Anthony felt like his brain had become disconnected from reality.

Professor Incanscino walked up to them. As she did, she looked over Anthony as though checking to make sure he was truly all right. Anthony could not tell what she was thinking, but after several seconds, the slight tension in her shoulders eased.

Professor Incanscino crossed her arms and tapped her foot, then seemed to think better of it and uncrossed her arms. She stood there, looking awkward for a moment, before finally huffing.

"It seems you all made it back safely," she said.

"We did," Anthony replied. "Sorry for worrying you."

Professor Incanscino looked away. "Who said I was worried? Anyway, you three had better follow me. There is a lot about this situation that I don't understand, and I would like to know what happened."

Secilia did not look like she wanted to come with this woman, but she wasn't given much of a choice. Even if she tried to refuse, Professor Incanscino could just freeze her in place. Anthony had once seen the professor affect the time around a person, trapping them within a single moment and forcing them to stand in front of the classroom with a bucket on their head.

They followed the professor through what Anthony could only assume was the Academy Island Private Security Forces' main headquarters. It was a multi-story structure that seemed to have been built underground. At least, he assumed so due to the lack of windows. It could just be a windowless building, but he somehow didn't think so.

There were numerous rooms in this place, and their uses varied. Anthony and the others weren't allowed in many of them, but they occasionally passed through areas that looked like training grounds for new recruits. One of the rooms looked like an urban zone with tall buildings and a lot of obstacles. The sounds of gunfire echoed from within those buildings. He wondered if they were doing live fire exercises.

It turned out Professor Incanscino had an office here. It wasn't anywhere near the level of ostentatiousness that her living quarters at the college possessed. In fact, her office was quite barren. Anthony guessed she didn't use it often.

The woman sat behind her desk, folded her arms, and leaned back as she gazed at the three. While Anthony and Brianna were able to meet her gaze evenly, Secilia looked away.

"It would be great if you three could tell me what happened any day now," Professor Incanscino said after a moment.

None of them spoke at first, but then Anthony sighed and stepped forward. "I can't say too much since I wasn't even conscious for most of it, but I'll at least tell you what I can."

"That's good enough." Professor Incanscino nodded and gestured for him to continue.

Anthony did his best to explain everything he could. He started from when Secilia drugged him, spoke about his meeting with Director Azrael after he'd woken up, then how he'd been drugged again and only woke up after Secilia gave him the antidote. He focused mostly on his and Secilia's escape from the maglev and the fight against the leonid, but that was only because he really didn't know what happened while he'd been drugged.

While he spoke, Anthony kept a close eye on both Brianna and Professor Incanscino, watching their reactions. While Brianna was clenching her fists, his professor looked like she was taking in everything he said calmly. Only the way her finger tapped against the desk betrayed her emotions.

"It seems like you went through something quite trying," the small woman said at last before turning to look at Secilia.

"Since it looks like Anthony doesn't have a full picture of the situation, I expect you to fill in the blanks."

Secilia trembled as though afraid of this woman, but then she took a deep breath and nodded.

"I'll tell you everything I can."

Like Anthony, Secilia started from when she had drugged him. However, her story wildly diverged from Anthony's soon after as she went into how she stole the antidote, how she and Luna tried to save him on the train, and how her mother had been killed trying to protect her.

Once she got to this part of her story, Anthony noticed how her body was shaking with emotion, so he reached out and grabbed her hand. It wasn't done through any conscious thought. He acted on instinct. Perhaps, he mused, it was his incubus nature acting out, though he didn't know for sure.

Secilia looked started when she felt his hand in hers, but then she squeezed it and managed to steady herself. She finished her story and grew quiet.

Professor Incanscino was silent for a time. She seemed to be absorbing everything Secilia had said, though Anthony also noticed how her eyes wandered to his and Secilia's conjoined hands.

Finally...

"I understand what happened now," Professor Incanscino began. "But what I want to know now is this." She looked at Secilia. "Why did you do it? It sounds to me like your actions resulted in more harm than good. Did you not realize this would be the outcome?"

"What else could I do?" asked Secilia, shrugging even as tears pricked at her eyes. "That bastard imprisoned my mother and used our safety as blackmail to force us into compliance.

If I did nothing, he would have killed Mom. I didn't... have a choice..."

"There is always a choice, but, well, I can't say I don't understand." Professor Incanscino leaned back in her chair as she tapped a steady rhythm on the desk with her small index finger. "While I understand Director Azrael forced you into compliance, you still broke the law. You will have to be punished."

"I understand," Secilia said quietly as she gripped Anthony's hand even tighter.

Brianna noticed the action and frowned, her expression conflicted. Anthony tried to pretend he didn't see it. They would talk about this when they were alone. Now wasn't the time.

"We'll get back to your punishment in just a moment. For the time being, I believe we should discuss Director Azrael," Professor Incanscino said. "I have already received a report ahead of time, but it looks like we lost track of him."

"That is correct," Brianna said. "We did check the train tracks for several miles, which led us to an underground bunker, but Director Azrael had long disappeared by the time we arrived. I'm guessing he realized he couldn't stay there and sent his therianthrope as a distraction while making his escape."

"Those are my thoughts as well. He's a wily one." Professor Incanscino sighed. "It's quite the troubling situation, but I intend to rectify this soon. I'll put out some feelers to see if we can track him down. While I can't leave Academy Island, I still have many contacts in the Americas who I can get in touch with. Once we know where he is, we can launch a covert operation to either capture or assassinate him."

Anthony was a little surprised to hear Professor Incanscino talk about assassinating someone so easily, but he was also aware that this woman was a lot older than she looked. At a glance, she looked like a middle schooler or maybe an extremely petite high schooler, but she was easily over one hundred.

Professor Incanscino narrowed her eyes. "You're thinking something rude right now, aren't you?"

"What?" Anthony blinked, startled. "No. Of course not."

"I'm pretty sure you're thinking about how I'm a lot older than I look," she continued, eyes narrowing further.

"T-that is absurd. Why would I think that? And even if I was, does it matter? It's not like it changes who you are."

"Hmph."

"A-anyway." Anthony coughed into his hand and tried to get this conversation back on track. "I have a favor I'd like to ask you."

"A favor?" The magic professor frowned. "What kind of favor?"

"When you find Director Azrael, I want me, Brianna, and Secilia to be the ones who take him out," Anthony said.

Silence reigned in the small office. Not only did Brianna and Secilia look shocked, but Professor Incanscino didn't seem to know what she should say either.

"I'm not sure that's possible," Professor Incanscino said at last. She raised a hand, stopping Anthony from saying anything as he opened his mouth. "You have to understand the situation you're in right now. Anthony, you are an incubus, a rare breed of demon that hasn't been seen in centuries. You're also something of an open secret. We don't know how many people know about you. Sending you outside of Academy Island could prove incredibly dangerous."

"I'm aware of all that, but I still want to go," Anthony said. "Also, while he'll probably keep the information about me being an incubus close to the vest, since telling others about me would mean he'd lose his chance to use me in his experiments, if we wait too long, he might sell that information to someone else in exchange for protection."

"You do bring up a good point. We *do* need to apprehend him." Professor Incanscino agreed with him on this point alone. "And if we can't apprehend him, then we have to take him out of the picture before he can sell that information on you. I'm just not sure if sending you is the right idea… but I will at least consider it. I understand you have a personal vendetta against this man now. Keeping you from getting justice might backfire on me."

Anthony knew that was probably the biggest concession he could ask for, which was why he didn't argue with her to concede completely. So long as she was willing to seriously consider letting him handle Azrael, it was fine.

Brianna finally stepped forward. "I agree with Anthony. While I understand the danger, I think letting us solve this problem would be better for you in the long run."

"And why is that?" asked Professor Incanscino.

"Because the Academy Island Private Security Forces are listed as a defensive private militia," Brianna said. "As a defense force, your role is not to attack others, but to defend your borders against attack. Your government has also signed a treaty with the Americas and other world governments that you won't use your military might to attack other nations. It's one thing to send a covert force into another nation to rescue one of your citizens. It's quite another to send in a covert force to secure or assassinate a criminal that's not a citizen of

Academy Island. Such an action could create a serious backlash against Academy Island if word got out."

"That is something I didn't think about," Professor Incanscino admitted. "Very well, I will give this a lot more consideration than I initially planned on doing. Now then, back to Secilia's punishment." Secilia stiffened as Professor Incanscino looked at her again. "Due to your extenuating circumstances, I'm not sure imprisonment is a good punishment, so for now, I'm going to have Brianna and Anthony keep an eye on you. I can trust them not to let you out of their sight until I've decided on what to do."

At the professor's words, all three of them had vastly different reactions. Anthony felt a little happy, but Brianna did not seem to enjoy the idea of watching Secilia like he did. Meanwhile the one being punished looked torn between joy and fear.

Anthony had a small inkling that he knew what Professor Incanscino was planning by putting Secilia in his care, but whether or not things turned out the way she wanted them to was another matter entirely.

***

Anthony opened the fridge in his kitchen and checked the contents. All he saw were pre-packaged meals with the Kitsune Kitchens logo on it. Most unfortunately, Anthony was not that great of a chef, so he preferred simply eating meals that he just had to heat up in the microwave.

He grabbed three packages labeled curry, set them on the counter, and placed one of them in the microwave. It only took a minute to fully cook. Once it was done, he placed the next one in the microwave, and then the next one. After the packaged meals were cooked, he grabbed some forks and took everything into the living room.

"Dinner's… ready…"

Anthony wanted to speak with some enthusiasm, but that died when he saw the situation in the living room. It also made him remember why he'd gone into the kitchen in the first place.

Brianna and Secilia were sitting on the couch. They were about as far apart as two people could be while sitting on the same piece of furniture. Neither of them looked comfortable with the situation, but Brianna appeared downright disgruntled and Secilia reminded him of a rabbit staring down the barrel of a shotgun.

He sighed. "Brianna, please stop glaring at Secilia."

"Why should I?" asked Brianna.

While Secilia flinched, Anthony remained unaffected—at least on the outside.

"Because if you keep glaring at her, I'll take away your food."

"So you're taking her side?"

When Brianna sent him a glare, Anthony did his best not to shy away. He knew looking the other way could be taken as an admission of guilt. That was why he met her harsh stare with an even gaze.

"This has nothing to do with taking someone else's side. Secilia is going to be living with us for the foreseeable future. The situation is already tense enough without you giving her that look that says you're going to stab her with your sword the moment she even looks at you funny."

His words were reasonable, and Brianna couldn't find any fault with him, which was probably why she huffed and looked away from Secilia. As the redhead stood up and made her way over to the dinner table, Secilia looked at him and mouthed "Thank you."

Dinner that night was an awkward affair. No one spoke. While Anthony had at one point been used to silent dinners, that was only because he used to live on his own. Ever since Brianna came into his life, breakfast and dinner had become a bit more lively. Sitting with two other people who absolutely refused to talk was just awkward.

"I think I'm going to take a shower," Anthony said at last, standing up from his seat after eating.

"I'll throw everything away." Brianna also stood up and grabbed his and her empty containers, plus their utensils. Anthony noticed that she did not grab Secilia's.

He sighed but decided to just ignore the girl's attitude for now. He understood that she was angry and needed to vent. He also understood the reason for her anger was because of what happened to him. Reprimanding her at the moment would probably do more harm than good.

Anthony took a quick shower in his square shower unit, which was so tiny he barely had any room to move. They could have gone to Brianna's room. However, Brianna did not enjoy the idea of Secilia staying in her apartment.

As he tried to wash his body in the small shower, Anthony wondered what he should do now, how he should go about dealing with those two. He didn't want Brianna and Secilia fighting. Was there anything he could do to make them stop? Could he convince Brianna to give Secilia a second chance? He really didn't know. Thinking about it was giving him a headache.

After taking a shower, Anthony wrapped a towel around his waist and headed outside. The bathing room was connected to a small hallway that had only two doors and a cupboard.

The sounds of the holographic TV echoed from the living room. It sounded like someone was watching an action-drama, which made him suspect that it was Secilia.

He entered his bedroom, closed the door behind him, then paused. His breath caught in his throat and his eyes widened.

Brianna was lying on the bed—naked. Her sensuous curves were fully emphasized as she laid on her side, one hand resting on her hip, the other being used to prop up her head. Anthony trailed his eyes from her small feet up her long legs and over the wide curve of her hips. Her taut stomach and small waist accentuated her hips and large breasts, which looked like a pair of teardrops.

Anthony had seen Brianna any number of times, but no matter how often he saw her, it never got old.

"Is this an invitation?" he asked, perfectly aware there could only be one reason Brianna would be waiting for him like this.

Brianna's cheeks, already lit up by a red blush, turned an even deeper shade of scarlet until they matched her scintillating crimson hair.

"I… it's been more than a day since we, er, since you were able to recharge your mana," she said. "Um, I thought… as your bondmate, this is kind of my duty, so… I read in a magazine that men like this pose, and, well…"

One of the cutest things about Brianna was that no matter how often they had sex, and no matter how forward she tried to be, the girl just couldn't do sexy. She didn't have it in her to act like a minx, and yet she tried so hard for his sake. It was endearing.

"I definitely appreciate the pose." Anthony licked his lips. "You look like a guaviare model."

He didn't think Brianna knew what those were, but even so, the blush on her face spread to her neck and even some of her chest.

Anthony chuckled as he dropped his towel and climbed onto the bed. The mattress shook as he crawled over to Brianna.

"Lay on your back please," Anthony requested.

Brianna, still embarrassed, turned over until she was lying on her back. She closed her thighs as though shy of showing him and covered her breasts with her hands. This shy act of hers actually turned him on a lot. He thought it was because she wasn't being like this on purpose. It was just how she was.

Anthony did not let her remain like that. He spread her legs apart, then lifted them into the air. Brianna squeaked as he shifted his hands until they were resting on the back of her knees. This caused her hips to lift partially off the bed and offered him a perfect view of her pussy and pink asshole.

"A-Anthony, this position is embarrassing!" Brianna said.

"Sorry. I wanted to try something new."

Brianna said nothing as she turned her head and clenched her eyes shut. Her body shivered. Even her pussy lips seemed to quiver, though he could tell through the bond that beyond her embarrassment, she was excited by the prospect of doing something different.

Anthony pressed his mouth against Brianna's snatch and gave her lips a long, languorous kiss. Brianna's breathing caught in her throat. A loud gasp escaped her lips as he pushed his tongue past her outer labia and began exploring her depths. With his nose pressed against the small hood of her pussy, he took his time exploring her folds and pushing his tongue even deeper into her. Brianna's breathing picked up.

"Ha… haa… Anthony… that feels… that feels… Ahn!"

Anthony shifted his grip from the back of her knees to her butt. Grabbing a handful of her plentiful flesh, he dug his fingers into each cheek and raised her hips even higher. This gave his tongue some extra reach. However, he soon retracted it in favor of working her small clitoris into the open.

"Hnnn! Ahn! Ah! Haaan! Hrrrn!"

Brianna opened her mouth wide as her gasps, moans, and pants mixed together. She gripped the bed sheets so hard her knuckles turned white. Anthony's actions caused her toes to spasm and her thighs to quiver as he suckled on her clit. Her breasts shook and jiggled with every action, while drool began leaking down her mouth.

"A-Anthony! I! I!"

The words were halted when Anthony ever so gently bit down on her clit. A soundless scream echoed from Brianna as she jerked her hips into his face, grinding her pussy against his mouth. Her juices flowed from her pussy, drenching his mouth, chin, neck, and chest. He tried not to spill, but it was impossible when so much was coming out.

All at once, Brianna's body went slack. Her ass would have slumped to the bed, but Anthony still had a hold of it. That said, her legs had fallen down and her thighs now rested on his shoulders. He gave her quivering pussy once last kiss before setting her down. As he did, feet slid off his shoulders and fell to either side of him.

Brianna seemed a little out of it, her breathing heavy, sweat covering her red skin. Even her chest was flushed. Anthony placed his hands on her thighs and massaged them, which caused Brianna to hum. Finally, he couldn't take anymore and grabbed his cock, scooting closer so he could place it on her pussy. He loved the way her lips folded around him; the sensation of her warm pussy engulfing him was incredible. He also noted, with some amusement, that his dick looked kind of like a hot dog situated inside of a bun.

He rocked his hips back and forth, lubricating his cock with her juices. Brianna moaned. With a smile, he leaned over until their noses were touching.

"I'm going to put it in, okay?" he said.

"Ah… o-okay," Brianna said, stuttering only a little.

Anthony leaned down and kissed her. Brianna released a content sound in the back of her throat as she wrapped her arms around his neck and kissed back. She opened her mouth wide and extended her tongue, playing with his as they shared saliva between them.

A stifled gasp escaped her lips as they continued to kiss, but that was because Anthony had plunged his dick into her pussy. He didn't start off slow either. Anthony didn't have the patience for that right now. He set a hard pace. The sound of his hips and balls slapping against her hips and ass mixed with the nasally gasps and grunts that slipped passed their still dueling tongues echoed around the room.

The feeling of Brianna's tight passage rubbing him was one of the best things Anthony had ever felt before. Her walls were like a vice that tried to milk him of his cum. It sucked him in and squeezed tight as he pulled out, but it wasn't painful. The pleasure of her pussy wrapping around his cock was unlike anything he had ever felt.

The sweat on their bodies mixed together as they continued to move. Anthony could feel her nipples rubbing against him as her chest found itself smashed to his. Brianna's arms tightened around his neck as she continued kissing him, her tongue almost desperately rubbing and caressing his.

Anthony could feel something building inside of him, and thanks to the feedback loop from their bond, he knew Brianna was close to cumming too. He grunted into her mouth as he kissed her harder and increased the pace of his thrusts. Brianna squealed into his mouth when he did this, then she wrapped her legs around his hips, hooked her heels together, and shoved him further into her pussy.

The walls of her tight passage seemed to clench as she orgasmed. Mana flowed into him through their bond the moment she came. He felt like he was being filled up.

This incredible sensation was enough that Anthony also lost control, shooting several loads of semen into Brianna's pussy. Even after he released his seed, neither he nor Brianna let each other go as they continued to kiss. It wasn't until Anthony felt his dick go flaccid that he pulled out and rolled onto his back.

"Ha…"

Brianna sighed as she rolled over and rested her head on his shoulder. Anthony wrapped an arm around her to pull her even tighter against him, which the redhead didn't seem to mind at all.

"I missed this," Brianna said.

"Me too," Anthony admitted. It had only been over a day, but he could honestly say that a day without Brianna sucked.

"Don't ever worry me like that again," Brianna added.

"I'll try not to."

"You had better not. If you do… I… I'll…"

When Brianna trailed off, Anthony looked down and smiled when he saw that she was asleep. He had wanted to speak with her about Secilia, but he guessed it could wait until tomorrow.

CHAPTER 9

Anthony woke up to the feeling of something wrapping around his dick. He groaned in a low voice as his body jolted and his hips bucked, electric surges of pure pleasure racing up and down his spine. Snapping his eyes open, he looked down to find Brianna between his legs, her chest on full display, hands pushing her breasts together as they wrapped around his cock.

He actually couldn't see his dick at all. His head was inside of Brianna's mouth. She was sucking on his head while sticking out her tongue and allowing saliva to dribble down his shaft, coating his dick in a natural lubricant that helped increase friction, allowing her to rub those magnificent breasts against him without rubbing their skin raw.

"Brianna! I—I'm—"

"Hmmm!"

Brianna hummed around his cock, then made a loud slurping noise like she was sucking the last bit of soda remaining in her cup through a straw. Anthony threw his head back and groaned as his dick twitched in Brianna's mouth.

He lifted his head, just watching Brianna's throat bob as she drank the cum he was shooting down her mouth. Not a single drop was spilled. That was kind of impressive actually. When she first started giving him blowjobs, she would always choke and had to cough his cum back up. But Brianna was stubborn. After her first failed attempt, she tried again and again and again. He didn't know what drove her to keep doing it, but after giving him head for over a week, she had become very experienced.

"Ha… that was quite the wake-up," Anthony mumbled.

"I… um… I thought you might appreciate this," Brianna said, cheeks flushing as she crawled up his body. Her breasts dragged against his stomach and chest before she laid on top of him.

Anthony placed his hands on her naked hips, relishing in their warmth. "I do appreciate it. And good morning."

"Good morning," Brianna mumbled before she leaned down and claimed his lips.

Anthony sighed into her mouth as her tongue darted forward, caressing him in all sorts of ways. As they kissed, Brianna ground her hips against his still erect cock. Anthony couldn't see it, but the feeling of his dick wedged between her pussy lips drove him insane. He wanted her. He wanted her so bad that he wasn't sure why his dick wasn't already inside of her.

"Brianna…"

"I… I want to be on top this time."

"Sure."

Brianna smiled as she kissed him again, but then she placed her hands on his chest, pushed herself up, and scooted back until his dick was now between her buttcrack. She raised her hips. Anthony placed his hands on either side of her waist as she slowly lowered herself onto his dick. With her hands placed on his chest, her breasts were smashed together as she moved lower and lower. He groaned when she took him inside of her, relishing in the sucking sensation of her walls pulling him in as their hips became connected.

"This is nice," Brianna muttered.

Anthony grinned. "Is it?"

"Ah! D-did I say that out loud?"

"You did."

Brianna's cheeks were already a little pink, but they suddenly turned bright red. "Well... I... that is... you know I enjoy being with you."

"I do know that. And I enjoy being with you."

"T-thank you."

"Anyway, I hope you're not just going to sit there."

Anthony bucked his hips slightly, and Brianna gasped when his dick churned her insides. She began moving almost without conscious thought, raising her hips, then lowering them. Her movements were slow at first, but she soon began getting into it. After only a few seconds, Brianna was roughly grinding her hips against him as she rode his cock, her tits bouncing with every thrust.

"Ha... ahn... ha...! Hyk! Ahn!"

Brianna wasn't the only one working. Anthony would never let her do all the work herself. He traveled deep inside of himself and felt out the connection between him and Brianna. It didn't tell him what to do in so many words, but through the sensations he received from the feedback loop between them, he knew what she liked and didn't like. He reacted accordingly.

"Oooohhhh!"

Sitting up, Anthony grabbed two handfuls of Brianna's ass, massaging the muscles by using Physical Enhancement to increase the strength of his fingers. Brianna released a long moan, then gasped when he used his hands to push her onto him, helping him reach even deeper inside of her.

"Anthon—hyk! Ahn! Anthony! I-I-I—ah!"

Anthony leaned down and began kissing her neck. He wasn't rough, but he wasn't gentle either. Having already thoroughly explored her body, he knew where she liked to be kissed and took advantage of that knowledge. It wasn't long before Brianna was incapable of speech and could only release nasally gasps and moans.

Feeling his balls tighten, Anthony knew his end was coming, so he stopped massaging her ass and placed one of his fingers into her mouth.

"Suck on it."

Brianna's juices flowed over his dick as she wrapped her tongue around his finger. It was a rather erotic sight, Brianna sucking on his finger, drool leaking from her mouth and dripping off her chin as she moaned and made incredibly loud slurping noises. The term "finger fellatio" came to mind.

Once his finger was coated in her saliva, Anthony removed it from her mouth, lowered his hand against her ass, and sought out the small hole. He found it and pressed his finger into her asshole. Brianna gasped as she wrapped her arms and legs around him, then shuddered when he pumped his finger into her. He timed his finger's thrusts into her asshole with the movement of his dick. The results were better than he expected.

Her pussy, legs, and arms tightened as she came. It was like all of her muscles were clenching him. Anthony held on for only another second before he came as well. Waves of pleasure caused his vision to go white. He would have fallen back onto the bed, but he placed a hand behind him. Brianna had no such strength and fell backwards once her energy was spent, though Anthony caught her with his other hand and pulled her to his chest as she shuddered against him like she'd been shocked.

His now flaccid dick slid out of her pussy with a plop. He could feel their combined juices also flowing out of her, traveling down her thighs and his crotch, but he didn't pay it any mind.

"Anthony?"

"Yeah?"

"I'm tired."

"You can't go to sleep."

"I know…"

With a sigh, Brianna unwrapped her legs from around his waist and climbed off him. She stumbled when her feet touched the floor, but caught herself at the last moment. Anthony admired her bare backside for a second before also standing up.

"We should take a shower," he suggested.

"Your shower is too small," Brianna sighed. "I'll head over to my apartment and shower."

"I guess… you're right."

Anthony hated the fact that his shower was so small. He needed a bigger place.

Brianna slipped on her panties and donned one of his shirts, which was several sizes too large. She left his bedroom, closing the door behind her. Anthony only realized after she left that he hadn't talked to her about Secilia. He sighed. He guessed it would be okay if they talked about it later today, but he really needed to speak with her soon.

Anthony took a quick shower in his small shower unit, then dressed himself in black jeans and a white shirt. They were some of the clothes he bought with Brianna after his big change. The clothing felt a little snug, but they were comfortable.

Secilia was awake when he entered the living room. She sat on the couch, eyeing him with a frown as he paused in the hallway.

"Is something wrong?" he asked.

"You two… don't know the meaning of the word discretion, do you?" she asked in return.

It took a moment to understand what she meant.

"Ah… were we too loud? I'm sorry." He scratched the back of his neck, suddenly feeling sheepish. "I wasn't trying to be loud or anything. As an incubus, I need to have sex a lot in order to gain mana. If I don't, I won't have enough mana to live."

"Yes, I know." Secilia crossed her arms and looked away. "I know that. Your species isn't that different from a succubus, so I read up on succubus a lot to prepare myself for… well… you know."

Anthony did know. Secilia's entire purpose in coming to Academy Island had been to seduce him, but he knew how guilty she felt over that, and he didn't want to bring up bad memories.

"Do you want breakfast?" he asked.

"Yes, please," Secilia said.

Anthony went into the kitchen and grabbed three containers, each labeled biscuits and gravy. He heated them up in the microwave, grabbed some forks, and brought them to the dinner table. Secilia looked at the containers and snorted in amusement as she sat down.

"So you still can't cook?" she teased.

"Cooking isn't something that ever interested me." He shrugged. "And you can't cook either, so you have no right to judge."

"I can at least follow directions."

"So can every person with at least a modicum of intelligence. Being able to follow directions doesn't make you special."

"Fine. One of these days, we will have to see who between the two of us can actually cook a meal using directions." Secilia grabbed her fork and stabbed it into a biscuit. "Winner takes all."

"All of what?" asked an amused Anthony.

Secilia looked like she was about to reply, but then her eyes widened as if she'd just realized something. Anthony tilted his head as he wondered what was wrong. As if his gaze was too much to bear, Secilia bit her lip and looked down at the table before quietly eating her food.

Anthony sighed. "Do you still feel guilty over what happened?"

"Of course I do," Secilia admitted in a morose voice. "I… I betrayed you. I drugged you, kidnapped you, and brought you to someone who wanted to experiment on you."

"You did it to protect your mother," he pointed out.

"And look at how well that turned out." Secilia gritted her teeth as tears threatened to fall from her eyes. "My mother is dead, Alex is dead… I betrayed someone important to me and ended up losing my family instead of protecting them."

As Secilia struggled to contain her emotions, Anthony moved to stand up, but just before he could, Brianna walked into the living room and sat down at the dinner table. She was dressed in street clothes. Her jean shorts were pretty skimpy, but she had thigh-high black stockings covering her legs. The red and black shirt stretched across her bust. It didn't show off her stomach. She never wore clothes that revealed her stomach because she still wore the battlesuit underneath it, even though she didn't need it anymore.

"Sorry it took me so long," Brianna said as she picked up her fork. "What were you two talking about?"

"Nothing," Secilia said before Anthony could respond.

"Hmmm… is that so?" Brianna eyed Secilia, who looked away in guilt, then shrugged. "That's fine then."

With those words, Brianna began eating, and after a moment, Anthony started eating as well.

The rest of breakfast was consumed in awkward silence.

***

Brianna thought they were getting more attention than usual on the maglev, but it was probably her imagination.

It was Monday. Anthony, Brianna, and Secilia were on their way to school. She had high school and Anthony and Secilia attended the Institution of Magical Sciences.

Despite how the entire incident with Anthony being kidnapped only consisted of Saturday and Sunday, to Brianna, it felt like a lot more time had passed. So much had happened in those two days. Anthony had been taken prisoner and smuggled out of Academy Island, Brianna had gone to Professor Incanscino, then joined a squadron from the Academy Island Private Security Forces and rescued Anthony.

As thoughts of Anthony passed through her mind, she glanced at the young man standing next to her and Secilia. He looked like he was protecting them from train gropers. His constant vigilance while they were on the maglev made her feel a little warmth in her chest, but then she glanced at Secilia and felt conflicted.

Secilia had kidnapped Anthony. She had betrayed his trust and delivered him to a man who planned on performing inhumane experiments on him. The anger she felt toward this woman was so great her vision turned red just thinking about how lightly Secilia was getting off—or it should have.

"And look at how well that turned out. My mother is dead, Alex is dead… I betrayed someone important to me and ended up losing my family instead of protecting them."

The words reverberated inside of her mind and made her heart quake. Brianna had heard the conversation between Anthony and Secilia, so while she didn't know the full story, she knew enough to make some pretty good guesses. She was still upset, but now she was no longer sure if Secilia deserved her hatred.

The maglev soon stopped at the Institution of Magical Science's station, the doors opening and hundreds of college students surging out.

Anthony turned to her.

"I'll see you later," he said, leaning down and placing a kiss on her lips. It was still embarrassing to kiss in public, but Brianna tilted her head and kissed him back.

"Yeah," she said after they parted. "See you."

"Come on, Secilia," Anthony said, turning his head to the dark-haired woman. "I'd hate to be late for class."

"That would be a shame, wouldn't it? I'd love to see how Professor Incanscino responded to you being late."

"Don't even joke about that."

Brianna did not know how she felt as the two exited the maglev, bantering like old friends. Secilia, for all the guilt she felt, easily fell into the familiar conversation as Anthony spoke to her without a hint of deceit or anger. Unlike Brianna, who wanted to hate Secilia for what she had done, he accepted what happened, forgave it, and tried to move past it.

Maybe she should do the same thing, but it wasn't so easy for her.

Those were her thoughts as she stepped off the maglev and walked to school.

"Brianna! Good morning!"

Brianna looked up as someone called out to her, a smile appearing as she spotted the familiar wolf ears, bushy tail, and cheerful face of Hana. The therianthrope girl ran up to her with a big smile.

"Hana, good morning," she greeted politely.

"Hiya! It's good to see you! How was your weekend?" asked Hana.

"It was… eventful," Brianna replied diplomatically.

Of course, Brianna couldn't tell Hana about what happened over the weekend. Lucretia Incanscino had told them that everything that happened was classified and they were to inform no one. Well, even if she hadn't told them the information was classified, she wouldn't have said anything. Brianna didn't want her first friend to get mixed up in her problems.

"Eventful, huh?" A sly look came to Hana's face. "I'm guessing you and your boyfriend had a good time together, then?"

Brianna felt her face burn as Hana's words made her recall both this morning and last night. Even recalling what she and Anthony did caused her body to shiver in phantom pleasure, but that also made her more embarrassed.

"Wow, Brianna." Hana giggled. "It seems you two really did get up to something naughty, huh?"

"That… what Anthony and I do in private is no one's business but our own!" Brianna snapped, huffing as she sped up her pace and walked through the school's entrance.

"Okay. Okay. I'm sorry for teasing you. Come on. Don't be mad at me," Hana said as she caught up to Brianna and clasped her hands in a pleading gesture.

Brianna huffed, but she forgave the girl easily enough. Really, though, couldn't this girl be a little more tactful?

***

"Depending on the strength and severity of the Magic Catastrophe, treating one can be something as simple as someone taking medicine for a period of time or as difficult as having several mages perform a large-scale magic ritual to cleanse the affected area," Professor Incanscino lectured the students in her class. "F and E rank Magic Catastrophes tend to be fixed very simply. Most of them only affect a single person and aren't harmful. The many pharmaceutical companies that now exist have created multiple kinds of medicine that can treat any number of Magic Catastrophes."

Anthony sat in the same place he always did, right in the middle, and typed away at his holographic keyboard as the woman spoke, diligently taking notes.

"Of course, sometimes even F and E rank Magic Catastrophes are not so simple to cure," the professor continued. "When a new Magic Catastrophe occurs, a new type of medicine needs to be made. You can't use a medicine that cures Novuperibitis to cure Turgesco. Each type of medicine is made to cure a specific Magic Catastrophe, which means new formulas are being created all the time."

As the professor's lecture continued, Anthony thought about his brother's circumstances.

Because no one knew what kind of Magic Catastrophe was afflicting Calvin, no one knew what kind of medicine to give him, or if medicine would even work. The doctors at the Academy Island Hospital for Magical Catastrophes had once said they were afraid to give him medicine because it might adversely affect him. Anthony personally didn't think it would be a problem. Could his situation be any worse than it already was?

"Medicine is usually created with the help of magicians," Professor Incanscino said. "Because Magic Catastrophes are magical in nature, only medicine made through the magic known as alchemy can cure them. This is also why magicians are called on to deal with areas that have been infected by Magic Catastrophes. Clearing away the poisonous miasma requires large-scale magic rituals that can take anywhere from several days to several weeks to complete."

Anthony wondered if there was any ritual magic that could be used to cure Calvin. Professor Incanscino had taken a look at Calvin before, but all she'd said was that his circumstances were unlike anything she'd ever seen. It seemed not even the most famous magician in recent history knew what was wrong with him.

When class ended, Anthony made his way down the stairs and stood before the lecture platform. A few of the passing students glanced in his direction. Unlike before, however, no one tossed him any glares. Even the girls didn't ogle him like before, though he did receive a few admiring glances and confused looks. Perhaps they were wondering why he seemed so different?

"Mr. Amasius," Professor Incanscino said. "Did you need something?"

"I wanted to know if you've made a decision on what to do with Secilia," he said.

"I thought you would have already realized what I plan on doing." Professor Incanscino grabbed her purse from underneath the lectern, placed it over her shoulder, and turned to face him. Her raised eyebrow and somewhat sarcastic glance made him shift. "Seeing as how you haven't seemed to figure it out, I guess I'll tell you. I don't plan on doing anything. No punishment will be given."

"It won't? Even though she broke the law?" asked Anthony.

"Do you want me to punish her?" asked Profess Incanscino.

"No. Of course not." Anthony shook his head. "I'm just surprised."

Professor Incanscino sighed. "There are a few people on the Board of Directors who did wish to punish Secilia. I'm not sure if you realize this, but the Board of Directors considers you their property. They didn't take it too well when they found out you'd been kidnapped."

Anthony didn't like being considered someone's property, but he knew nothing could be done about that right now. The Board of Directors was the ruling body of Academy Island. They were in power and made all the decisions.

"I managed to convince them that punishing Secilia was a bad idea, and that it would be a better idea to let you look after her," Professor Incanscino said, shocking Anthony.

"How did you convince them of that?" he asked.

"I just told them that if she became your bondmate, she'd have no choice but to obey you. A bondmate cannot betray the one they are bonded to. If they tried, the magic involved in the bonding process would create a backlash and kill the bondmate," Lucretia told him. "I don't think Secilia knows this. If you two had bonded and she tried to kidnap you like her original plan was, she'd have died in the attempt."

A shiver ran down Anthony's spine. He was suddenly very glad Secilia hadn't become his bondmate yet.

"In either event, you should hurry up and sleep with her," the professor continued. "The longer you wait to make her your bondmate, the more uncertain the Board of Directors will become."

"You say that like it's easy." Anthony noticed the blank look on Professor Incanscino's face and waved his hand. "I just mean I need to make sure Brianna is okay with it before I can do anything. After what happened, I don't think she's keen on letting Secilia join us, and I don't want to do something that would make her mad."

"I suppose you wouldn't at that." Professor Incanscino suddenly smiled at Anthony. "That's just like an incubus."

Anthony didn't know what Professor Incanscino meant by that, but he didn't have time to ponder it because his next class was starting in five minutes.

The rest of the school day passed by quickly. Anthony eventually met with Secilia at the entrance to Building #1, and the two of them traveled to the maglev station.

Anthony remembered a time when Brianna would be waiting for him so they could travel home together, but that didn't happen now that she had school. No one was waiting for him and Secilia when he arrived.

The two of them entered the maglev with everyone else. All the seats were already taken, and it was so crowded that the two of them were forced into close quarters. Hemmed in from all sides, Secilia's chest was pressed against his. She wasn't much smaller than him. They were almost the same height, in fact, which meant her chest really was squishing into his. Her breasts weren't as big as Brianna's, but they weren't small either. Her modest chest, clad in a white bra, was just barely visible when he looked down and glanced at it through the hem of her shirt.

Unlike Brianna, who always blushed when they were pushed together like this, Secilia showed no embarrassment. Instead, she looked ashamed.

"Sorry about this," Anthony said, leaning down to speak in her ear. Everyone else on the maglev was also talking, which meant it was hard to converse without needing to speak over the noise. That was why he spoke into her ear instead, even though it meant their position was far more intimate.

"It's okay," Secilia said back, though she certainly didn't look like it was okay.

Anthony decided not to push this conversation while they were on a crowded maglev. The station they normally got off at to travel back to his apartment was several stops away, but when it finally came time for them to get off, Anthony grabbed Secilia's hand before she could leave. She looked at him curious. He, however, merely shook his head as though telling her not to get off.

"Are we not going to your place?" she asked.

"I want to visit my brother," he said.

"Oh... are you sure it's okay for me to come with you?"

"Why wouldn't it be?"

"It's just… no. It's nothing. Please forget I said anything."

Anthony frowned before leaning down to her ear again. "You know, if you're going to be like this, I feel like I should spank you."

"Hmph. Feel free if you can. We both know you don't have the guts to spank a woman in broad daylight."

"That was before I came into my powers as an incubus. I feel like I've become a lot more skeezy these days."

"Skeezy enough to spank a woman in public? I didn't realize sexual harassment was part of an incubus' modus operandi."

"It's only sexual harassment if she doesn't want it."

Anthony felt relief as Secilia's lips curved into a sharp smile as she traded wits with him. This was how their relationship was supposed to be. He hated how this woman kept walking on eggshells with him, letting her guilt dictate her actions. He knew she couldn't help it. Had their positions been reversed, he would have been the same, but that didn't mean he couldn't do something to help her out. Even if he could only distract her for a little bit, that was better than nothing.

They soon arrived at the Academy Island Hospital for Magical Catastrophes. Anthony greeted the receptionist and, ignoring the somewhat lascivious look she sent him, got himself signed into their database as a visitor. He planned to have Secilia sign in as well, but she shook her head.

"You go on ahead. I'll wait here."

"You sure?"

"Yes." She smiled at him. "I think it's important for you to have this time with your brother. I'll wait for you."

Anthony debated on what to do, but in the end, he only nodded. "Okay then. I'll try to be quick."

Secilia shook her head. "Take your time. I'm sure you have a lot to tell him."

Since he couldn't convince Secilia to come with him, Anthony went up to the room where his brother was being kept.

The room looked the same as he remembered. The large bed that looked more like a cryotube meant to keep someone in a state of suspended animation was still hooked up to all kinds of medical equipment. Anthony ignored the soft whirring sounds of machines as he sat on a chair next to the bed and looked at his younger brother, who looked a lot like him.

"Sorry it took me so long to come back and visit you," Anthony apologized. "A lot has been going on. I know. I know. I used that excuse before, but I'm serious. You'll never believe what happened to me this time. I ended up getting kidnapped by Secilia and…"

***

Secilia sat on one of several chairs in the hospital's waiting room, her left leg crossed over her right one. She wished she had a machine to tinker with. However, she hadn't thought to bring one. Had she known in advance that Anthony wanted to visit his brother, maybe she would have brought something, but it was too late now.

Several nurses had come up and asked her if she'd been helped. Secilia had to tell them that she was merely waiting for her friend to finish visiting his brother.

As she sat there and waited, the hospital doors opened and someone walked in, though Secilia didn't pay attention. Plenty of people had walked through these doors. She continued to sit there and stare blankly at the floor until a set of shoes appeared in her vision. Blinking several times, she let her gaze travel from the shoes to the knee-length socks, up the skirt, the shirt, and finally, onto the face of Brianna.

"Brianna? Did Anthony tell you he was visiting his brother?" asked Secilia in surprise.

"No." Brianna shook her head. "I have a familiar tracking Anthony whenever he goes somewhere without me. It'll let me know if something happens to him."

Secilia nodded. She remembered the familiar that Alex had destroyed. That was probably how Brianna was able to respond so fast to Anthony's kidnapping.

Brianna sat down on the seat next to Secilia, shocking her.

"Are you not going to go up and visit Anthony's brother?" she asked.

"I'll let Anthony have this time with Calvin," Brianna said. "I actually want to speak with you anyway."

"With me? What did you want to talk about?"

Secilia would admit to being curious. Up to this point, Brianna seemed to want to have nothing to do with her, but of course, Secilia didn't blame the girl. After what happened, after what she had done, Brianna's hatred for her was completely natural.

"I wanted to know… exactly why you kidnapped Anthony," Brianna said. "I never gave it any thought until this morning, but I can't help but feel like you had a reason for doing what you did, so I'd like to know what it is, if you don't mind."

So that was it. Well, it wasn't like Secilia didn't understand Brianna's curiosity. However...

"Does it really matter what my reasons were?" asked Secilia, looking at her hands. "It doesn't change the fact that I betrayed Anthony's trust. He told me he wanted me to become his bondmate, and I responded by stomping on those feelings."

"But... you did it for your mother, right?" When Secilia snapped her head over to Brianna, eyes widening in shock, the redhead gave her a somewhat apologetic smile. "I'm sorry. I overheard your conversation with Anthony this morning." She placed her hands on her lap and looked at the crowd of people in the hospital, her expression a little conflicted. "I don't have any parents. War Maidens like myself are just orphans Custodes Daemonium takes in. I can't say I understand exactly how you feel... but I think if my instructor was being imprisoned and someone was threatening to kill her if I didn't do what they said... well, I can't say I would betray Anthony, but I can't say I wouldn't either."

Secilia didn't say anything for a moment, choosing instead to study the young redhead. Despite being several years older than this girl, Brianna seemed far more mature than she was, which maybe was because she'd been trained in combat since birth. Maybe it was that warriors grace she possessed that gave her such a mature demeanor.

"What are you trying to say?" asked Secilia.

"I'm trying to say that while I think you made a terrible decision, it isn't an unfixable one." Brianna shrugged. "If you really feel guilty and want to make it up to Anthony, then give yourself to him. Become his bondmate and never betray him again. That will be enough to atone for what happened."

Brianna's words left Secilia stunned. However, she wasn't able to say anything because Anthony walked into the waiting room at that moment. He looked around before spotting them. With a smile, he walked over. Meanwhile, Brianna stood up and smiled at him.

"I didn't realize you knew I was here," Anthony said. "Do you have another familiar following me around?"

"I do," Brianna admitted without shame. "Did you have a nice conversation with your brother?"

"I did. I feel like I still have so much more to tell him, but… well, this is enough for now."

"Then why don't we go home?"

"That sounds like a good idea." Anthony reached out and grabbed Brianna's hand, then looked at Secilia and offered his other hand to her. "You coming?"

Secilia stared at the hand being offered to her, conflicted emotions rising within her chest, making it difficult to breath. Did she really deserve to take this hand? Did she deserve to be forgiven? Just as her thoughts turned negative, she remembered Brianna's words from just now, about how she should atone for the sins she committed against Anthony by giving herself to him.

Slowly, hesitantly, she reached out and placed her hand in his. It was much bigger than her own, but his hand was also a lot softer. It didn't have the callouses that her hands possessed from working on machinery all the time, and yet, while his hand seemed soft, it was also strong.

"Yes," she said. "I'm coming."

Anthony pulled Secilia to her feet, and the three of them left the hospital together.

CHAPTER 10

It was evening when they returned home. Anthony microwaved a set of packaged dinners for them the same as always, and they all sat down to eat. This time it was Swedish meatballs with pasta.

Dinner was fairly quiet once again, with neither Brianna or Secilia saying much of anything. They would glance in his direction while they ate. He would catch them. Then they would look away.

He wondered what was going on.

"I'll throw these away." Anthony grabbed the empty food containers. "You two can get ready for bed if you want, or you can watch TV or something."

"I'm actually going to be in my apartment tonight," Brianna said as she stood up. "I have a lot of homework I need to finish."

"Do you need any help?" asked Anthony.

Brianna shook her head. "I'm fine. See you both later."

Anthony trailed after Brianna with his eyes, watching as she slipped on her shoes and exited through the door. It took him a moment to realize she had said goodbye to both him and Secilia. He remembered seeing them talking together when he entered the waiting room after talking to his brother, but he hadn't known what they had talked about. Was it possible Brianna had let go of her anger toward Secilia?

"You can get ready for bed or relax and watch some TV if you want," Anthony said to Secilia as he went to the trash can, dumped the containers inside, and placed the forks in the washing machine.

"Actually," Secilia began, "I was hoping we could talk."

Anthony came back into the living room and looked at Secilia as she stood by the table, a nervous expression marring her face. She glanced at him, looked away, and wrung her hands together. All were telltale signs of anxiousness.

"What did you want to talk about?" asked Anthony. "Wait. Something tells me we should be sitting down for this conversation."

He went over to the couch and sat down, then looked at Secilia, who hesitated for a moment before sitting on the couch next to him.

Anthony didn't know what she wanted to talk about. Well, he had a few guesses, but those were all he had. While he was relatively certain he knew what she wanted to talk about, he'd be embarrassed if his guess ended up being way off base.

"Brianna talked to me while you were in the hospital visiting your brother," Secilia said at last. "She said that what I did to you was horrible but not unfixable." She placed her hands on her lap and clenched them. "Ever since we got back to Academy Island—no, even before then, I had been thinking about how I can make up for what I've done. I didn't think I was worthy of becoming your bondmate. How can I be when I betrayed you to Director Azrael? But Brianna said if I was really sorry and wanted to atone, then I should give myself to you."

Anthony's breathing caught in his throat, though he still didn't say anything, but now it was because he wasn't sure what to say.

Secilia turned to face him, hands still in her lap. He'd never seen her look this nervous. Even so, despite looking like a rabbit that might run away at the slightest sign of danger, she took a deep breath and looked him square in the eye.

"I don't think I'm worthy of becoming your bondmate, but if… if you'll have me, then I promise to do everything in my power to atone for what happened," she said, then in a much quieter voice, added, "I promise to never betray you again."

The sun was dipping beyond the event horizon. Reds, oranges, pinks, and yellows streaked through the clouds covering the atmosphere, casting warm hues of light through the window and into the room.

Anthony had so many things he wanted to tell Secilia; he wanted to tell her that she was worthy of becoming his bondmate, that he understood she hadn't betrayed him because she wanted to, and that he wasn't upset over what happened. He didn't though. Secilia's feelings on this matter weren't so simple that a few words could make her feel better. The guilt she felt was not something that could be fixed with a single conversation.

"Are you saying you'll become my bondmate in order to atone, or do you actually want to be my bondmate?" asked Anthony. "I have to be honest. If the reason you want to become my bondmate is solely to atone for what you believe is a transgression against me… then I'm not sure I can accept you." Secilia paled, but Anthony continued before she could voice her concern. "I like you, Secilia. Even after what happened, I still like you. That's why I don't want you to feel like bonding with me is a form of atonement. I want you to become my bondmate because it's what you want to do, and if it isn't, then there's no way I can accept that. Becoming my bondmate is permanent, you know. Once it's done, it can never be undone."

Anthony had thought long and hard about the criteria for what sort of women he wanted to bond with. Of course, he wanted women who were strong and capable. His life would likely be a dangerous one, so he couldn't bind himself to someone who wasn't able to take care of themselves; but more than that, he wanted women who earnestly wanted to be with him because they loved him. He didn't want to force himself on someone, nor did he want to be with someone who didn't have any actual interest in him as a person.

Secilia took a slow, shuddering breath. "I understand. Anthony, I can't say part of the reason I'm doing this isn't because I want to atone. It is. But it's not like that is the only reason." She bit her lip, then smiled. "Do you remember all the times we shared this past year? Some of my greatest memories are from those times. Going out to eat, playing VR laser tag, arguing late into the night over TV shows and passing out on the couch... they are some of my fondest memories... because you are in them with me. Look. What I'm trying to say is that, yes, I want to atone for what happened, but that isn't the only reason I'm doing this. I also want to be with you."

Anthony felt the tension in his shoulders ease as he listened to Secilia talk. He'd been worried. While he knew Secilia had feelings for him—she'd never disguised it—there had been a part of him that feared it was all fake, that she'd only done it to get close to him. He felt bad about that, but, well, it was hard not to have that concern after what happened.

Now that she had told him otherwise, Anthony felt a lot better.

"So… you want to become mine?" asked Anthony.

"I do," Secilia said.

Anthony leaned over and pressed his lips to Secilia's without any warning. Despite her surprise, Secilia did not reject his kiss, instead tilting her head and kissing back.

Her lips were soft. Anthony remembered how he would sometimes find himself staring at those lips and wondering if they felt as soft as they looked. Now he knew. Secilia's lips were warm and delicate, pliant as he took her lower lip between her teeth and gently nibbled on it.

Secilia gasped in surprise as he pushed her onto the couch and continued to kiss her, irregularly switching from one lip to the other. As their actions continued, Anthony felt a greater need growing inside of him, and he didn't resist. He slipped his tongue into her mouth and deepened the kiss.

Her taste intoxicated him.

He wanted more.

Anthony stopped kissing her lips, but that was only so he could begin kissing her neck. He pressed his mouth to her throat, trailed his lips along her skin, and listened to her breathing as it hitched.

He soon discovered that Secilia preferred harder kisses to soft ones. Her neck was sensitive and her responses were more enthusiastic when he was being rough. Secilia's stilted breathing mixed with her gasps and pants as he spent however many minutes he could finding each and every point on her neck that made her arousal spike.

"Anthony…" A soft moan reached his ears. "I can't… take it. S-stop teasing me… like this…"

"Sorry. Guess I lost myself there."

Anthony sat back up and took a moment to admire the woman underneath him. Secilia's fair skin was flushed a light shade of pink, and her breathing was heavy, which caused her chest to move, though her breasts were currently confined by a bra. Her shirt had ridden up to reveal her cute stomach. She wasn't fit like Brianna, who had been trained in combat since birth, but Secilia did exercise. She needed to be strong to work on heavy machinery.

"I've always thought you were gorgeous," Anthony said in a soft breath. "But wow. You look…"

"Stunning?" asked Secilia.

"I was going to say erotic."

"I'm not sure that's a compliment."

"You say that, but aren't you smiling?"

"Am I?"

"You are."

Secilia wore a wide smile, her eyes half-lidded as she stared at him with a seductive quality Brianna didn't have. It was that expression on her face, more than anything, that broke any resolve he might have had left to resist her.

Dipping his head back down, Anthony didn't go for the lips this time. He went down to her stomach. The way her tummy twitched as he pressed his lips and tongue to her soft skin made his already hard dick swell even more. He began kissing her stomach in earnest, working his way up toward her solar plexus. Secilia's soft moaning reached his ears. He wondered what other sounds he could get her to make.

He pushed her shirt over her chest, revealing her white bra, which fortunately had a front hook. He undid the clasp and her breasts sprang free.

Secilia's chest was not as large as Brianna's, but they were more than a handful. They were also sensitive. As he grabbed one of her boobs and gave it a firm squeeze, Secilia's spine arched as she opened her mouth and released a soft cry. Her nipple had stiffened. Staring at it made his mouth go dry. He didn't resist the compulsion to lean down and take it into his mouth.

"Nnnggg! Anthony! That feels—oh!"

He swirled his tongue around her nipple. As he licked and flicked the now hardened point, he reached down to her pants and undid the buttons and zipper with one hand, then slipped his hand inside of her pants and underwear. He moved lower until he found her warm pussy, already wet with her juices.

Anthony cupped a hand to her crotch, not doing anything yet, but just admiring the warmth coming off her. Her lips were soft and squishy. Just pressing his fingers lightly against them let him know of their elasticity. It was an amazing feeling.

"Are you… are you just going to keep your hand there… and not do anything?" asked Secilia, her breathing raspy as she reached out and threaded her fingers through his hair.

Anthony couldn't answer her with words, as his mouth was still full of her nipple, but he pressed his index finger against her outer labia, letting his finger become wedged between her lips. He rubbed up, then down, and then repeated the process.

"Ha… ahn… ha… A-Anthony! S-stop teasing—ahn!"

As he switched from one breast to the other, Anthony pressed his index finger inside of her, slowly working his way into her pussy. He rubbed his finger against the walls of her vagina. He began pumping his finger inside of her, then quickly added a second one. As he rubbed his fingers along her walls, Secilia released a loud squeal as he bucked her hips into his hand.

"Oh. It seems I found something," he muttered.

He stopped playing with her nipples and kissed his way back down her stomach. When he reached her pants, he removed his hand from inside. His fingers came back wet, but he sucked those clean. She tasted sweet. He wondered if it was because she liked drinking soda, but those were thoughts for another time.

He grabbed her pants and underwear, hooking his fingers inside of them, then moved them down her hips. Secilia raised her hips so he could slide them off. When they were around her knees, Anthony lifted her legs and removed them. He tossed her pants and panties to the ground, then looked back up to admire Secilia.

Now dressed only in a shirt and a bra that had been undone, Secilia struck an erotic image that became burned into his mind. Her skin was covered in a light layer of sweat. It caused her to sparkle a little. He wanted to lick the sweat off her skin, but there was something else he wanted more.

He bent down between her legs, spread her legs apart, and placed them over his shoulder, then pressed his mouth against her pussy and kissed it.

"A-ah-ahn!"

Secilia threw her head back as he spread her lips apart with his tongue. He used his thumb to work out her clit and began rubbing it as he explored her depths. One of Secilia's legs fell off his shoulder, striking the floor with a dull thud that echoed around the room. He glanced down at the sound to find her toes spasming. Her clit throbbed under his touch as Secilia's gasps reached a crescendo. All at once, her body seemed to stiffen as she squirted her juices all over his face. He jerked back in surprise, watching as nectar squirted from her pussy sort of like… like one of those old-fashioned water guns.

After cumming, Secilia's body relaxed on the couch. Anthony admired the stains that would have to be cleaned at some point. He wasn't sure he'd want anyone sitting there until after he cleaned it off, but he shook the thought away and scooped Secilia into his arms.

The woman stirred as he held her like a newlywed bride and walked into his room. The couch simply wasn't big enough to have sex on, and he wanted her first time to be more comfortable, though it wasn't like his twin bed was much bigger.

He was glad the door to his bedroom was automatic. As it slid shut behind him, he wandered over to the bed and placed Secilia on it. She had recovered from her orgasm now and watched as he removed his clothes, first his shirt, then his pants. Anthony looked over to find Secilia's eyes glued onto his chest and stomach.

"I hope that look means you like what you see," he said with an only slightly embarrassed smile.

"I certainly can't say I dislike it," Secilia admitted shamelessly. "I've always liked you, but I will admit you weren't as attractive back when you were scrawny. You looked so unhealthy."

"Gee, thanks. You're so kind."

"I'm just telling it like it is," Secilia said.

Anthony finally removed his boxers and tossed them to the floor. When his dick sprang free from their confines, Secilia gaped at him.

"What kind of monster is that?!"

"Excuse me?" Anthony asked.

Secilia pointed at his dick. "Have you been impaling Brianna with that beast?"

"I'd appreciate it if you didn't call my dick a beast. He has feelings too, you know."

"So you say…" Secilia kept her eyes locked on his dick as he climbed onto the bed. She looked wary. "Is that even gonna fit inside of me?"

"It will fit," Anthony assured her.

"How do you know?"

"Men's intuition."

"Men don't have an intuition."

"Now that is just sexist."

Anthony didn't give Secilia a chance to retort as he grabbed her shirt and removed it, followed by her bra. He placed his hands on her shoulders and pushed her back onto the bed. Now both naked, he hovered over her, his hands on either side of her head.

"This is your last chance to back out. You sure you want this?"

"I'm sure." Secilia must have realized he wasn't joking because she wrapped her arms around his neck. "I've wanted this for a long time now. You don't have to worry. I won't regret my choice. Not now. Not ever."

"Good. Because I'm about to start."

"Wait. What? Now?"

"No time like the present."

"Hold on! At least let me prepare fir—oooh!"

Secilia's words turned into a drawn out moan as Anthony pushed his cock inside of her. Her back arched off the bed as she threw her head back and closed her eyes.

He once heard someone say no two vaginas were the same. The person who'd been speaking was an idiotic braggart who claimed to have slept with dozens of women, and Anthony honestly thought the man was blowing smoke up everyone's asses, but he couldn't deny that Secilia and Brianna felt very different. Brianna was tight. Her pussy was like a vice that sucked him in and refused to let go. Secilia was looser. He guessed it was because she wasn't as fit as Brianna. It felt like her soft inner walls were gently rubbing against him. The sensation was no less pleasant. Just different. Also…

"No hymen?" he mumbled in surprise.

"C-clones… don't have hymens… for… for some reason," Secilia gasped as she calmed back down. Her body twitched and shuddered as if she was experiencing mini-orgasms.

"Huh. I did not know that. You learn something new everyday, I guess." He paused. "How do you feel?"

"Like someone shoved a cucumber up my pussy." Secilia glared at him. "You could have warned me."

"Didn't I say I was sticking it in?"

"That wasn't a warning. Cruel and unusual. That's what you are."

Anthony gave her a cocky grin as he leaned down until their noses and foreheads were touching. From up close, Secilia's dark eyes were even more dazzling than normal. He stroked her cheek, causing those eyes to close as Secilia unconsciously nuzzled into his hand.

"You say I'm cruel, but we both know you enjoy surprises."

"I can't deny that," Secilia admitted in a whisper.

"Right. So how about another surprise," said Anthony before he leaned down and kissed her.

Secilia wrapped her arms around Anthony's neck as they kissed. Before he could consider deepening it, she stuck out her tongue and pushed it into his mouth.

Anthony jerked his hips back, then thrust them forward, setting a steady pace. He grunted a little, but the noise was muffled by Secilia's tongue in his mouth, and he wasn't the only one making noise. Nasally gasps escaped the woman beneath him as she pistoned into her.

Sweat formed on their naked bodies as they pressed so close together not even a sheet of paper could have slipped through. The feeling of her breasts pushed against his chest, of her warm insides conforming to his cock, and of her tongue in his mouth was a sensation Anthony never wanted to get used to. All of it felt incredible. He'd even go so far as to say it was mind blowing.

As they continued to have sex, Anthony felt something inside of him opening up. It was just like that time with Brianna. It was as if a small space inside of him had suddenly appeared, or maybe it had suddenly been unlocked. Within that space, he felt emotions that weren't his. They were Secilia's. And right now, those emotions were all over the place, an odd combination of joy, guilt, and pleasure.

It wasn't just Secilia he felt either now. A small thrill was running through him from the space that belonged to Brianna. The pleasure he felt coming from there told him she might be masturbating, though he had no way of confirming that.

The connection between him and Secilia solidified as he continued pounding into her. Lewd sounds, the sound of his balls smacking against her ass, of grunts and groans of passion, echoed around the room. The scent of their mixing sweat was enough to drive Anthony crazy.

Their kiss had become open-mouthed and passionate. Their tongues entwined together, a slippery dance that neither of them was eager to end, though Anthony soon found himself wanting to change positions.

He leaned back. Secilia whined in complaint, until he flipped her onto her stomach. Then she squealed in surprise.

Before she could ask him what he was doing, Anthony grabbed her hips and raised them. Now with her ass sticking in the air, he pressed his dick to her pussy once more and, as she had so eloquently put it, impaled her.

"Hyk!"

Secilia's spine arched as he thrust his dick all the way to the hilt. Her toes curled, her thighs flexed, and her ass clenched as he began pounding her pussy from behind. The gasps she released as he took her from this new position were louder than before. He grabbed her beautiful buttcheeks and massaged them as he set a much harder pace.

"Ahn! Ah! Ahn! Hyk! Haht! Haaang!"

Perhaps she was trying to keep quiet, but Secilia buried her face into his pillow and bit down on it, though even that couldn't muffle her cries of pleasure, which grew louder the longer he fucked her like this.

Anthony eventually ceased massaging her ass and placed his hands on her sweaty back, kneading the muscles there. Secilia groaned as he combined screwing her from behind with a back massage. He placed his thumbs on her shoulder blades and pushed down, erasing the tension that came from working on heavy machinery. For whatever reason, this made her pussy quiver.

"Ahn! Hang! Hyrk! A-Anthony!" Secilia cried out. "I-I'm cumming! I'm cumming!"

Her body shook as she came, once more squirting her juices against him. They drenched her thighs and the bed beneath her. He felt her mind explode inside of him, filling him with pleasure and mana, but even though she had cum, he didn't stop. He continued thrusting his cock inside of her.

"Anthony! Anthony! Haak! Ahn!"

Secilia gripped the bed sheets tightly, turning them into twisted fabric. The scent of sex hung heavily in the air. Anthony breathed it in as he kept moving, kept thrusting. Secilia came again.

"Ha… ha… ahn…"

Leaning down, he placed a hand against Secilia's cheek and turned her head towards him. He kissed her, and she kissed back, her tongue once more engaging with his.

Anthony stood up and took Secilia with him. Now on their knees, with her back against his chest, he slowed his pace but continued to thrust his hips as he kept one hand on her cheeks and brought the other down to her pussy. He sought out her clit and stimulated it with his middle finger. Secilia screamed into his mouth as she came again.

That was Anthony's breaking point, and as his mind became inundated with mana and pleasure, he released his seed inside of Secilia.

Because they were upright, his spunk mixed with Secilia's love juice as both ran down her thighs and drenched the bed. As they came down from their high, Secilia seemed to lose strength. Her sweat-coated body fell forward. Anthony caught her before she could faceplant and gently lowered her

onto the bed. He rolled her over and admired Secilia as she gasped for breath, her glistening breasts jiggling, goosebumps forming around her hard nipples.

"My body… feels so hot," Secilia mumbled as her eyes began shutting. "Anthony… I feel… so warm…"

Anthony watched as Secilia closed her eyes and fell asleep. He wasn't sure if he could fall asleep quite yet. His body was brimming with energy. However, even if he wasn't tired, Anthony settled down next to Secilia.

As if she could sense him next to her, Secilia rolled over and moved closer. He slid an arm around her and pulled the woman into him, letting her rest her head on his chest and shoulder. She wrapped her legs around him, hooking her legs with his until they were tangled.

Like that, Anthony enjoyed the sensation of Secilia's body against his until sleep eventually claimed him.

***

Anthony was filled with energy when he woke up the next morning. Secilia was still fast asleep. Cuddled into his chest, the woman released soft snoring sounds that he thought were pretty darn cute.

After taking a shower, he went into the living room to find Brianna setting out three containers of food. It was bacon and eggs this time. She looked up as he wandered into the room and smiled.

"I'm guessing last night went well?"

"It did." Anthony went up to Brianna as she set the last container on the table, wrapped his arms around her waist, and pulled her to him. "I don't know what you said to Secilia, but thank you."

"I only did this for you," Brianna mumbled, blushing as she turned her head.

"That's why I'm thanking you."

He placed a hand under her chin, tilted her head, and kissed her. Brianna released a sound like a kitten's meowing as she kissed back. Her hands came up and grabbed his shirt, though she let go as the kiss ended.

"I'm guessing Secilia is still asleep?" Brianna said as she and Anthony sat down.

"Yeah…" Anthony felt a small trickle of sweat run down his face. "I, uh, may have been a little too enthusiastic last night. I think I exhausted her."

"You didn't have sex with her until she passed out, did you?"

"I don't think so… I mean, she did fall asleep, but it's not like she passed out."

"Hmmm…"

"W-what is that look for?! Don't look at me like you think I'm lying. I'm being honest here!"

The skeptical expression on Brianna's face changed into a smile as she turned her head. "You say that, but I know how carried away you can get."

Anthony groaned. "That only happened one time…"

As they continued to talk and eat, the sound of the shower starting caused them to stop for a moment. About twenty minutes after the shower began, it stopped. By that point, Anthony and Brianna had already finished their meals, which left Secilia as the only one who hadn't eaten.

Secilia came out of the small hallway a few minutes later. Her hair was still wet, she didn't look fully awake, and she walked with a slight limp. She was also wearing one of Anthony's shirts and some of his pajama pants, which were several sizes too large. That made him remember how they didn't have any of her clothes. They'd have to make a stop by her apartment after school and grab her outfits.

"Goooood mooorning," Secilia said, prolonging her words as she yawned.

"Good morning," Brianna greeted softly.

"How do you feel?" asked Anthony.

"Like I was fucked unconscious," Secilia said immediately.

Brianna gave him a stare.

"It didn't happen like that!" Anthony swore to her.

Brianna sighed but let that go. As Secilia sat down at the table and began eating, her pace slow as if she still wasn't fully awake, she changed topics.

"Now that you two have bonded, we need to see what powers you've gained. Also, Secilia should be able to use your power as well. We need to make time to test that out."

Anthony nodded in agreement, but Secilia seemed shocked.

"Wait. You're saying I can use Anthony's power?"

"My understanding is that you can only use one of his powers," Brianna said. "When a woman becomes an incubus's bondmate, she unlocks one of his abilities. Whatever ability she unlocks is also the ability of his that she can use. Since we don't know what that ability is, we will need to test it out."

Anthony raised his hand. "I actually do know what that ability is."

"You do?"

"Of course I do. It's my ability." He shook his head. "I can't fully explain how I know, but it's like I am just instinctively aware of what I can do."

"So what's your new ability?" asked Secilia.

"Farsight," Anthony said. "It seems I have the ability to look into the future. That said, while I do know what my ability is, I don't know how far into the future I can look. I only know that I can."

"Which means we'll have to see how well you can use this ability during training," Brianna said, pausing as she placed a hand against her chin. "Still, I'm surprised this is your next ability. Farsight is a rather advanced spell used by Custodes Daemonium. We don't have a monopoly on the spell, of course, but very few people outside of the organization know how to use it. Also, I've noticed that this one is also a supplementary ability like Physical Enhancement."

"I've noticed that too," Anthony said. "And I think I have a theory on why my ability isn't attack magic like elemental manipulation or something similar."

Secilia finished eating and took the container into the kitchen. She came back out after throwing it away and sat on the couch beside Anthony. Perhaps she was still tired. After tucking her feet underneath her bottom, she leaned over to rest her head on his shoulder and closed her eyes.

"What is your theory?" asked Brianna, frowning at Secilia.

"I think it has something to do with the women who become my bondmates," he said, placing a hand on Secilia's hip and stroking it. Brianna's cheeks swelled as she pouted. "Because my mana comes directly from the women bound to me, I think the magic I can use also comes from them. Farsight must be an ability that Secilia should be able to use with training even if she wasn't bound to me."

"Maybe," Brianna admitted, still glaring at Secilia. "But if that's the case, then the magic that came from me should have also been Farsight. It's the ability I'm best at."

"Maybe not," Anthony refuted. "You might not have mastered Physical Enhancement when we first met, but I bet you were still better at using it than most people your age."

"Well… that is true," Brianna said, then sighed. "I guess you bring up a good point." She stopped talking for a moment to stare at him and Secilia, who released soft noises that sounded suspiciously like purring. Her eyes went blank. "By the way, just how long do you two plan on remaining like that? You know we have school, right?"

***

While the day seemed to pass by slowly, school eventually came to an end, and Brianna took Anthony and Secilia to an empty park. She put up a barrier like the one they had been using while sparring. Once it was put in place, she turned to them.

"Anthony, you and I are going to spar," she said. "Rather than using Physical Enhancement, we're going to use Farsight."

"Sounds good," Anthony said.

Brianna turned to Secilia. "I want you to also use Farsight. Try to see if you can use it to determine what we're going to do before we do it."

"I'll do my best," Secilia said. "Though I'm honestly not sure how to use Farsight. How am I supposed to activate it?"

It was only after she had spoken that Anthony and Brianna realized the problem. Secilia had no magic training. She wouldn't know how to activate Farsight. What's more, she had never been trained to use mana, meaning she probably didn't know what it felt like.

"Well, this is a problem," Brianna sighed. "I guess… we'll put training in Farsight on hold until Secilia can use mana." She turned to fully face Secilia. "Sit down and cross your legs."

Secilia sat down and crossed her legs, then Brianna sat down in front of her. Anthony stood back and watched.

"Hold out your hands, please," Brianna instructed. When Secilia did as told, Brianna grabbed her hands and held them in a firm grip. "Okay. I'm going to channel my mana into your hands. I want you to close your eyes and focus on the feeling of my mana flowing through you. Once you have a firm grasp on how it feels, I want you to search for that same feeling inside of yourself. It might take awhile to feel out your mana, but we'll keep at it until you've found it."

"Are you sure you shouldn't be training Anthony?" asked Secilia.

But Brianna shook her head. "Anthony is already fairly strong. Right now, you are the weakest link since you don't have any powers. We need to change that. You should especially want to change that if you'd like to take revenge on Azrael."

At the mention of Azrael, Secilia's lips became a thin line and her eyes hardened. She nodded once. After taking a deep breath, she closed her eyes and relaxed. Brianna also closed her eyes and took a deep breath.

Anthony was still standing some distance away from them. As he studied the two, he felt a strange surge coming from Brianna. He couldn't see anything. No ethereal flames appeared on her body. There was no physical indication that anything was different. However, the air had suddenly become charged as if positive and negative ions were clashing together.

"I think I feel something," Secilia said excitedly. "It feels like electricity! No, it's like energy rushing through my body!"

"That's my mana you feel," Brianna said. "Make sure you memorize that feeling. Once you know how it feels, you should be able to find your mana simply by imagining this feeling."

"I got it." Secilia's brow furrowed as she concentrated. "I think I have it."

"In that case, I'm going to let you practice on your own." Brianna released Secilia's hands, stood up, and turned to him. "Are you ready to begin training?"

"I believe so," Anthony said.

"Good." Brianna smiled as she walked back to their sparring ground, which was just a small patch of dirt. She slid her feet against the ground, the sound of shifting gravel echoing around them, and set her hands in a basic martial arts stance. "In that case, let's get started."

Anthony narrowed his eyes and activated Farsight. His mana surged through his body and rushed into his eyes. As it did, Brianna's body seemed to split in two. One of them was moving at him while the other stood still, though it wasn't long before both were moving. It was hard to explain what he was seeing, but it was almost like… like Brianna's image was being overlapped with another image that was happening several seconds ahead of the first.

The first Brianna came at him with a punch, and he moved to dodge, but then the second Brianna shifted into a thigh kick. While he was able to avoid it, a third Brianna suddenly appeared and threw a punch at his chest. He avoided it, but then a fourth, fifth, and sixth Brianna split off from the first and unleashed different attacks. Anthony had no idea who to dodge or block and could only stand there in indecision.

Stars exploded in his vision as something struck him in the face. He stumbled back.

"W-what was that?" asked Anthony, holding a hand to his bruised cheek.

"That was the drawback of Farsight," Brianna said, letting the hand she'd punched him with come to rest at her side. "Farsight is an amazing ability that lets you look several seconds into the future. However, the future is always in motion. Farsight calculates shifts in the future to show you what is going to happen before it happens, but since the future is always in motion, it is hard to predict which future will actually happen. There is also the issue of knowing what's going to happen and not being able to do anything about it. You might be able to see what's coming, but if you aren't fast enough to react to it, then being able to see into the future won't matter."

As Brianna finished her explanation of the Farsight ability, Anthony felt a little depressed.

Farsight sounded like a great ability. How many people didn't wish they could see into the future? It sounded like such a useful power, but listening to Brianna, he could tell it took a lot of hard work to master.

"So how do you get better at using it?" asked Anthony.

"By constantly practicing with it," Brianna said. "To use Farsight, you must learn how to focus your mind and capture the moment in time that you wish to see. Just now, you probably saw several different futures instead of just one, which is why you couldn't react to my attack. Once you master the basics of Farsight, you will only see one future, which we call the True Future. It is the future that will happen out of the many different possible futures that could happen. The better you get at using it, the further into the True Future you'll be able to see."

Anthony ran a hand through his hair. This sounded like a really complicated power, but he thought he understood the gist of it. He had to train his ability to find that "True Future" out of the many possible futures.

A good example would be if he was sparring Brianna and she ran at him. There were a lot of attacks she could use. She could kick him, punch him, or even grapple him. Just from this one action, there were at least three possible futures. Of course, the futures further branched off after that. What kind of kick would she throw? Would she punch him with a jab or a hook? How would she grapple him? Once he thought like that, Anthony realized the possible angles of attack she could unleash were endless, which meant there were an endless number of possible futures.

The goal of practicing Farsight was not only to look further into the future, but also to find the future that would happen out of those many possibilities.

"Let's try that again," Anthony said.

"All right." Brianna smiled as she adopted her martial arts stance once more. "Here I come!"

Anthony activated Farsight once more, and once more multiple Brianna's appeared the closer she got. Once more, Anthony found himself trying to respond to multiple possible futures, only for him to become breathless when Brianna slammed a knee into his gut.

As he stumbled back and held his stomach, Anthony understood that training to use Farsight was going to take a lot longer than using Physical Enhancement.

That didn't mean he was going to give up.

It just meant he was probably gonna get beaten up a lot more before he mastered it.

Whoever created that saying about no pain, no gain must have gone through something similar.

CHAPTER 11

Anthony narrowed his eyes as he watched Brianna close the distance between them. It looked like there were two, but he understood the one in front was actually a projection of what she would do .5 seconds from now. While he kept most of his attention on the projection, he didn't neglect Brianna, who could change the projection's future with her own actions. He had to focus.

Mana flowed through his eyes as he waited until Brianna was on him, then raised his arm in front of his face and moved it right. The back of his hand struck Brianna's fist, pushing her straight jab to the side, redirecting it. He rotated his whole arm and locked her arm underneath his armpit. Once she was secured, he diverted energy into the palm of his left hand and thrust it out. He was aiming at her solar plexus.

Brianna proved her talent by leaping into the air and twisting her body. Her arm was still locked within his grip, but it rotated along with her as she brought her leg down—or up?—on his head—or tried to. Anthony saw it coming thanks to Farsight and backed away, letting go of her arm in the process.

He was unable to back away far enough, however, and Anthony felt a tug on his shirt as Brianna grabbed a fistful of it. He tried to fend her off. Yet even though he saw it, he was not fast enough to respond. She landed on the ground, her hand full of his shirt, then rotated on the balls of her feet and lifted him into the air.

"Whoa!"

The world became inverted as Anthony was flipped upside down. It only lasted for a moment. Then the air was rushing from his lungs as his back hit the ground, kicking up sand and depriving him of oxygen.

As he lay there, gasping, Brianna's brilliant green eyes, beautiful face, and red hair filled his vision. She was smiling at him.

"You're getting a lot better at using Farsight. You lasted a full thirty minutes against me."

"But I'm still not good enough to beat you," he said with a groan.

Brianna held out her hand to him, and Anthony accepted it. As she pulled him up, several cracking noises echoed from his back. He groaned again. It felt like his back was popping.

"I've been trained in combat since I was just six years old," Brianna reminded him. "You might have some really good instincts, but you were never formally taught how to fight."

"Well, Orion did teach me a little…" Anthony rubbed the back of his head, trying to rid it of sand. Brianna also patted him down to get the sand off. "… but he only taught me how to fight without wasting too much energy and how to deal more damage to people."

"Which is why we are sparring like this," Brianna said as they began walking. "Not only are we training you in how to use Farsight, we're helping you refine your fighting style even further by pitting you against someone who has been trained to fight demons from a young age. I'll whip you into shape in no time."

"I think I'd prefer you whipping me in bed," Anthony said with a strained voice as he stretched his arms above his head. He winced as the muscles in his back, arms, and shoulders tightened.

"I'm not really one for whips," Brianna whispered with a fierce blush. "Is that something you would like?"

"I was just teasing you."

They made it onto a small, paved walkway, which led them out of the park and onto one of the roads. Earlier this morning, there had been no one on the streets. Now, however, there were hundreds or maybe even thousands of people walking around.

Anthony pulled Brianna close as a pair of men in business suits walked past them. A couple of vampire children raced by on their other side, traveling toward the park he and Brianna had just vacated, the kids harried parents catching up seconds later. As they walked past a gaggle of school girls in casual clothes, Anthony caught a whiff of overpowering perfume. The girl who was wearing it, a young woman decked in gaudy clothes and bleach blonde hair, winked at him while her friends giggled.

Brianna sighed. "You aren't even emitting pheromones anymore, but women still look at you."

"It can't be helped." Anthony shrugged.

"I know, but it still annoys me."

With his arm still wrapped around her, Anthony enjoyed the feel of Brianna's body as they walked.

"You don't need to worry. I'm not interested in girls like that."

"I know." Brianna sighed as she looked away. Her ears were red, meaning she was probably blushing. "I just think it's rude."

"If you say so."

Brianna turned her head back and glared at him, though there was no heat within her eyes.

"I do say so."

Within the bustling metropolis, Anthony and Brianna looked like any other couple. They traveled through the streets and eventually reached the maglev station. As they walked up to the entrance gates, the pair separated and walked up to the small gates. Anthony accessed his student ID from his wristwatch and held it up to the scanner. A soft beep issued from the gate as it opened and he stepped inside. Over at the gate next to him, Brianna did the same thing.

There were a number of maglevs coming and going. Anthony stood with Brianna on one of many platforms as the one they were waiting for arrived, then hopped on with her. They found a secluded spot to stand as far from the crowd as was possible in such a crowded place and quietly conversed.

"So what do you think Secilia is making?" asked Brianna.

"She said she was making weapons," Anthony said, shrugged, then continued. "During my fight with that leonid, I was only able to fight him to a standstill. I couldn't beat him because I didn't have a weapon of my own. I believe Secilia wants to create a weapon I can use to rectify this particular problem. She's also planning to make some weapons she can use… though I have no idea what weapons she'll make for herself."

"Secilia has been training really hard in Farsight," Brianna said as she tugged on a strand of her red hair. "Her talent at using it is probably even better than mine. Given how well she can use it and how good her vision is, I think a long-range weapon would suit her best."

"I think so too."

Secilia had always been good at VR Laser Tag, which was all about shooting people from a distance. She was a great sniper, but she was also talented at dual-wielding pistols.

Of course, Virtual Reality Laser Tag was not the same as wielding an actual gun. The weapons they used in laser tag did not have any recoil and only fired low-intensity lasers that couldn't even shoot an eye out. Still, if she trained in how to fire actual guns for a while, Anthony suspected Secilia would become a great marksman.

The maglev soon reached the Institution of Magical Sciences's stop. Anthony and Brianna moved with the flow of traffic as they exited, stepping onto the station and beginning their walk toward his college.

Five buildings loomed over them as they walked along a paved walkway, and though they were not the largest buildings Anthony had seen, they were big in their own right. The one they were heading to was Building #4, located on the eastern side of the campus.

Since Building #4 was dedicated to magical engineering, most of the rooms were composed of labs and workshops where students could build machines that used both magical and non-magical components. They passed by a number of rooms that had holographic signs like *Robotics*, *Magical Armaments*, *AI Development*, and *Prosthetics*.

The room they ended up traveling to was unmarked. All the hologram said was *Private Workshop*, basically designating it as a workshop being privately used by one of the students. Anthony used his Student ID to unlock the door, then walked inside with Brianna.

There was a lot of equipment inside of the lab, large contraptions that looked like engines, boxy machines that had a lot of arms with different tools attached to each one, and other devices that looked like something a madman might create. While this space was littered with numerous creations, each piece of equipment had been neatly organized so as not to clutter the place.

They found Secilia in the back of the room next to a workstation. The rectangular table was about ten feet long and five feet wide. An array of tools sat on the table.

Secilia was entirely focused on the device before her, which Anthony realized as he came closer was a gun of some sort. Longer than a standard rifle, it reminded him of a sniper rifle. What let him know his guess was probably on the mark was the unusually long length of the barrel, the stock designed for firing from a prone position, a telescopic sight, and the presence of a bipod next to the rifle itself. It looked like Secilia was taking the gun apart at the moment.

"So this is what you are working on," Brianna said as she looked at the gun. "Isn't this a Longinus R700?"

At the sound of Brianna's voice, Secilia spoke even as she continued removing the stock from the gun. It looked to Anthony like she was replacing it with a different stock. The one she was replacing it with had a different curvature, which looked like it was designed for someone with smaller shoulders.

"I'm surprised you recognize this. I didn't realize you knew much about guns."

"Custodes Daemonimium does not use guns, but we have to know what weapons are currently being used by the many different nations and various factions," Brianna answered as she watched Secilia work. "The business tycoon, Alexandros Ross, has a militia that uses the Longinus R700 for covert operations because of its accuracy and penetrating power."

"The Academy Island Private Security Forces also use it," Secilia said. "I was able to convince Lucretia—Professor Incanscino—to let me have one."

"I'm surprised she gave one to you just like that," Anthony said.

"I wouldn't say she gave it to me," Secilia muttered. "I have to do something for her in return, but she also knows I need a weapon if I'm going to be of any use to you when a fight breaks out. Aside from this modified Longinus R700, I've also got two Vulpine 22s, which have already been heavily modified by yours truly."

"The Vulpine 22 is an automatic pistol, right?" asked Brianna.

"That's right," Secilia said. She kept working, attaching the new stock and adding a different telescope. "The Vulpine 22 is basically a submachine gun that looks like a pistol. It fires anti-magic rounds that can penetrate the magical defenses of various demons, including the tough skin of a therianthrope and the magic shields of a vampire. Of course, I can also switch the magazine out for regular bullets if need be. It has very little recoil, which makes it great for dual-wielding."

"You always did love your dual-wielding," Anthony said.

"Damn straight, I do."

Secilia finished putting her sniper rifle together and hefted it up. Now that she had completed it, the weapon only vaguely resembled the Longinus R700. The body was the same, the barrel was the same, but the stock, telescope, and magazine were completely different. One thing Anthony noticed was how the weapon seemed to have its own magic circuits, which meant this device used mana in some capacity.

"All done! I still need to test it, but this weapon should have more power and be easier to use than the Longinus R700."

"And how are you going to test it?" asked Brianna.

"Well, I'll have to ask Professor Incanscino if she can let me use a shooting range at the Academy Island Private Security Forces' main base." Secilia let the gun's long barrel sit on her shoulder. "I'm sure she'll oblige. After all, I'm helping build a state of the art spa for her house."

Anthony could feel the droplet of sweat trickle down his scalp as he realized what Professor Incanscino was getting in return for purloining a state of the art sniper rifle and two automatic pistols. The idea of trading weapons for a spa sounded ludicrous. However, knowing the professor as he did, it also struck him as something she would do.

"I've also got a weapon for you, Anthony," Secilia said as she set the sniper rifle back down.

"You do?"

"Yup."

Anthony was surprised as Secilia led them over to a storage locker, which she opened with an access code. She reached in and pulled out a case that was smaller than he would have expected. Moving back over to the workstation, she set it down, undid the locks, and opened it.

What lay inside looked like nothing more than a simple cylinder. Secilia picked it up and handed the object to Anthony, who looked at it in confusion alongside Brianna. Neither of them knew what to make of this.

"Channel your mana into it," Secilia said.

Anthony did as he was told, only to make an exclamation of shock when several artificial magic circuits began flowing along the surface. An extension shot from one end of the cylinder a second later. It grew to about two feet in length. This was a truncheon. Like the base, the length of the weapon was covered in glowing magic formulas connected by several magic circuits.

"I thought long and hard about what kind of weapon I should make for you, and I decided to eventually go with something simple but effective," Secilia said with a happy smile. "This truncheon has been infused with artificial magic circuits that have been tailored to your mana, meaning no one else can use this but you. The magic I applied to the magic formulas is a combination of Physical Enhancement and the spatial magic, Negation." She glanced at Brianna as she said this. "Since it is a blunt weapon, it's not effective at cutting like your Geminius Sword, but it will negate the magic of anything it touches... provided Anthony channels enough mana into it. It isn't perfect. In order to negate the magic, Anthony must overpower the mana being used in his opposition's magic, meaning if he isn't stronger than his enemy, he won't be able to negate the magic."

"It sounds like this might not work on everyone, but it's still a lot better than not having a weapon," Brianna said. "Actually, this is some pretty amazing stuff. I'm shocked the Academy Island Private Security Forces haven't strong-armed you into working for them."

"I'm sure they would if they could, but not only was I working for Nametech before this, Professor Incanscino won't let them," Secilia said.

"Ah."

"Now that you've made these, I guess we should take them out," Anthony said as he stopped channeling magic into the truncheon and watched as the extendable section retracted back into the base. "I don't think it would be a good idea to keep weapons like this inside of a school. Actually, I'm surprised you're even being allowed to modify weapons here."

"This is my personal workshop," Secilia said with a huff. "No one but myself, Professor Incanscino, and you are allowed inside."

Since Secilia was finished working, she quickly dismantled her sniper rifle and placed it inside of a carrying case. Her modified Vulpine 22s were also placed within their own case. She slung the sniper case over her back and held the case with her automatic pistols.

"Do you want me to carry anything for you?" asked Anthony.

"No, I've got it," Secilia said with a smile as she adjusted the sniper case. "How do you like the truncheon? I call it the Uredine Staff."

"The Blasting Staff?" Anthony raised an eyebrow at her use of Latin. "Well, it sounds like a useful weapon. I'll have to test it to see how well it works, but I think it has a lot of potential."

"In that case, once you've tested it and given it your approval, I'd like a reward."

"I don't see a problem with that. What kind of reward are you looking for?"

With Secilia now in tow, the three of them left the private lab. Secilia locked the door behind them. Then the three of them made their way toward Building #4's front lobby. As they walked down the long corridor, Secilia hummed in thought before grinning.

"I want to try bondage tonight."

"Bondage?" Anthony blinked several times while Brianna blushed bright red. "You want to be physically bound while we're having sex?"

"No." Secilia shook her head. "I want you to be physically bound while we have sex."

"Huh…"

Anthony's brain nearly froze when he heard Secilia wanted to tie him up during sex, but he didn't dismiss the idea out of hand. He didn't think he had any real desire to be bound up. At the same time, he wanted to please Secilia, so he didn't think he'd necessarily mind.

While he didn't mind, however, there was someone who did.

"W-what a perverse idea!" Brianna shouted, her voice echoing down the corridor. "You can't honestly—to bind Anthony and have your way with him… that's—"

"What's wrong with that?" asked Secilia. "So long as he consents to it, I don't see the problem."

"But… that's so perverted," Brianna muttered, her cheeks glowing.

"Says the woman who has been having sex with Anthony at least twice a day," Secilia countered. "Just because I want to experiment in bed doesn't mean I'm any more of a pervert than you, Ms. Moans-So-Loud-Even-the-Neighbors-Complain."

At the mention of how loud she was, Brianna clammed up, her face turning an even fiercer shade of red. While she didn't say anything, the glare she sent Secilia said enough.

The relationship between Brianna and Secilia was an odd one. They were both his lovers, but they didn't necessarily get along. They both worked hard to help him, and they did *sometimes* agree on things, but they also argued. A lot. A lot a lot. Sometimes their arguments were over simple matters like who got to sleep with him. At other times, their arguments were over issues like morality and sex.

Brianna was a lot more straightlaced and by the book, while Secilia was willing to bend and even break rules if she thought it would get her what she wanted. Their personalities also affected their sex life.

As they were leaving Building #4, Anthony's wristwatch began ringing. He stopped walking. Secilia and Brianna, walking on either side of him, stopped and looked at him curiously, but he ignored them as he pulled up a holographic screen.

"Professor Incanscino is calling me," he told them as he pressed on her name. "Professor?"

"I'm glad you're so prompt," a soft and girly voice with a sharp edge spoke directly into his mind. *"I want you, Brianna, and Secilia to head over to the Academy Island Private Security Forces' main headquarters right now."*

"Did something happen?" asked Anthony, feeling a tingle run down his spine.

"Something did indeed happen," Professor Incanscino said. *"I can't speak of it right now since this is an unguarded channel. Anyone with telepathy magic can listen in. What I can tell you is that it involves the person responsible for last week's incident."*

As Anthony was reminded of last week's incident, in which he had been kidnapped and Secilia's mother (progenitor) and half-brother were killed, he narrowed his eyes. It sounded like Professor Incanscino had finally discovered a clue regarding Director Azrael's whereabouts.

Or so he hoped.

***

After traveling to the Academy Island Private Security Forces' headquarters and showing the guards at the front gate their student IDs, the group of three was allowed to enter. It appeared Professor Incanscino had told the guards to expect them.

They were met at the front entrance by a young woman dressed in black and blue military fatigues. She had dark hair, brown skin, and seemed quite fit. She also looked a little annoyed.

"So you three are the ones I've been waiting for?" She eyed them with a disgruntled expression, though she did pause to look Anthony up and down once. "Well, come on. I was asked to lead you to Commander Lucretia's office. Let's not waste time here."

The woman turned around and entered the base. Secilia grimaced.

"What a pleasant disposition this woman has."

Neither Anthony or Brianna said anything, even though they both agreed.

They entered the base and followed the woman as she led them through several halls, a number of rooms, and finally stopped in front of two large double doors. Unlike the doors to Professor Incanscino's private residence, the doors here were state of the art, automatic doors made from composite alloys. Anthony couldn't tell how thick they were, but these doors looked like they were made to withstand explosions.

The door opened when the woman held out her wristwatch to a scanner. She led them inside, stopped, and snapped off a smart salute.

"Commander Lucretia, I've brought the three people you've requested."

"Thank you. You're dismissed," Commander Lucretia said.

The woman grimaced, but she still nodded and left. As the door slid shut behind her, Anthony studied his diminutive professor and the person with her. While Professor Incanscino looked the same as always, the woman sitting in a chair before his professor's desk was someone he wasn't familiar with. She looked like she was in her late forties or maybe her early fifties, with a mixture of black and gray hair. Despite being older, the way she carried herself, with her back straight and her shoulders set, made her seem much younger.

"Instructor Noel!" Brianna said in surprise.

"Hello, Brianna."

Instructor Noel smiled at her. It was one of those grandmotherly smiles, though it brought neither Brianna or Anthony any comfort to see. After all, this woman had been the one who ordered Brianna to execute him.

"What are you doing here?" asked Brianna. "What's going on?"

Instructor Noel raised a hand, silencing the redhead. "I'm sure you have many questions. I will answer them one at a time. Why don't you three sit down first?"

Anthony did not know how he should feel about meeting Brianna's instructor for the first time, but as Professor

Incanscino summoned three more chairs for them, he knew they couldn't just leave. Something had happened regarding Director Azrael. That this woman was here meant she was somehow involved.

Out of concern for Brianna, Anthony glanced at her to find the redhead staring at her instructor with mixed emotions. She looked pained, like something was tearing her apart from the inside out, threatening to break free. He was certain she had no idea what to think right now. He could feel the torrent of emotions flooding his mind. This woman had ordered Brianna to kill him, but rather than killing him, she had saved his life. More than that, she had become his bondmate. It was a direct violation of the orders she'd been given.

"First, I believe I should introduce myself. My name is Sarah Fortis Noel. I am a War Maiden General working for Custodes Daemonium and Brianna's instructor. If you're curious, Fortis Noel is the name bestowed upon me by our leaders. Now then, I'm sure you three must be curious to know why I'm here, especially you, Brianna," Instructor Noel said, still wearing that placid smile of hers.

"I am a little curious," Brianna said, shifting as she sat on the chair to Anthony's right. "After becoming Anthony's bondmate, I expected my funds to be cut and for Custodes Daemonium to send someone else to kill both me and Anthony. That never happened though."

Instructor Noel nodded. "Do you know why we chose you to deal with the incu—sorry, I mean Anthony? Do you mind if I call you Anthony?" she suddenly directed a question toward him.

"Feel free." Anthony shrugged.

"Thank you."

"Now that you are here, I think I have an idea as to why, but I'd like to hear the reason from you," Brianna said, brow furrowing, eyes narrowed. She was understandably cautious.

"About five hundred and fifty years ago, another incubus appeared. Back then, Custodes Daemonium had only heard about how powerful incubus could be. Our organization feared what would happen if we let an incubus roam free, and so we tried to kill him. We cornered the incubus and his harem, fought against them, and managed to kill one of his bondmates." Instructor Noel's smile turned bitter. "It was an incredibly foolish decision on our part. Up to that point, the incubus had been fighting conservatively. We later learned that he was actively trying not to kill us. However, once his bondmate died, the incubus flew into a rage and slaughtered the entire battalion we'd sent after him. After that, he and his remaining harem charged into the main headquarters and began slaughtering everyone in sight. We managed to kill them by wearing him and his harem down, but before they were killed, we lost more than three hundred thousand people. Four people managed to kill three hundred thousand of our finest warriors at the time. Even our leader back then was killed."

Anthony and Secilia had known nothing about this, but Brianna seemed to at least know the basics, though she still looked a little surprised. During that time, Noel glanced at Professor Incanscino. The woman nodded at her, as if allowing her to continue.

"This is something of a closely guarded secret, so we never tell people about exactly what happened, not even our own," Instructor Noel continued. "To be honest, if you hadn't become Anthony's bondmate, I would not have even told you this, but circumstances have decided that you should know about what happened."

"And what does that have to do with me and Anthony?" Brianna's frown was growing larger by the second.

"When we learned that Anthony was an incubus, we had three options," Instructor Noel said. "We could ignore him, kill him, or have one of our own become his bondmate, thereby tying Anthony to our group as an ally instead of an enemy."

"And that's why you sent Brianna," Anthony said. "As a woman who just completed her training, you sent her to me, knowing the likely outcome would be her becoming my bondmate."

"We wouldn't have complained if she had killed you," Instructor Noel confessed. "However, we thought it would be better if she became your bondmate. Custodes Daemonium did extensive research into your personality before selecting Brianna for this mission. We learned about your temperament, your goals, your younger brother, and about how you were originally one of Lilith's bondmates. After that, we selected Brianna to carry this mission out, figuring she would either successfully kill you or would be seduced by you. Either outcome would have worked."

It sounded like Custodes Daemonium had decided not killing him would be more beneficial to their cause. He now understood that Brianna had been essentially offered up to him as a sacrifice. She was, in a sense, the ball and chain that bound him and Custodes Daemonium together. They knew of the loyalty incubus had for their bondmates from experience. Now they were using that experience to their advantage.

Anthony glanced at Brianna, who was clenching her pants so hard that her knuckles were turning white. Her arms shook, her shoulders trembling, and her face was red with emotion. This was not a blush. She was angry.

He placed a hand over hers. The trembling stopped as Brianna looked in his direction. Anthony smiled and rubbed her hand, soothing her frayed nerves. Brianna relaxed.

Instructor Noel had been watching the interaction between them, a complicated smile making her face twitch.

"I understand that you are angry, Brianna," she said. "Truth be told, you do have every right to be angry. However, you should also realize that we War Maidens are and always have been weapons to be wielded against Magic Catastrophes. Anthony is still classified as an S-rank Magic Catastrophe. It is just that the manner in which you were selected to deal with this threat differs from how our organization normally operates."

Brianna's expression became pained, like she didn't know whether she wanted to cry or scream, rage or break down into tears. However, she was also a highly trained warrior. Taking several deep and calming breaths, the redhead settled down.

"I understand," she said in a soft voice.

"Well, I don't," Secilia said suddenly. "You basically used Brianna as a sacrificial lamb. That's pretty fucked up. I should know since the director of Nametech tried to use me the same way."

"I do not disagree with you." Instructor Noel shrugged her shoulders in a helpless gesture. "However, it is just like I said. We are weapons to be wielded by our leaders in service to humanity. If we are told to kill, we kill. If we are told to die, we die. We cannot disobey our orders."

"What concerns me is not that you ordered her around, but that you told her only to kill me and didn't leave her room to refuse," Anthony said. "Brianna spent this entire time worrying about what would happen when your organization finally decided to make a move, and now you are telling us there was never a need to worry because it all went according to plan? That doesn't sit well with me."

"I understand your feelings, but we needed to make it look like what happened was unintentional." Instructor Noel set her hands on her lap as she explained this all to them. "You must understand that the plan to make Brianna your bondmate was made in secret. Nobody but our leaders and myself were aware of it. To keep it that way, we needed to make it seem like what happened was the result of an accident. After we confirmed that Brianna had become your bondmate, we 'deliberated' over what to do before announcing that we'd 'use you' for the betterment of humanity. We did this to quell potential dissenters."

Anthony couldn't lie and say the plan wasn't well thought out. It sounded like they had done this to cover all their bases. Even so, he didn't appreciate the emotional turmoil they put Brianna through. The only reason he didn't lash out at them was because he was sure Brianna would become even more upset if he did something like that.

"Now that you three are up to speed on this matter, I believe it is time for us to speak about the real reason I summoned you here," Professor Incanscino said, finally speaking.

"I'm guessing it has something to do with Director Azrael?" Secilia asked.

"Correct." Professor Incanscino gave her a chilling smile. "Thanks to Custodes Daemonium, we have discovered the location of Nicolas Azrael, the director of Nametech. We are planning a joint operation to take him out. Given what happened with you three, I thought it would be a good idea to let you take part in this operation."

"Can you even do that?" asked Anthony.

Professor Incanscino waved her hand. "I'm the commander of the Academy Island Private Security Forces. If I want to temporarily make you members of our forces to participate in a joint operation, who is going to stop me?"

While the woman spoke arrogantly, she did bring up a good point. Anthony glanced at Brianna and Secilia to see what they thought.

"I'm in," Secilia said. "Director Azreal took my mother and half-brother from me. There's no way I can leave dealing with him to someone else."

"If you're going, I'm going to," Brianna said with a sigh. "You are Anthony's bondmate just like me. I can't let anything happen to you."

"How thoughtful of you."

"Shut it."

"Anthony?" Professor Incanscino asked.

"I don't think you need to hear my answer to know that I'm going." Anthony shrugged.

Professor Incanscino nodded. "In that case, you three should prepare yourselves. The operation will take place in two days. I'll inform the other professors that you two will be exempt from school that day, so come straight here first thing in the morning."

The conversation was more or less concluded. Anthony had a lot more information now, about himself, about Brianna, and about incubus in general, but he tried putting that out of his mind for the moment. Knowing all this wouldn't help him. He needed to focus on their upcoming operation.

Anthony didn't consider himself a vindictive person, but he wouldn't deny that he wanted Director Azrael to pay for what he had done to Secilia.

And he was going to be the one who forced the man to pay up.

CHAPTER 12

The stealth plane they were in had been loaned to them by the Academy Island Private Security Forces thanks to Professor Incanscino. The Board of Directors had been against it, from his understanding, but his diminutive professor had somehow forced them into capitulating to her demands. It made him wonder about what kind of power she wielded.

If he didn't include their pilot, it was just the five of them going on this mission. He was, of course, including Instructor Noel, who had told them she was going with them to supervise her student. Anthony didn't know if that was her real reason for tagging along. In either event, the woman was now sitting next to them on the plane and asking him all kinds of invasive questions.

"So you and my student have a lot of sex, right?"

"INSTRUCTOR!!!"

"What? I'm just curious. He's an incubus, so you and he must obviously be fucking like rabbits during mating season."

"T-that is none of your business!"

Anthony had yet to actually speak since Brianna was getting defensive over every question Instructor Noel asked. He had actually spent most of his time simply watching the interesting shades of red Brianna's face could become. Part of him thought it would be appropriate to force the older woman to stop, but another part secretly thought Brianna was adorable when she blushed.

Instructor Noel might be bringing out his inner-sadist.

"Those two have sex at least twice a day," Secilia said. She was sitting on Anthony's other side. Her weapon cases were located in a storage locker right next to the bench.

"Don't tell her that!" Brianna screeched.

"Why not?" asked Secilia. "It isn't a big deal. Besides, if you don't tell her, then she's just gonna keep pestering you. Might tell her and get her to stop."

"But… but…"

Brianna glared at Secilia with tears in her eyes. Anthony finally decided to take pity on the redhead, who was a lot more pure than either Instructor Noel or Secilia… despite how often he had sex with her.

"That's enough, you two," Anthony said. "Rather than talk about this, we should discuss the upcoming mission. Miss Noel, you said Custodes Daemonium has located Director Azrael of Nametech. Can you tell us more about his location? I'd like to know what we're getting into."

"Of course," she said.

Instructor Noel reached into her breast pocket and pulled out a disc-shaped device with a single button on top, which she pressed. The moment she did, a holographic projection appeared in the air before them, a map detailing what appeared to be a relatively large city, though it wasn't close to being the same size as Academy Island.

"We tracked Nicolas Azreal to Nash, a large city located in the east of the Americas. This city belongs to a faction of demons called the Underworld's Rejects," Instructor Noel explained.

"The Underworld's Rejects?" Secilia wrinkled her nose. "That's such a lame nickname."

"Lame or not, this faction is powerful enough that they own several cities within the eastern Americas and aren't people we can afford to underestimate," Instructor Noel said. "That said, they also shouldn't make trouble with us since this is Custodes Daemonium business. So long as we get in, do our job, and get out, we should be able to avoid dealing with them."

"What about Azrael?" asked Brianna. "Where is he in this city?"

"I'm getting to that. Don't be so impatient." Instructor Noel pressed the button on her remote again and the map zoomed in, focusing on one specific building, which was a large skyscraper that was several stories tall and looked gaudier than any building Anthony had ever seen. "Currently, Nicolas Azrael is holed up in this hotel. The Nash Ritz Country Resort. It's owned by the Underworld's Rejects and is home to the largest gambling parlor in this region. Of course, gambling is just a cover. It's really used for black market transactions. We believe Nicolas Azrael is planning to sell the information about Anthony to a woman named Elizabeth Tepes."

"Isn't Elizabeth Tepes one of the Vampire Warlords?" asked Brianna, leaning forward.

"She is," Instructor Noel said.

"I thought so," Brianna murmured, then glanced at Anthony and Secilia. "I've actually met with Elizabeth Tepes before. She's a pacifist who believes in coexisting with other races, which often put her at odds with Warlords like Vlad Dracul and Cane, who believed in fighting with other races and using humans as walking blood banks. But why would she come all this way to buy information on Anthony?"

"She might not know what information she is buying." Instructor Noel shrugged. "But it could also be that she's interested in acquiring more power. She might be a pacifist, but she is also the weakest of the three Vampire Warlords. You can't uphold your ideals if you don't even have the power to protect your people."

"Do you think we will have to fight her?" asked Anthony.

"Not if we can kill Nicolas before he has time to make contact with Lady Tepes," Instructor Noel said.

"So how are we going to kill him?" asked Secilia, an almost eager look on her face. Anthony wasn't surprised. If their positions had been reversed, he would have been eager to get revenge as well.

"Anthony and Brianna are going to head into the casino using a disguise and locate Nicolas. Once they do, they will follow him and await an opportunity to dispose of him." Instructor Noel began laying out her plan. "Meanwhile, you and I will find a secure place to watch the hotel from a distance. Should the mission go south, it will be our job to provide cover and support while Anthony and Brianna retreat."

"Wait. So I'm not actually doing anything?" asked Secilia. "I'm just providing backup?"

"You are their long-range support. What did you expect?" asked Instructor Noel, shaking her head as if this should have been obvious.

Secilia opened her mouth to object, but Anthony placed a hand on her thigh, which caused the woman to immediately snap her mouth shut. She glanced at him. He shook his head, grimacing only slightly when Secilia's lips became a thin line.

Secilia looked away with a huff. He sighed.

"In any case, we have disguises for you two," Instructor Noel said to Anthony and Brianna as she handed them a set of bracelets. "These bracelets use light bending magic to create an illusion around your bodies. They will make you look like someone else. However, be careful not to get them wet or broken. Your cover will be blown if that happens."

"I understand," Brianna said as she took both bracelets and handed one to Anthony.

He slipped the bracelet onto his wrist, watched as it lit up, and then noticed how his hand became slightly older. That must mean he no longer looked like himself. When he looked at Brianna and saw that a middle-aged woman with blonde hair had taken her place, he knew the devices were working.

"I guess it's about time to get started," Anthony said, smiling just a little.

His blood was beginning to boil with anticipation.

✳✳✳

Secilia wanted to scream.

"I hate this," she muttered.

She was standing on the roof of a building that was about ten stories high. A chilly wind swept over the rooftop. She shivered as goosebumps broke out on her skin. While it wasn't the largest building in the vicinity, it was the building with the greatest view of the hotel.

The Nash Ritz Country Resort stood before her, a gigantic skyscraper of blazing neon colors, gaudy signs, and the statue of a large cowboy strumming on a guitar next to it. Dozens of people were walking in and out of the entrance. All of them were decked to the nines, dressed in snazzy tuxedos and extravagant gowns.

"You mean you hate being up here with me?" asked Instructor Noel.

"I hate not being down there," Secilia corrected. "I hate the fact that I'm stuck up here, while Anthony and Brianna are down there, dealing with Director Azrael. That man took my brother and mother from me. I should be the one who kills him."

"Would killing him make you feel better?"

"Damn right it would."

"Hmmm…"

Instructor Noel was silent for a time, which Secilia used to set up her sniper rifle. She wasn't what anyone would call an expert, but she did have a good deal of knowledge on this weapon thanks to having taken it apart and made numerous modifications. This weapon was something she'd designed so even an amateur like her could use it.

"I cannot say that revenge would not make you feel better," Instructor Noel said at last. "But you must understand that having long-range support is important. You are our sniper. Having you watch from a distance is a tactically sound decision."

"I know that," Secilia growled.

She flipped on the scope and pressed her eyes against it. This scope was rectangular instead of square and made for two eyes instead of one. The soft rubber surrounding the scope conformed to her face as the HUD display appeared within the scope, giving her information on distance, wind speed, and a targeting reticle.

Once she had finished setting up the sniper, she continued talking, "but just because I know how important my job is doesn't mean I have to like it."

"I suppose not," Instructor Noel agreed. "But just know that Anthony and Brianna are counting on you for support."

"You don't have to tell me twice," Secilia said softly as she watched the entrance and area surrounding the hotel.

She wanted to be down there with those two, but beyond that, she wanted to keep them safe; she didn't want to lose anyone else, and so she rested on that tall building with Brianna's instructor, waiting and hoping for a chance to help the man she was bonded to.

✲✲✲

Anthony had been to a few casinos before, but it had always been with Lilith and his brothers.

It was pretty well-known that Lilith had been a hardcore gambler with a serious addiction. It had also been well-known that Lilith's luck at gambling was terrible. She often lost a lot of money. Anthony and his brothers had always been the ones who made that money back for her.

As he looked around at the blackjack tables, the people playing roulette, lottery machines, and the gamblers having the time of their lives, a somewhat nostalgic feeling enclosed around him. Sharp pain jabbed at his chest as he remembered those times.

"Are you okay?" asked Brianna, holding his arm.

"I'm fine," Anthony said with a sigh. "Just remembering the past."

Brianna didn't say anything for a moment. Several demons—therianthropes—walked past them and moved over to a blackjack table.

"I've heard that Lilith loved casinos."

"She did." He smiled, but it was filled with pain. "Gambling was one of her favorite past times."

"Do you still miss her?" Brianna asked.

"There will always be a part of me that misses her," Anthony answered honestly. "But I know I can't live in the past." He reached out with his free hand, placing it over one of hers. "I have you and Secilia now, and I love you both very much."

Brianna smiled but didn't say anything. Perhaps his words were enough to satisfy her. Perhaps they weren't.

Looking for one person in such a massive casino was difficult but not impossible. Anthony and Brianna went over to some of the tables, sometimes watching, sometimes playing, all to blend in as they kept their eyes open for Director Azrael, who was supposed to be somewhere inside of this casino to enact a black market transaction.

There were many different sights, sounds, and scents pervading this place, which caused Anthony a bit of trouble. A pair of therianthropes wandered past, smelling of wet dog. It mixed with the perfume of a pureblood vampire and created a pungent odor.

Numerous chandeliers hung from the ceiling. Lights reflected off the many crystals, which were like prisms that captured and released multi-colored light that dazzled his eyes.

The sound of lottery machines beeping, coins spilling from their mouths, and people shouting blended together to create a cacophony of sound that assaulted the ears. It was all very nostalgic.

"I've found him," Brianna said suddenly as Anthony was playing—and winning—at blackjack.

"Where?" asked Anthony, not looking up from his cards.

"Sixteen yards to our left," Brianna answered. "He is heading toward a room with several dozen men in black suits. There's a man at the front. I don't know him, but he looks like a vampire noble."

Anthony kept playing blackjack as he discreetly looked in the direction Brianna had indicated. He was just in time to see Director Azrael and a dozen men—vampires—slip through a door. There was a security guard, a human with a bald head and sunglasses, standing guard.

"Let Instructor Noel know we've located him and ask for directions," he said.

"Already done," Brianna answered as she tapped a finger against her ear.

Anthony kept up the charade of playing blackjack and won two more times before Brianna gestured for him to follow her. He folded his hand and didn't bother claiming the reward as he left the table, to the shock of those who had been eagerly watching him.

"I'm just in it for the thrill," he said to the awed crowd as he and Brianna walked away.

They traveled through the casino, mindful of the numerous guards stationed inside the building. Brianna led him toward a restroom that was close to the door Director Azrael had slipped through.

Anthony felt a little awkward standing in the women's restroom. It was fortunate no one else was inside at the moment. Brianna didn't seem to care as she pulled him into the middle stall.

"I need you to let me stand on your shoulders," she said, pointing up. "That's our way to Azrael. This ventilation shaft apparently leads to the room he is in."

"Right."

Anthony clasped his hands together. Brianna stepped on it, then stepped onto his shoulders. He grabbed her legs to keep her from losing her balance, her dress falling over his face and making it impossible to see. Even if he could see nothing, he at least heard the sound of Brianna undoing the vent. Metal scraped against metal. Then Brianna's weight left his shoulders and the dress blocking his vision disappeared.

"Get up here," Brianna said.

Anthony looked up as Brianna moved away from the ventilation shaft's entrance. Letting a trickle of mana run through his body to activate Physical Enhancement, Anthony leapt into the air and reached the shaft, grabbing it with both hands and pulling himself up. Once he was inside, Brianna pushed the grating back in place.

"Follow me," Brianna said as she turned around and began moving.

Anthony followed after her, staring at her ass, which he could see quite well through the thin fabric of her red dress. He wished he could have enjoyed the way her butt moved as she crawled through the vents. It was most unfortunate that their situation did not let him admire the view.

After numerous turns, Anthony eventually heard voices coming from one of the vents. He couldn't make out what they were saying at first, but the closer he and Brianna got, the more coherent they became.

"An incubus, you say? You had better not be lying about this," a voice said. It was a little nasally, and held the kind of arrogance Anthony remembered from the aristocrats Lilith would occasionally meet. "Lord Vladd will not be pleased if he finds out you're lying."

"I'm not lying," Director Azrael's voice reached them. "All the information on the incubus is in this hard drive."

"We'll be the ones who determine whether or not you're lying."

Anthony and Brianna finally reached the vent and looked through the gaps, peering at the group of vampires and one human down below. Director Azrael was standing to one side, the vampires on the other. One of the vampires, who Anthony now understood was a vampire noble working under the Vampire Warlord Vlad Dracul and not Elizabeth Tepes, reached out his hand to grab the disc the director was holding out, but the man pulled it back.

"I want the payment first," Director Azrael said.

The vampire noble narrowed his eyes. "You demand payment from us when we haven't even checked the contents?"

"Do you think I'm stupid?" asked Director Azrael. "Once I give you this, you won't even have a reason to pay me. Give me the money first. Then I'll give you the hard drive. If you don't give me the money…" Director Azrael held up a small device that looked like a detonation switch. "I'll blow up all the contents with the bomb I planted inside."

The vampire noble bit his lip and debated what to do. Only after several seconds passed did he nod toward one of the other vampires, who came forward bearing a briefcase, which she opened to reveal what must have been hundreds of thousands of dollars. She closed the case and handed it to Director Azrael.

"The hard drive," the vampire lord said, holding out his hand.

Director Azrael reached out to place the hard drive in his hand, but Anthony and Brianna decided to act at that moment.

Brianna removed a small knife from a holster strapped to her thigh. The knife began glowing a light blue as she used it to slice through the vent. She dropped through the opening and twisted her body around as she fell. With her sword arm raised, she brought it down and cut through the hard drive and Director Azrael's hand.

"Aaaaaaaahhhhhh!!!"

Director Azrael screamed as his fingers fell to the ground. He held his bleeding hand to his chest and stumbled back in shock. All the fingers had been cut clean off. The ruined remains of the briefcase clattered to the ground.

"The hard drive!" The vampire noble's eyes widened in shock before narrowing in anger. "I do not know who you are, but you will pay for what you've just done."

"Hmph. The only ones who are going to pay is you," Brianna said as she stood up and flicked the blood off her knife, which was now glowing with thousands of magical circuits.

"Get her!" the vampire noble shouted.

The eleven other vampires all charged forward to attack. That they weren't using magic was enough to let anyone knowledgeable about vampires know they were not purebloods. They were probably dhampirs.

Brianna bent her knees, waited until one of the vampires leapt to attack, then raised her leg in a powerful kick that caught the creature under the chin. Her body was glowing blue as mana flowed through it. With her physical abilities enhanced, the vampire didn't stand a chance. His head snapped back, breaking, and the man fell to the floor, twitching several times as his muscles underwent death spasms.

Knowing better than to watch while still surrounded, Brianna spun around, slashing her knife across the throat of another vampire. Blood spilled from his throat as she sliced open his trachea.

With all the vampires now distracted, Anthony dropped from the vent, mana overflowing from his body as he used Physical Enhancement, glowing blue lines appearing all over his skin. He landed on the shoulders of a vampire attacking Brianna. Gravity did its job, bringing the man to his knees, the floor cracking underneath him.

Anthony leapt off the vampire. Rotating his body, he extended his leg and kicked another vampire in the face. His attack was so strong the vampire's face caved in, bones breaking, blood spewing from her nose and mouth. The woman went down with a scream. Anthony didn't show mercy just because she was a woman and stomped on her throat, crushing it.

Four vampires had already gone down, which meant there were only eight left. However, those eight surrounded him and Brianna, who now stood back to back.

"You two have made a terrible mistake in coming here," the vampire noble said.

"Really? I don't think we've made a mistake at all," Anthony said as he took a step forward.

The vampire noble frowned at him, then looked at Brianna.

"You are… a War Maiden," he said at last. "I do not know what you are doing getting involved with this, but it's too late for you now. Custodes Daemonium has overstepped its bounds here."

"You are the one who has overstepped your bounds," Brianna said. "The incubus is listed as an S-rank Magic Catastrophe and therefore falls under our jurisdiction. That you are trying to acquire information about him is like declaring your intent to fight against us."

"Hmph! I see talking to you is pointless," the vampire noble said. "Kill them both!"

Seven of the eight vampires charged forward while the vampire noble vanished into his own shadow.

Anthony clicked his tongue when he saw the man disappear, but he knew there wasn't much they could do.

Ducking under a punch, Anthony removed the truncheon hidden inside of his pocket, activated it with mana, and swung. He smashed the weapon against the vampire's face, tearing through it. His eyes widened as the vampire's head cracked open and spilled blood and brain matter onto the floor, but he didn't have time to get sick over the sight as two more vampires attacked him from either side.

He stepped forward and spun around, tearing through an arm with the truncheon and raising his other arm to block a claw swipe. A yelp escaped his mouth as the vampire's clawed hand tore through his forearm. His pained cry, however, was drowned out by the howling of the other vampire, who was cradling the stump of his missing arm.

Since one of them was in too much pain to fight, Anthony moved on the one who had injured him. He swung the truncheon, hoping to bash the vampire's face in, but the man moved back with a grace befitting his species. It seemed he had learned from watching the other two vampires go down that his weapon was not something he could take headon.

Gritting his teeth, Anthony pushed Physical Enhancement to the limit, causing the glowing blue lines on his body to flare up. Then he activated Farsight, which caused the present to overlap with an image of the vampire .5 seconds into the future. It was thanks to his vision that he knew the vampire was going to thrust a clawed hand at his face. He twisted out of the way, then swung his truncheon upward.

The vampire was fast and managed to retract his hand, but Anthony also knew he would do that thanks to Farsight. He was already changing his attack from an upward swing to a thrust. He smashed his truncheon into the vampire's jaw, not just breaking it, but tearing straight through it. Anthony grimaced as blood covered his weapon and arm.

While Anthony took care of three of the eight vampires, Brianna dealt with the remaining five. Like Anthony, she used Farsight and Physical Enhancement to boost her abilities, but she was far better at using both than he was. With the ability to see five seconds into the future, she was capable of predicting what her opponents would do with plenty of time to spare and used that to her advantage.

The first vampire died after raising her hand to slash open Brianna's face. Brianna had seen it coming and moved forward quicker than even a vampire's eyes could track, jabbing her knife forward and impaling the woman through the throat. Blood spurted from the wound as Brianna removed the knife. None of it got on her, however, as she moved out of the way, shifting behind the dying vampire and shoving her into one of her companions.

Both went down in a tangle of limbs.

With one dead and one down, Brianna moved on the other two. They attacked at the same time, but she shuffled across the floor, avoiding their attacks with unparalleled ease. She swung her knife once, shearing off a hand. As the vampire screamed, she silenced him with a kick to the throat. The other vampire tried to attack while her leg was still raised, but Brianna leapt into the air with the power of just one leg and threw her knife as she passed over him. The weapon pierced the vampire's head, killing him instantly.

By this point in time, the last vampire had gotten out from underneath the corpse of the first vampire Brianna killed. He saw what had happened to his companions and tried to make a break for it.

Brianna wouldn't let him.

With Physical Enhancement boosting her to well past human limits, she rushed over and thrust out her palm, which was glowing a bright blue as she gathered mana into it.

"Fulgur Percutiens!"

Anthony didn't know what kind of attack that was, but Brianna slammed her palm into the vampire's back. The vampire's scream was lost as lightning exploded from where her palm came into contact with his body. He flew forward, struck the ground, his body smoking as he struggled to get up. Brianna quickly walked over to where he had fallen and slammed another palm into his neck.

"Fulgar Percutiens!"

Mana flowed through her palm and slammed into the vampire. Anthony almost winced when the lightning attack instantly killed the man.

Brianna stood up and walked away from the smoking corpse. She went over to the one with the knife in its head, removed the knife, and cleaned the blade on the dead vampire's shirt. It was such a smooth action that Anthony shivered.

"It looks like Director Azrael escaped while we were battling the vampires," Anthony said.

"Seems that way," Brianna sighed. "And the vampire noble also escaped. The briefcase is gone too."

"We should let Secilia know."

"You are right. With luck, Secilia will be able to spot the man as he's leaving." Brianna placed a hand to her ear and spoke. "Secilia, can you hear me?"

***

"Secilia, can you hear me? Director Azrael escaped during our battle with the vampires. He should be coming out of the hotel through a back entrance."

"I hear you," Secilia muttered, though she knew Brianna couldn't hear her right now. Her communicator was only set to receive right now.

She swept her rifle around the hotel, searching for the familiar features of Director Azrael. There were a lot of people around the hotel, which made it difficult to look for one person, but Secilia did have the help of her HUD, which had a facial recognition program she'd installed into it. The program worked by hacking into the international registry, which contained a list of every person ever born (this did not include people who hadn't registered, which was considered an international crime).

Her eyes narrowed when she finally caught sight of Director Azrael after performing a sweep of the area. His name appeared over his head as he came out through an entrance on the side. It looked like he was trying to slip out through an alley.

Not on her watch.

Thanks to the HUD's information, Secilia was able to aim her sniper perfectly. She even enhanced her aiming by using Farsight to look at where Director Azrael would be two seconds into the future. Calculating her aim based on all the information she was receiving, Secilia pulled the trigger and was rewarded by seeing his arm fly clean off as her bullet tore his shoulder apart. The man stumbled forward, still alive somehow, and tried to keep moving. Secilia pulled the trigger again. This time she was rewarded by seeing a hole blow open on his torso.

Blood and guts splattered across the ground as Director Azrael went down. Secilia saw all this and suddenly felt her stomach rebel against her. She jerked her face away from the scope and puked out what little food she'd had for lunch that afternoon. Continuing to wretch as the sight of gore stained her vision, Secilia tried to overcome how shaken she was by what she'd just seen, by what she'd just done.

"I'm guessing you killed Director Azrael?" asked Instructor Noel. Secilia couldn't talk. All she could do was nod. "And how do you feel?"

"I feel like I'm going to throw up again," Secilia finally managed to say, though it came out in a low rasp.

"That usually happens after your first kill," Instructor Noel said with a nod. "And do you feel better now that you've got your revenge?"

"Not really," Secilia admitted with a sigh. She wiped her mouth and sat back up. "I know killing Director Azrael isn't going to bring back my mom and Alex." She sighed and closed her eyes. "While I don't feel much better, I do feel relieved knowing that he can't reveal Anthony's secret to anyone."

"That's actually the best way to look at this situation. If you can think like that, then you'll be fine." Instructor Noel held out her hand. "Come on. Let's head to the extraction point."

Grasping Instructor Noel's hand, Secilia let the woman help her up. Then she dismantled her sniper, put it back in her case, and set the case on her shoulder before following the much older woman off the roof and into the building.

EPILOGUE

There was something surreal about taking part in a covert operation to kill the director of a large corporation, getting into a fight with a group of vampires, and then going to school the next day. Brianna probably had it worse since she was still in high school, but Anthony felt like his life had become very unrealistic in the last few days. He felt like a character in a science fiction movie.

When the end of the day came, Anthony waited inside of the Building #4 lobby. There were a couple of seats for guests to use. He sat down and did his best to ignore the giggles, ogles, and glares coming from various people who walked past him. Even without his pheromones active, he still attracted attention. This, he supposed, was just another part of life he'd have to accept.

Fortunately, the wait was not long. Anthony stood up as Secilia emerged from a hallway, a case slung over her shoulder.

"Secilia," Anthony greeted as he grabbed the case from her.

"Look at you, being all gentlemanly," Secilia teased him.

"I have been known to act like a gentleman on rare occasions," Anthony joked along. "How are you feeling?"

They walked out of the building together, under the watchful eyes of several whispering students. Just what those people were whispering about would forever remain a mystery. Anthony didn't care enough to listen in.

"I'm… well, I wouldn't say I'm okay, but I feel a lot better thanks to you," Secilia said, her teasing look turning into a warm smile. "Thank you for last night."

"You've got nothing to thank me for." Anthony shook his head. "You know I'm always up for cuddles."

"I do now. I never realized you were such a snuggle bug."

As they waded through the crowd, just another pair of students on their way home from college, Anthony reached out with his free hand and laced his fingers through Secilia's. He didn't use an excuse like, "So we don't separate." Granted, it would be easy to get separated in this crowd, but Anthony liked to think he wasn't so juvenile that he had to justify why he was holding hands with his bondmate.

It wasn't long before the two reached the station and hopped onto a maglev that would take them home.

"Professor Incanscino talked to me today," Anthony said.

"Oh?" Secilia raised an eyebrow and prompted him to continue.

"It looks like the public isn't aware of what happened last night," he continued. "Custodes Daemonium sent some people to clean up the bodies of Director Azrael and the vampires he was trying to sell info to. The only people who know what happened are us, Custodes Daemonium, and the vampire who escaped. Fortunately, I don't think he's aware of who we are since Brianna and I were in disguise."

"So, basically, we're safe," Secilia said.

"More or less."

"That's good."

Secilia breathed a sigh of relief.

What happened last night had been classified by both Custodes Daemonium and the Academy Island Private Security Forces as a covert operation. He, Brianna, and Secilia had been sworn to secrecy. It seemed neither side wanted anyone knowing they had teamed up. If it did become known, it could cause a huge shift in the power balance between nations as other countries and organizations scrambled to form alliances.

"By the way, what do you want for dinner tonight?" asked Anthony.

Secilia gave him a bland look. "What do you mean: 'what do I want?' All you have to eat are those terrible packaged meals."

"T-that is true... but I bought some new flavors." Anthony scratched the back of his neck and looked away.

If there was one thing Secilia refused to let Anthony live down, it was how he couldn't cook and only bought packaged meals—not like she was any better. Still, the woman made it a point to mercilessly tease him about his lack of cooking abilities all the way home.

Brianna was not present when they arrived home. The two slipped out of their shoes, set their bags down, and made it over to the couch.

"What's first on the agenda?" asked Anthony.

"Kicking your ass at Gun Gate Online."

Anthony narrowed his eyes when Secilia flipped her hair over her shoulder and gave him the smuggest smile he'd ever seen.

"Is that a challenge?"

"Damn right it is."

"You're on. Loser has to… heat up our dinner."

"Laaame." Secilia vetoed his proposal with a thumbs down. "How about this? Loser has to strip in front of the other."

"Deal."

While Secilia sat back, Anthony went to the holographic TV and set up his game system. It was just a simple system called an NC2022, which used controllers and VR helmets. The game they were playing, Gun Gate Online, was a FPSMMO. People started off in towns, but they could leave towns, go exploring, enter tournaments, take on quests, go on raids, and even create their own tournaments.

Anthony and Secilia ended up taking their characters to the arena, where the two spent nearly half an hour battling it out, Anthony with his assault rifle and Secilia with her dual-wielding sub machine guns.

Unfortunately, Secilia had gotten way better than him at FPS for some reason. He wondered if she was cheating by using Farsight. She claimed she wasn't, but until recently, they had been pretty even.

"You're just being a sore loser," Secilia said. "Now, come on. Strip for me."

"Tch."

Anthony clicked his tongue as he stood up and removed his shirt. Secilia catcalled him, but he merely sent her a mock glare as she clapped. He sighed and reached for his pants…

"Hold on!" Secilia raised a hand to stop him.

"What?" asked Anthony.

"Dance."

"Huh?"

"Come on." Secilia gestured at him, her eyes gleaming. "If you're going to strip, you should also do a little dance to go with it."

"Absolutely not."

"Who is the victor here?" asked Secilia. "It isn't you. I'm the one who won, so I make the rules for this bet. You are already stripping. What's the harm in doing a little dance?"

Anthony released another tired sigh, but then he did his best to start dancing. He wasn't sure what to do, so he shook his hips a little. It felt awkward, and he was sure his face was red, which Secilia in no way helped with her laughing. He growled at her, cheeks burning as he slid his pants off and tossed them at her face. Secilia didn't even seem to mind as she kept them and continued to laugh at his expense.

Just as Anthony was about to remove his underwear, the door opened and Brianna walked in.

"Sorry I'm a little late," the redhead said. "I had to stay after school for a project. So what's... what's... um..." Anthony stopped dancing as Brianna trailed off, eyes slowly going from lively to deadpan. His heart stopped cold as the girl glared at him. "What is going on?"

"Nothing," Anthony said.

"Anthony is doing a striptease," Secilia said as she patted the spot beside her. "Come on over and watch. I'm sure you'll enjoy it."

Anthony was sure Brianna would tell the two of them to stop fooling around, that now was neither the time or the place for them to do something so indecent. Much to his surprise, shock, and consternation, however, Brianna merely walked over and sat on the couch.

"I'm interested in seeing this striptease as well," she claimed as she stared at him, hard.

"You heard the girl!" Secilia cheered. "Get to stripping again! Come on!"

Giving them both a frustrated glare, Anthony grimaced and, once more, began slowly peeling off his clothes.

That said, he only had one article left to remove.

It was a short striptease.

~Fin

AFTERWORD

Hello. I hope you all enjoyed reading Incubus 2. If you did, please consider writing a review. Books live and die by their reviews, so I would greatly appreciate it if anyone who enjoyed this volume can write one so the book can reach more readers.

With the end of Incubus 2, Anthony has found his second bondmate and is well on his way to becoming a Harem King. Considering his species, that is probably a good thing. The poor women in his harem won't get a moment's rest unless he can bond with five more women.

Incubus is definitely the most erotic series I have ever written. While some of my other stories have sex scenes, there isn't a single story I've written that has so many within a single volume. That is because the sex is as much a part of this story as everything else. Like, you can't have a series about a creature who needs sex to survive without writing a couple dozen sex scenes. Right? Right.

This particular volume focused heavily on Secilia, which makes sense considering she was the woman that Anthony bonded with in this volume. When I was creating her character, I wanted to make someone who followed the standard archetypes of the magic academy genre of anime, but who was also different. A homonculus who happened to also be an engineering genius with the ability to hack into any database and build complex machinery sounded like a good gimmick, so I went with it. I'll admit, I used Asagi Aiba as a basis for Secilia, but I think she's also different enough that people can enjoy her for what she is rather than who she was inspired by.

Like the previous volume, this one has a heavy emphasis on a loved one betraying Anthony for reasons that I hope to God make sense because this will suck if it doesn't. This will also be the last time I use this particular subplot in Incubus since I believe it has worn its welcome with me. The rest of his harem will be acquired through less dark and treacherous means.

Saying that, I do hope you guys enjoyed Secilia's backstory and personal dilemmas. I really wanted to up the angst factor with her. While Brianna fell in love with Anthony relatively quickly, Secilia has been in love with him for years, so her quandary is far more potent than Anthony's first bondmate.

Now, I'd like to give a few last minute thank yous before heading out.

First, I want to thank my beta readers, editor, and proofreaders. They found a large number of continuity issues, sentence structure mishaps, homonym errors, and so on within this volume. I'm grateful to them because my writing would suck without them. Seriously. It'd be bad.

I also want to thank Orendi Laran for doing all that marvelous hentai art. I'm a huge fan of hentai, in case you couldn't tell, and Orendi does an amazing job. This artist also works on visual novels, which explains why the art for this series has such a wonderful VN feel.

Finally, I would like to thank all of you. Thank you reading this story, for writing reviews on sharing them on whatever site you bought this from, and for sharing it with your friends and fam—well, maybe not sharing it with your family, but at least your friends? Maybe? I hope. Anyway, thank you very much.

I hope everyone who enjoyed this volume will stick around for Incubus 3! I plan on introducing a vampire to the harem!

~Brandon Varnell

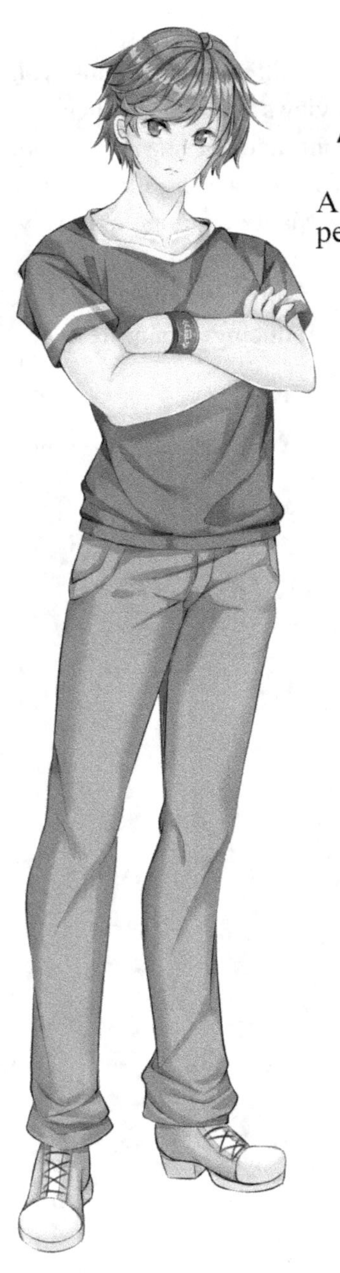

ANTHONY AMASIUS

A 19 year-old college student. He just happens to be the world's only incubus.

BRIANNA

A War Maiden of Custodes Daemonium. She's 18 years-old and
well-versed in magical combat.

SECILIA

Anthony's friend. She attends the same college as him. Well-known for her sarcasm and sharp tongue.

LUCRETIA INCANSCINO

Known to her students as the lolita teacher because of her youthful appearance, Lucretia is also an Attack Mage working for the Academy Island Private Security Forces.

Did you know that Brandon varnell is adapting the american kitsune series into a manga on patreon?

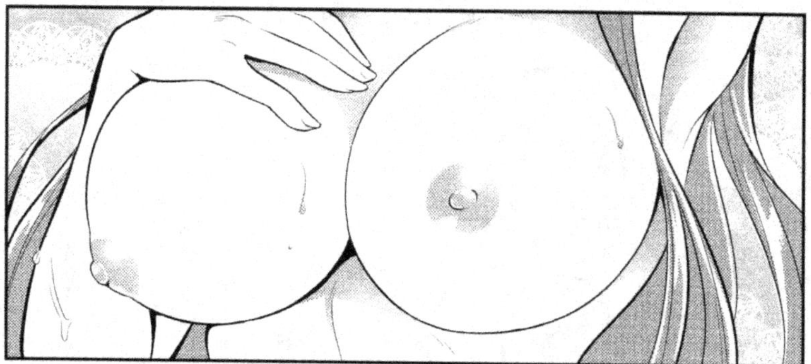

HAVE YOU EVER EXPERIENCED ONE OF THOSE LIFE-CHANGING INSTANCES? AN EVENT SO MOMENTOUS THAT, YEARS LATER, YOU'RE STILL MARVELING AT HOW IT CHANGED YOUR LIFE?

I HAD ONE OF THOSE. IT HAPPENED A WHILE AGO

EVEN TO THIS DAY, THROUGH ALL THE CHANGES THAT HAVE HAPPENED, THROUGH ALL THE EXPERIENCES THAT I'VE BEEN THROUGH, I STILL CAN'T BELIEVE HOW THIS ONE MOMENT CHANGED MY LIFE FOREVER.

NO MATTER WHAT CAME AFTER, OUR FIRST MEETING IS SOMETHING THAT I'LL ALWAYS REMEMBER.

ESPECIALLY SINCE, AT THE BEGINNING OF THIS TALE, I THOUGHT SHE WAS NOTHING BUT AN ORDINARY FOX WITH, UNORDINARILY ENOUGH, TWO BUSHY RED TAILS.

LIFE

.
.
.
.
.
.
.
.
.

IT HITS YOU WHEN YOU LEAST EXPECT IT TO.

coming soon!

Hey, did you know?
Brandon Varnell has started a Patreon
You can get all kinds of awesome exclusives
Like:

1. The chance to read his stories before anyone else!
2. Free ebooks!
3. exclusive SFW and NSFW artwork!
4. Signed paperback copies!
Er... maybe we don't want that last one, but the rest is pretty cool, right?

To get this awesome exlusive conent go to:
https://www.patreon.com/BrandonVarnell
and sigh up today!

WIEDERGEBURT

LEGEND OF THE REINCARNATED WARRIOR

catgirl doctor
Buy volume 1 on paperback, kindle, and Kindle Unlimited!

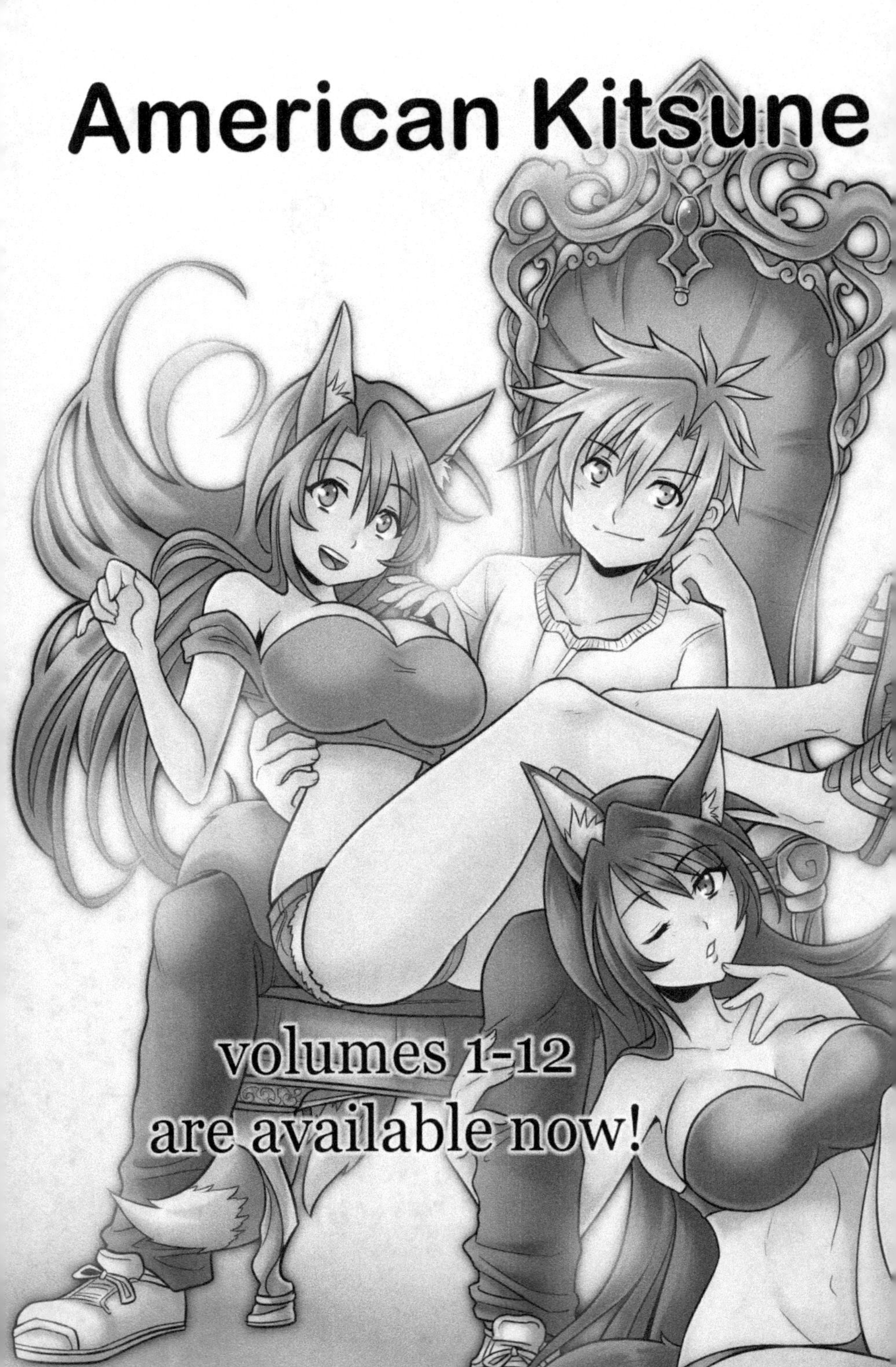
American Kitsune
volumes 1-12
are available now!

Volumes 1-7
are available now!
A Most
Unlikely
Hero

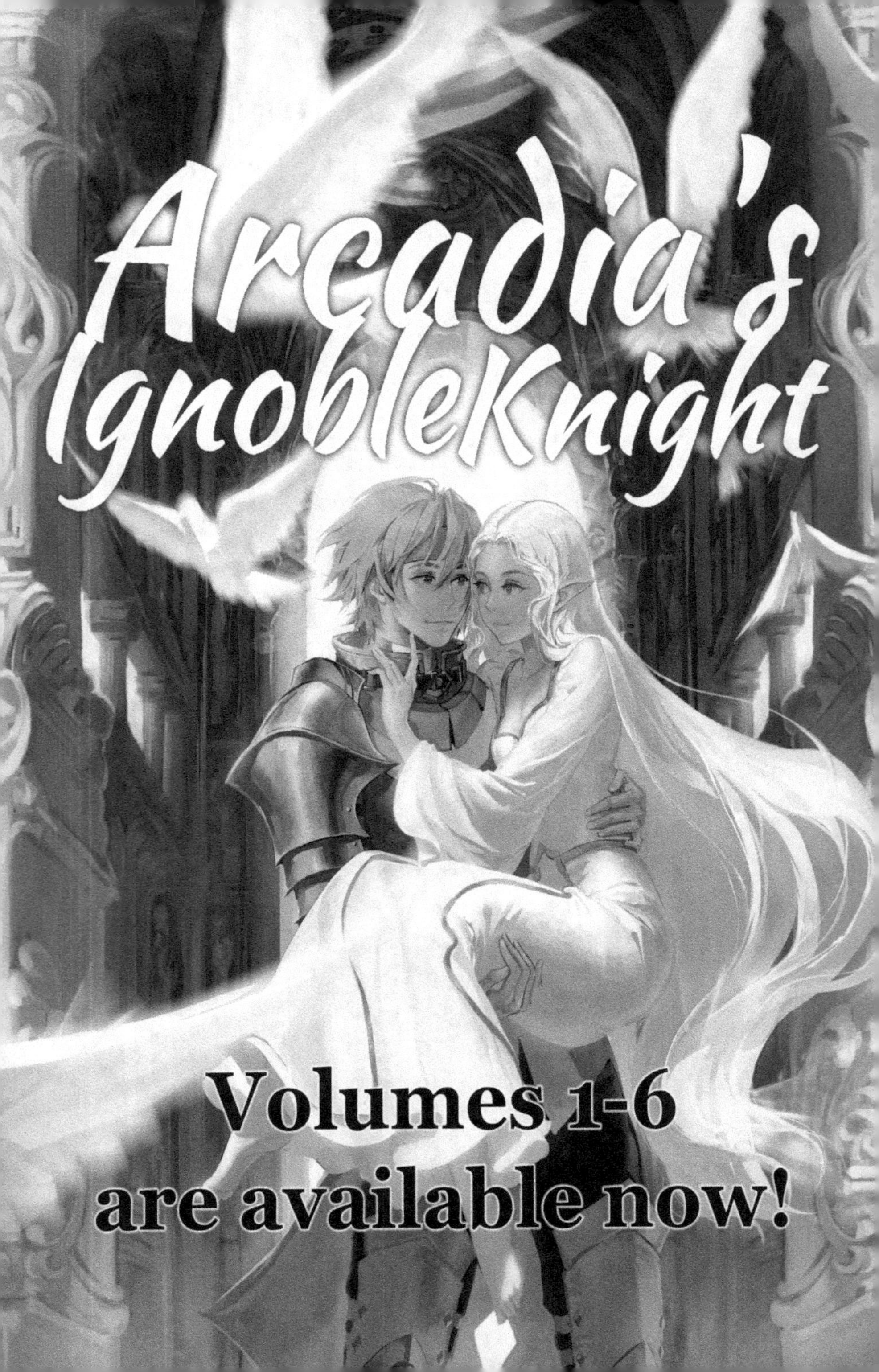
Arcadia's
IgnobleKnight
Volumes 1-6
are available now!

Volumes 1 & 2 are available on
paperback,
Amazon,
and Kindle Unlimited
Swordsman
Of the
Rift 2

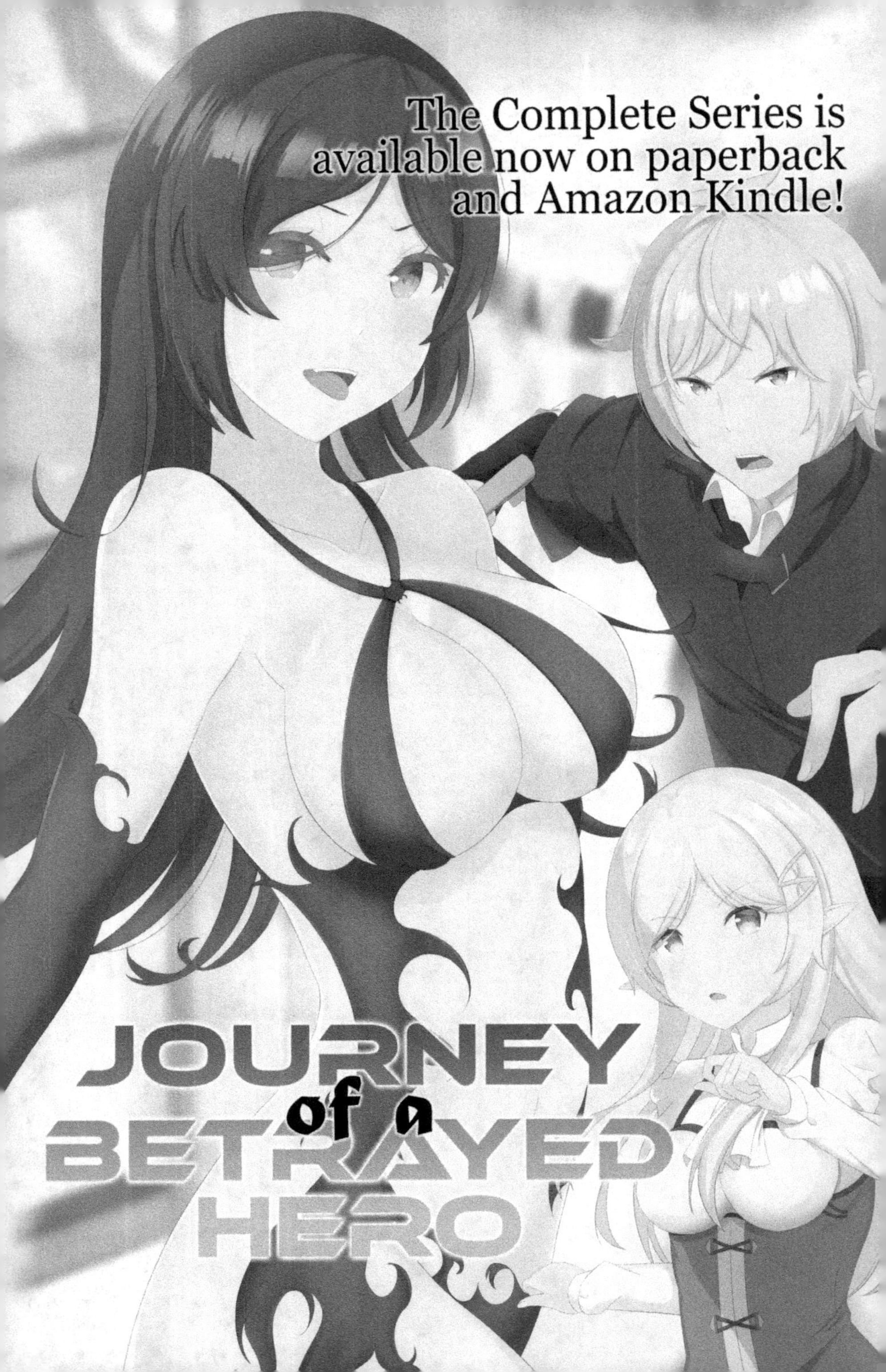

The Complete Series is available now on paperback and Amazon Kindle!
JOURNEY of a BETRAYED HERO

The Executioner Series
The complete series
is available now!